MASCARA AND MOSCATO

SHAKELA JAMES

D1570103

Acknowledgements

First and foremost, I want to thank God for giving me the opportunity to live out my dreams. It is through Him that I have the strength and patience to continue to write these books. I thank God for blessing me with a gift that allows me to entertain and inspire others. I give Him all the glory.

Princess Kamryn, you are everything to me. You give me so much strength, motivation, and joy that I wouldn't know what to do without you. I hope I make you as proud as you make me.

Michael: my biggest fan. Thank you for being an amazing husband and supporting me through all my endeavors. You make this process a whole lot easier. I love you so much.

To my family and friends: thank you all for your continued support. It means the world to me. There are too many of you to name, but know that I wouldn't be where I am without you.

To my granny, Rita: I love you more than words can express. Thank you for everything you've done for me throughout my entire life.

Yolanda and Alyce: Thank you both for all the time, dedication, honesty, and advice you two give me each time I release a book. I couldn't have chosen two better people to help me along this journey. I will always be grateful that I met you two both even though y'all some messy ass bullies (lol).

Carmen, you work every single nerve in my body. (lol) You're so petty, but I wouldn't trade you for the world. Your advice is very much appreciated.

To all of my readers, THANK YOU! Every single one of you inspires me to continue to write these stories. I take all of your suggestions, criticism, and praise and learn from them to become the best author I can be. Thank y'all for taking a chance on me and continuing to stand behind me.

Sheila Robinson, Javonti Barnes, Micheala Benjamin, Glenda Coats, Brittany Si'mone, Maria Sanchez, Rocio Reyes, Fredricka Williams, and Fareeda Abdullah: your continued excitement and support does not go unnoticed. Thank you guys so much for the messages, posts, shares, etc. Y'all are truly the best.

Tajuana Smith, Jody Andrews, Joan Brooks, Tura Billingslea, Dawnyale Peeks, and Betty Holloway: Thank y'all for going HARD for this book.

Ashley Robinson: You know that you're my girl. Thanks for the support.

If I forgot anyone, charge it to my head and not my heart. Every person in my life is here for a reason and I appreciate all of you for putting up with all of me.

Shakela James

"If you're going through it, just know it's called going THROUGH it. You're not gonna get stuck, you're not gonna die; you're gonna survive."

- **Tina Knowles**

CHAPTER 1

"Have fun this weekend, but not too much fun. I expect to see you all here Monday," Nina called out as she prepared to shut down the office for the day. She was the sales manager at a call center in Downtown Houston, but by the way she worked, you would think she was the VP of the company.

"Bye, Nina. See you Monday," her employees said.

Nina waved before locking up the office. She couldn't wait to get her three-day weekend started. The Fourth of July was on a Saturday this year, so that meant the turn up would definitely be real. Not only was she ready for the ratchet festivities that were sure to take place, Nina was excited about Mascara & Moscato night. She got together two Fridays a month with her best friends, Allie and Chanel, for all things girly. It had been a while since they all hung out together.

When Nina made it to her Nissan Maxima, she didn't waste any time sliding off her heels and turning on the radio. She began taking out the bobby pins that held her bun in place. Her golden brown hair fell freely down her shoulders. Nina had a light skin color but she wasn't considered a "yella bone." She stood 5'7", about 180 pounds. She wasn't exactly fat, but she sure had a little extra meat on her bones in the right places.

She buckled her seatbelt and turned up the radio even louder. As she rode down Highway 59, she rapped along with Wale, who was paying homage to the *Illest Bitch Alive*. She listened to the song at least twice a day, just to remind herself that she was sho nuff a bad motherfucker.

Nina saw flashing lights and quickly looked out the rearview mirror, trying to figure out what she did wrong. When she didn't see anyone behind her, she remembered that her niece Tiffany switched the settings on her phone to where the light would flash if she got a call or text. She grabbed the phone and glanced at the screen. She frowned, not recognizing the number.

She hit ignore and continued rapping. An unsaved number could only mean bills or drama, and Nina didn't have time for either one. When the number called right back, she decided to answer.

"Hello, Nina St. Claire speaking," she answered, just in case it was a business call.

"About time, what if there was an emergency?" asked the voice on the other end.

Nina shrieked. "Sweetie, is this you? Oh my God, where are you?"

"I'm in Houston. For good," answered Sweetie. Sweetie was another one of Nina's childhood friends. About a year ago, Sweetie got married and moved to Austin with her husband. They kept in contact the first few months, but eventually lost touch.

"Yes, this is perfect timing. The girls and I were planning on starting a Mascara & Moscato night again, starting tomorrow. Travis and I are also cooking for the Fourth of July," said Nina.

"We'll be there. Well, I'll check back with you later. Make sure you lock me in and tell the girls I said hello. I'll see you tomorrow," said Sweetie before hanging up the phone.

As soon as Nina put her phone down, it was buzzing and lighting up again. This time, it was her husband Travis calling. Nina was only twenty-four years old but she had been married to Travis since she was twenty-one. They'd met through Chanel's boyfriend Jaheim only six months before they'd gotten married. She could admit that their union was sudden, but three years later, they were still going strong.

"Hey baby," she answered.

"Sup bae, I was just making sure you were okay. I haven't heard from you since your lunch break earlier," he replied.

"I'm fine babe, I was going to call you, but between Sweetie calling me and Wale, I sort of forgot," she answered honestly.

"Nina," he said, sternly.

"I'm sorry," she retreated. Travis could be overbearing at times but Nina understood that it was only because he cared. "Sweetie's moving back!" she quickly changed the subject.

"That's what's up. Alright babe, I'll see you when you get here. I love you," said Travis.

"Love you too, bye!" she replied as she threw her phone down for a second time.

Nina couldn't wait to call and tell the girl the good news, but first she had to sing her song all over again since she was so rudely interrupted.

"*Illest bitch alive, realest bitch alive...*"

CHAPTER 2

"What do you mean I'm not eligible for graduation?" asked Allie as she fought the urge to bring out the hood side of her. Yeah, she was pursuing her nursing degree but was still from Third Ward in Houston and seconds away from catching a case.

"I'm sorry but there was a problem with your transcript. It shows you never took a Health and Wellness course," said Dr. Thornton, who was the department chair.

"You guys didn't have that in my degree plan!" she cried.

"Look Alyssa, I'm sorry. I don't know what to say. These new board members are really cracking down on us," he tried to reason.

Allie dropped her backpack and tried to keep a poker face. Though she was seconds away from having an emotional breakdown, she didn't show an ounce of emotion. She glared at Dr. Thornton and wanted to jump behind the counter and beat his bald ass. "So, I have to suffer because your faculty fucked up?"

"Watch your language, Ms. Spencer," Dr. Thornton warned, wearing a scowl that showed he meant business.

Allie quickly realized that she was fighting a battle she couldn't win. She dropped her head in defeat. "I can't afford to not graduate this fall," she said on the brink of tears.

"Look, if you can find someone certified to train you in the state of Texas, we'll sign off on it as an approved course. You will need to have them document your hours for verification. The only issue is that this trainer needs to be found by Monday because you must start by Tuesday."

Allie looked at him like he'd lost his mind. *Monday*? It was Thursday, so all she had was three days to make the impossible happen. She sighed and picked back up her backpack before muttering okay. She had no other choice; she had two kids who needed her to win. Allie's kids, Jeremiah and Jerricka, were her world. When she'd gotten pregnant four years ago with Jeremiah, she'd promised herself that she would be successful no matter what. When she had her daughter Jerricka two years later, she became determined to push herself to give her children the life they deserved.

Allie worked as a freelance makeup artist in order to get by. Her baby's father, Spade, was the store manager of an upscale restaurant but had recently gotten fired for failing a random drug test so naturally, money was tight. Allie didn't know where she would get money for a trainer but she had less than three days to figure it out.

Allie left her school's campus and drove home silently. She just couldn't catch a damn break. She wanted to call Spade to vent to him, but knew they would end up arguing. Allie and Spade were high school sweethearts. Everyone knew that they would grow to be the perfect couple and live the perfect life, but reality hit like a ton of bricks when Spade got another girl pregnant right out of high school. The girl ended up losing the baby, but it was then that things changed between the two of them. They fought through the pain, but things never got back to the way they were. Allie became slightly insecure and Spade started drinking more and more. Once Allie gave birth to their son, things seemed to get better but after Jerricka was born, it was back to the drawing board. They were constantly fighting, Spade's drinking got worse, and Allie just became fed up. Nine years, two kids, and zero rings was enough for Allie.

As soon as Allie pulled into the driveway of her three-bedroom home, her phone started to ring. Before she answered it, she looked in the mirror and tried to wipe any evidence of tears away from her face. At the age of twenty-three, Allie felt like she had the weight of the world on her shoulders. She wiped her eyes, noticing the bags that were there. Her once beautiful glowing skin now looked pale. She looked at her hair, which was thrown into a ponytail, and shook her head. "I'm really letting myself go," she muttered as she grabbed her backpack and stepped out of the car.

As she reached for her phone, she noticed a missed call from Nina. She quickly called her back before walking into the house because she knew it would be nothing but chaos from that point on.

"Talk quick, I'm about to walk in," said Allie as she leaned against her old Toyota Corolla.

"Just wanted to confirm that we're still on for Friday night and also let you know that Sweetie moved back," replied Nina.

"Really? When?" asked Allie, surprised by the news. She talked to Sweetie often and she had never mentioned moving back to Houston.

"I think she moved back already. She's coming over Friday night," answered Nina.

"Okay, great. I can't wait to see all of you," Allie replied. Her response was genuine but she couldn't help but feel a twinge of jealousy. Since middle school, it had been the four of them but her and Sweetie was thick as thieves, same with Nina and Chanel.

She took a deep breath before walking into her home. As suspected, Spade was laid out on the couch in nothing but his basketball shorts. The TVs volume was so loud; he didn't even hear Allie come in. Jeremiah was playing with his toys in the middle of the floor, while Jerricka was resting comfortably in a clothesbasket. As soon as she closed the door, her kids stopped what they were doing and shot over to her.

"Mommy, can I have some food?" asked Jeremiah as she hugged her leg tightly.

"Eat-eat mommy," said Jerricka as she followed in her brother's footsteps and clung tightly to Allie's other leg.

"Why didn't y'all tell Daddy that y'all were hungry?" asked Allie, glancing over at Spade who had yet to even acknowledge her presence.

"Well, I did but he ignored me," answered Jeremiah. That immediately infuriated Allie, but she chose not to say anything. She walked into her kitchen and noticed a sink full of dirty dishes. Spade's ass has been home all day and hadn't even attempted to clean up. Exhausted, Allie put on her big girl panties and started to clean her kitchen. If she didn't do it, it wouldn't get done.

Allie searched her freezer for something quick to make for her kids. She decided chicken nuggets, macaroni, and roasted carrots would do. Once she put the nuggets in the oven, Allie washed the dishes and cleaned off her counters.

"Mommy, can I take out the trash?" asked Jeremiah as he watched his mother clean.

"We can take it out after dinner, okay?" she replied with a smile. She was unsure about a lot of things, but knew for certain she was raising her kids the right way.

After she fed and bathed her kids, she sent them to bed after reading them their favorite story. Once Allie got into the shower, she broke down and cried. After ten minutes of wallowing in her sorrows, Allie sucked it up and prepared to go to sleep so she could take on another day.

Meanwhile, Spade was lying on the couch cursing himself out. He wanted to be more help to Allie but he was going through a really dark time. Normally, when he wasn't in good spirits, he could smoke a blunt and drink a few beers and be okay; lately the darkness he felt was starting to consume him

Nothing satisfied him. Not his woman, not his children, and not the alcohol in which he normally found solace. He felt lower than low for dropping the ball like he did. After he lost his job, he no longer felt adequate. He knew Allie deserved the world and everything in it, but he wasn't in the position to provide that. He didn't want her to have to worry about bills and stress things, but he couldn't do anything to take those worries away. Deep down inside, Spade was trying to detach himself from Allie because he knew that one day he would lose her to somebody worthy of having her. He wanted to talk to her and express his feelings but once he saw her outside sneaking on the phone, he knew he was losing his family.

Allie lay down in bed and wondered when things would get better. She wondered if this was as good as it got or if there was something great out there waiting on her. She fell asleep only minutes after lying down. Allie was just plain tired.

CHAPTER 3

"Yes, baby. Right there," purred Chanel. She was so close to reaching orgasm, so in between moans she was praying that Eric wouldn't move. With her luck, of course, he moved and her growing orgasm faded away. He picked up his pace and Chanel knew he was about to climax. She began shaking and screaming his name, feeding his ego.

"Yeah, baby cum on this dick," muttered Chanel's baby daddy.

"I'm cuuu-uuu-minnnnnng," faked Chanel. Eric smiled at the mother of his child as he dug deeper and deeper into her.

Chanel continued putting on a show until Eric's body was laying limp on top of hers. "That pussy still good," said Eric as he eased himself out of Chanel.

Chanel walked into his restroom and cleaned herself up. As she wiped away the sperm of her child's father, she felt guilty knowing she was about to go home to her boyfriend Jaheim. She started dating Jaheim about six months ago and they've been rocking tough ever since; however, Chanel had a soft spot for her baby daddy. Although he kicked her out and denied paternity of their son in the beginning, Eric was starting to be a more active figure in Eric Jr.'s life and Chanel was fine with that.

Chanel watched Eric get dressed and wondered whether or not she wanted to be petty. She decided she would be and discreetly slid her earring under the pillow where his wife slept. All hell would break loose once his wife found out that her perfect little husband was still the same dog he'd always been. Chanel would never admit it, but she was so jealous of Talia. She didn't understand what was so special about the bitch that he would never leave her.

"You want to check the bed and make sure there's nothing there?" Chanel asked sarcastically. Eric chuckled at her smart remark. A few weeks back he'd told her that he didn't trust her to keep their secret sex life between them. He had a feeling that one day, Chanel would try to throw it in Talia's face.

"Nah, we good." He had already checked the bed while she was washing off. Chanel rolled her eyes at him and then stuck her hand out. Eric walked over to his wallet and peeled off five one hundred dollar bills. Chanel took the money and stuck it into her nude Steve Madden clutch. She then stuck her hand out again.

Eric laughed as he hit her open palm. "What you still got your hand out for?"

"These five hundred dollars are for me. Where's the money for E.J?" Chanel asked.

"That's more than enough," Eric countered, trying to understand where all this was coming from. He had been giving Chanel five hundred dollars every two weeks for child support.

"That's not nearly enough, Eric," Chanel said, not trying to hear any of the bullshit Eric was talking.

"Since when? I've been giving you a thousand dollars each month since he was born, why is it such a big deal now?"

"I spend five hundred dollars on my hair, I mean...you can't support a child with a thousand dollars a month," Chanel countered. She didn't understand why he just won't give her two grand a month so they could all be happy.

"Then get a fucking job if it's not enough. I pay for his daycare, which is a pointless bill since you don't do shit all day. I still buy shoes, clothes, diapers, and whatever else he needs. I'm holding up my end of the bargain and if you can't, give him to me," Eric spat.

15

Chanel almost lost it but she reminded herself that she needed to keep calm. She wanted Eric to see that she had changed. She wasn't the crazy, hot-tempered girl she once was. Chanel had keyed Eric's car, started drama at his job, and stalked him a little but she had changed within the last year. Besides, he always came back to her, so that must meant he loved her. Right?

"Eric, I'm very capable of taking care of our son. I appreciate all that you do but I need more money. Are we going to do it the easy way or the hard way?" she asked, staring him down.

"You know what, Chanel, fuck it! File child support!" Eric threw his hands in the air. He was at his wits end with Chanel's threats. Eric didn't have a real job, he was into street pharmacy and he didn't need the courts all in his business. Someone told him that since he was legally married to Talia, they could garnish her wages to pay his child support. Eric didn't know how true it was, but he didn't want to take any chances. That's why he'd been dishing out a thousand dollars a month since his son was born a little over a year ago.

"That's fine, I'll be at the attorney general's office Monday morning," spat Chanel as she walked out of Eric's bedroom, one with he shared with his wife. "Tell Talia to get her wallet ready."

Eric was fuming on the inside but he knew Chanel was intentionally trying to push his buttons and he refused to play her little game. He walked out of the bedroom calmly as Chanel continued to make smart remarks. Once they got to the door, he opened it so she could step out.

"Stop bringing up my wife's name, Chanel. Jealousy doesn't look good on you," Eric smirked.

Chanel put on her Dior shades and flipped her Cambodian hair. "Jealous? I'm a way badder bitch than Talia and you know that."

"You are," Eric agreed. Chanel was glad her back was to him because she couldn't stop the smile that spread across her face. She shot him a seductive look over her shoulder.

"I'm glad you know it," she smiled, well aware that Eric found her sexier than his wife.

"You're a badder bitch but that's it, Chanel. But guess what, my brother got a bitch badder than you, and somebody got a badder bitch than that. What else do you have to offer? Let me tell you something about my wife. She's a go-getter. Whether she has me or not, she gonna get shit done. She's loyal as fuck, and to be honest, I don't deserve her. But she loves me and I love her for the beautiful woman she is, I just slip and fuck a few bad bitches from time to time," he said before walking back into the house.

Chanel was glad he walked away because she didn't even have a comeback for his ass. Chanel was a gorgeous girl, standing 5'11 with long, toned legs. Her dark skin was rich and smooth, while her jet-black hair caused her to look like she could be foreign. Though she wore weaves on a consistent basis, the length and texture of Chanel's hair could put any bundle to shame. Chanel felt like she was the closest thing to perfection and didn't mind letting others know too.

Chanel smiled as she got into her 2015 Mercedes Benz. Although Eric had just read her like a book, all she heard was that he acknowledged that she looked better than his wife. Chanel was determined to get her man back but she was being patient and Jaheim was helping her pass time.

Jaheim was sexy as hell. He was just her type. Tall, dark, and stacked in both departments: pockets and pants. He worked at the gym as a personal trainer on top of coaching a little league football team. He was so sweet and caring. He was everything she wanted, except for Eric. If she could give Eric some of Jaheim's traits, she would be a happy woman. Chanel felt kind of bad for cheating on Jaheim because he took great care of her and loved her son to death, but the heart wants what it wants. And Chanel's heart was stuck with Eric.

When she arrived home, she saw that Jaheim was already there. Chanel had her own apartment but she had recently been staying with Jaheim. Her son E.J. was at her mom's house for the weekend so she was ready to let loose. As she walked into the condo, Chanel got completely naked and walked towards the bedroom. She quickly realized Jaheim was in the shower and decided to join him.

She quietly slipped into the shower and placed her arms around Jaheim's strong shoulders and kissed his back.

"Did I scare you?" she questioned as Jaheim turned around and hugged her tightly.

"I ain't scared of nothing but God," replied Jaheim as he rubbed on her plump ass. Chanel's body started to quiver the second he touched her.

"I could have been a robber," she said with her eyes closed, resting her head on his chest. Jaheim was 6'3" and built like a grown ass man. Muscles peeked out everywhere on his caramel toned body.

"Nah, ain't no robbers gonna move as slow and graceful as you did," he replied, kissing Chanel on her neck. Jaheim was really feeling Chanel. He knew she had a lot of growing up to do, but he was willing to help her grow.

Chanel let out a moan and grabbed Jaheim's manhood. She smiled at him seductively knowing he was about to finish what Eric had started.

CHAPTER 4

"Jameka, we haven't even got settled in yet and you're running to your friends' house?" asked Noah as he watched his wife lotion her body. She had just gotten out of the shower, looking as beautiful as ever.

Jameka, affectionately known as Sweetie, shook her head at her husband. "Noah, it's been over a year. I miss them."

Noah knew how much her friends meant to her but he would rather her stay at home with him. He didn't like her around other women too long; they started to get in her head.

"Please, baby?" he pleaded.

Sweetie looked at the expression on Noah's face and went over to kiss him on his sexy lips. "I'll leave early, but I promised I would be there. Oh, and we're going to Nina's for the fourth, okay?"

Noah nodded his head and kissed Sweetie back. Sweetie loved her husband so much, but she needed a break and girl's night was just what she needed.

She and the girls came up with Mascara and Moscato night a few years back. It was a day for them to vent, bitch, laugh, cry, pig out, and freely drink wine. Sweetie walked over and pulled out a pair of silk pajamas.

Noah smiled to himself, happy that she was staying in tonight. When she got dressed and picked up her keys, he got confused. "Where you going?"

"To Nina's," replied Sweetie, not sure of why he was acting lost.

"In that?" he asked, referring to her purple pajamas.

"Yes, that's the theme tonight," answered Sweetie. She saw a beautiful silk gown she wanted to wear, but she knew Noah would trip so she settled on a two-piece pajama set.

He stood up and stretched, never taking his eyes off of Sweetie. He glared so hard she began to feel uncomfortable.

"What?" she asked.

"I just don't understand why a bunch of grown ass women would want to sit around in their pajamas," he replied.

"I didn't pick the theme, babe. I think it's cute," she said, looking at herself in the mirror.

"Is Travis going to be there?" asked Noah, watching his wife check herself out.

"No, he won't be there. He never is," replied Sweetie.

Noah had a tendency to be very jealous and overprotective. Sweetie did her best to make sure that he always felt secure. She loved him so much and wished he'd just trust her more.

"Noah, the girls miss me. And I miss them. I won't stay long, okay?" Sweetie kissed his lips and moved down to his neck. Noah slowly caressed his wife's back as he got lost in her kisses.

Sweetie smiled at him and got up to leave. If she and Noah had to fight about this later, then so be it. She needed a break and she wasn't going to let Noah prevent her from taking one.

Noah and Sweetie had been together for four years, married for one. They had a two-year-old daughter named Dallas, who was with Noah's parents for the weekend. They recently moved back to Houston because Noah was offered a promotion.

When it came to her marriage, Sweetie would bend over backwards and jump through hoops. All she wanted to do was make her man happy because he took such good care of her. At the lowest point in her life, Noah loved her and gave her the confidence to feel beautiful again. She vowed that no matter what, she would stick by his side.

She had flaws of her own, so Noah's insecurities really didn't bother her. She actually found it quite flattering that he was somewhat afraid to lose her. Noah was the most handsome man alive to Sweetie. Standing 6'4", 245 lbs., Noah was a rock solid man. Between his wavy hair and his pretty teeth, Sweetie felt like her husband was a prize and she would do what she had to do in order to make sure she kept him.

CHAPTER 5

Nina pranced around her kitchen, singing as she prepared the food for her girl's night. She focused on making everyone's favorite. There was shrimp pasta, which was Chanel's favorite, boneless wings for her, mini burgers for Allie, and meatballs for Sweetie.

Nina had such a nurturing personality but refused to have kids any time soon. It was a topic her and Travis argued about often. Nina was too career-driven. Once she was settled into her career, then she could think about having kids. Hell, a husband wasn't supposed to be in the picture until she was thirty, so Nina felt like Travis should be grateful.

As Nina checked on her Jell-O shots, she heard the door open. Seconds later, Travis appeared.

"Hey baby," he greeted her with a kiss on the cheek.

"Eww, you stink baby," replied Nina, frowning. Travis didn't even get mad at her because she looked so cute whenever she crinkled her face the way she did.

"I ain't trippin. I'll be stank all the way to the bank," he joked before heading to their room to shower.

Nina continued to prep for the party as Travis got cleaned up. She wondered what he and his boys had planned for the night. Minutes later, Travis appeared again, this time walking toward the stove.

"What are you doing?" asked Nina as she popped Travis's hand. The meatball he'd just retrieved fell back into the pot with a thud and barbecue sauce splashed into her face.

"What you do that for?" Travis retorted, sucking the remnants of BBQ sauce off of his finger.

"Why are you touching the food?" she snapped, wiping her face with a napkin.

"Cus I'm hungry. Fix me a plate please, baby," he pleaded. Travis grabbed Nina by the waist and kissed her neck softly. She removed his hands and scowled at him.

"This is for tonight. There are sandwiches and noodles in there to eat," she offered as she walked over to the dining room to set up.

Travis looked at Nina in utter disbelief. "Wait a minute, you mean to tell me I come home after twelve hours of busting my ass and I can't get a home cooked meal?"

Nina stopped in her tracks and turned around to face her husband. "Seriously, Travis? If you were hungry, why didn't you stop to get food?"

Travis loved his wife to death but she was so selfish sometimes. Nina turned back around and started setting the table without a care in the world.

Travis walked over to the cabinet and pulled out a plate. He walked over to the stove and fixed himself a hearty plate of shrimp pasta. When Nina returned to the kitchen, she let out a small shriek. "Travis, why?"

He waved her off as he continued to eat. "This my fuckin' house. I pay bills in here. The fuck I look like eating noodles while my WIFE is in here cooking five-star meals for her friends?"

Nina instantly became annoyed with Travis. She didn't see what the big deal was, seeing that he knew she was organizing her girl's night. "Travis, you knew what I was doing tonight."

"And you knew your husband would come home hungry after a sixty hour work week," he yelled. He was trying to keep his composure but Nina was looking at him as if he was speaking a foreign language.

"There's a Jack in the Box right around the corner if you were that damn hungry," Nina snapped. She put her hands on her hips and watched her husband as he stared her down.

He nodded his head before getting back up. He grabbed his plate and walked back over to the stove where he scraped the remaining food off his plate and back into the pot. "You're right; let me go spend extra money on fast food. Shit was nasty anyway," he muttered before walking away.

Nina looked at the pot in disgust and couldn't believe her husband was acting that way. She did her best to scrape up his leftovers as she shook her head. Travis had been on edge lately and she wasn't sure why.

A blaring sound came from the living room. She took a deep breath before following the sound. Travis was sitting on the couch, with a bag of chips in his hand.

"You know I'm using this space for tonight," she said slowly.

Travis continued chewing his chips without even looking at her. Nina marched in front of their 62" TV and placed her hands on her hips. "What is wrong with you?"

Travis looked at her, and then back at the TV without muttering a word.

"Hellooooo," Nina exaggerated, while waving her hands.

"What's wrong with you, Nina? You go above and beyond to take care of everybody but your man."

"Because I didn't cook for you?" she questioned.

"Not just because you didn't cook for me, Nina! You- you know what, never mind," he groaned, getting up. He decided to walk away before he said something he shouldn't. He headed down the hall to his man cave and slammed the door. He had to take his aggression out some way.

Travis loved his wife but she knew how to push every button he had. He didn't understand how a woman could be so selfish and inconsiderate. When he married her, he knew she had some growing to do and was willing to help her do that, but it got to the point where he wasn't sure if she even wanted to help herself. Travis often felt like she only married him just to say she was married.

Travis heard footsteps and hoped his wife would come in to apologize or at least attempt to make up with him, but when he heard the shower running, he knew if he wanted reconciliation, he would be the one to make the first move. *Fuck that*, he thought as he laid out on his futon and watched SportsCenter until he dozed off.

CHAPTER 6

Allie was the first to arrive at Nina's place. She desperately needed a break and couldn't wait to unwind with her girlfriends.

When Nina opened the door, the two hugged each other until they cried. It had been about four months since they'd seen each other face-to-face. Sure, they would call and Facetime often, but it was nothing in the world like being in the presence of your best friend.

"Allie Cat, I missed you so much!" Exclaimed Nina, as she stood to the side and let her in.

With her makeup kit in tow, Allie stepped into Nina's house instantly loving the peace and quiet.

"I missed you too," replied Allie. "You need help with anything?"

Nina gave her a look that said, *Bitch please.* Allie didn't even know why she asked. Of all the girls, Nina was like the mother, which was ironic because she was the only one of them without kids.

"Where's the alcohol?" questioned Allie as she walked towards the kitchen.

"Jell-O shots are still freezing, make some Pink Panties, please," replied Nina as she grabbed wine glasses from her cabinets.

Shortly after the drinks were made, Sweetie and Chanel showed up, ready to party. Nina invited all the girls to the kitchen, where the drinks were being served.

"Did you miss the memo, Allie? It's a pajama party," Chanel commented, referring to Allie's attire of a t-shirt and sweatpants.

"Then why are you wearing lingerie?" Allie shot back.

Chanel let out a small laugh. "What's wrong Allie? Jealous that you no longer can wear lingerie?"

"That's enough," scolded Nina. Allie and Chanel went at it constantly but she knew they loved each other. Sometimes, though, it could get intense and Nina wanted to stop the bullshit before it even started.

"Relax, Nina, "retorted Chanel as she flopped down on the couch. "Allie knows I'm just messing with her."

Allie shot her a nasty look and rolled her eyes. Sweetie looked on in silence, hoping tonight would be fun.

"Sweetie, why didn't you tell me you were moving back? We talked last week and you didn't mention it," Allie pointed out as she poured all the girls drinks.

"It wasn't planned. Noah got the promotion and we packed up and left with no warning," answered Sweetie.

Allie and Chanel shot each other glances that said they didn't believe it, but they decided to leave it alone. After all the girls were seated, and Allie changed into the proper attire, the girls' night began.

"Okay, so are we bragging or venting first?"quizzed Nina, excited to have all her girls around her.

"Venting," replied Chanel, as she smacked her lips dramatically. "Cus a bitch has a lot to vent about."

Nina rolled her eyes and shook her head. Chanel was the dramatic diva of the group for sure.

"So, right after me and Eric finished fuckin-" Chanel started.

"Chanel! What about Jaheim?" Nina asked. Travis and Jah were best friends so she wasn't comfortable knowing Chanel was still sleeping with her baby daddy.

"What about him? He probably doing the same thing," shrugged Chanel.

"Chanel, that ain't right!" Exclaimed Nina.

Chanel looked at Nina and rolled her eyes. "Are you going to continue to be Mother Goose or can I finish my story?"

Nina rolled her eyes back and sat back on the couch. "Continue."

Chanel smacked her lips dramatically again and finished her story. "Well, like I said before being rudely interrupted by a certain Judgmental Judie, after I finished fuckin my baby daddy's brains out, he finally admitted that I was badder than his wife," she bragged proudly.

Allie frowned her face in confusion. "And what else?"

"Can we focus on one point at a time? He finds me more attractive than he does his wife. Let's relish in that for a few seconds. He probably fantasizes about me when he sleeps with her," smiled Chanel.

Nina shook her head at her best friend. Chanel could definitely be vain. Sweetie couldn't believe Chanel was proud to be sleeping with a married man.

"Anyways, so right after he basically told me that I was the shit, he told me all I would ever be was a bad bitch and nothing more," admitted Chanel. She recapped the event to her girls.

Allie couldn't contain her laughter. "I'm sorry; bitch but he read you your rights!"

Nina and Sweetie couldn't hold their laughs in any longer and joined Allie. As much as Chanel wanted to be mad, she found herself laughing too.

"I don't know what it is, but I can't leave his ass alone," whined Chanel, sipping her drink. She really wanted to move on from Eric but every time he called, she came running.

"He's married, Chanel. That should be good enough reason. A man will never leave his wife for the bitch on the side," Sweetie spat.

All of the girls looked at Sweetie. Her words were laced with venom and there was a distant expression in her eyes.

"Well, damn Sweetie," scoffed Chanel, feeling some type of way about Sweetie's outburst. She knew it was true but damn her delivery was harsh.

"Sorry, Nel," Sweetie apologized, feeling bad about hurting Chanel's feelings but the truth was that she didn't like the fact that Chanel was sleeping with a married man; baby daddy or not.

"Well, I guess my only venting would be about Travis," interjected Nina. "He's so pushy lately. It seems like everything I do pisses him off."

"That man wants a baby, Nina," Allie said as she stood up to go make herself another drink. "Anyone want another drink?"

Chanel held up her cup. Allie walked over to get it and continued talking to Nina as she poured glasses of Moscato. "He always throws little slugs about wanting a baby."

"Well, that's on him. I told him I didn't want babies right now. We have plenty of time for that. I want to travel and build a career first."

"I understand what you mean, but that's the only thing he asks of you Nina," reasoned Allie.

"I don't see an issue with it. It's her body and her life," interrupted Chanel.

"When she got married, it became THEIR life and body," Allie shot back.

"That's bull shit," Chanel retorted, rolling her eyes. "If you don't want to push out no babies, don't fucking do it."

Nina watched the scene before her and shook her head. "I just feel like we can wait on that. He has to respect that."

Allie shrugged her shoulders, clearly not wanting to argue any further. She really wanted to tell Nina how selfish she was being but she decided to keep her mouth shut. Leave it to Nina and Chanel; the women wore the pants in their household. And Sweetie... Allie didn't know what to think of Sweetie, who had been so distant lately.

Allie exhaled and decided to vent about her own problems. "Well, I found out that I may not be graduating in the fall after all."

"What? Why?" asked Sweetie. She was so proud of Allie's determination. Even with two children, Allie managed to make it almost to the finish line. She would be the first of them to obtain a degree.

"Some bullshit about me not taking a health course. So, Dr. Thornton told me I have to find a personal trainer by Monday and do that for five weeks so I can graduate," explained Allie, sadly. Disappointment was written all over her face.

"Well, that shouldn't be too hard to find," reasoned Sweetie. "At least there's hope."

"I suppose," Allie shrugged, not feeling very hopeful.

"You'll graduate, boo. Don't stress about it," Nina chimed in. "How's everything with Spade?"

Allie sighed yet again. "I don't know. He's been so down since he lost his job. He doesn't want-"

"Lost his job?" spat Chanel. "When did this happen?"

Allie rolled her eyes at Chanel's excitement. "A few weeks ago. Like I was saying, it's like he doesn't want to do anything. He is just lying around and it's pissing me off."

"That has to be hard on him, continue to be patient with him," encouraged Sweetie. She believed in the power of love and she had experiences Allie and Spade's love firsthand. They were made for one another.

"I'm trying," Allie replied sadly.

"I wouldn't be taking care of no grown ass nigga with no job. Sorry, she ain't doing it," said Chanel, referring to herself in third person.

"Chanel, this has been her man for nearly a decade. Stick it out, Allie," urged Nina.

Chanel rolled her eyes. It seemed like the girls always went against what the hell she said. Chanel waved her hand and continued drinking. "Forget all that. Couldn't be me," she shrugged.

"That's why you can't keep a man," Allie chuckled.

"Bitch, clearly you can't either. Neither one of us has a ring on our finger," spat Chanel, wiggling her fingers.

"Come on, y'all. Really?" frowned Nina. She didn't understand why they were constantly at each others' necks.

"I'm just saying, don't act like you better than me, "Chanel ranted while giving Allie the evil eye.

Allie wanted to give Chanel a few choice words, but she bit her tongue instead. Clearly they were two totally different calibers of women. Allie had only slept with Spade in all twenty-three of her years. Chanel probably slept with twenty-three men in the last two years. Allie looked Chanel square in the eye."Don't speak on my man. I'm taking care of shit the same way he's been doing while I've been in school. You stick to your mistress handbook and I'll stick to the one that has kept my man around for nearly a decade."

"Moving on!" yelled Nina looking at Chanel and Allie like they were crazy. Those two could never get along and Nina couldn't figure out why."Sweetie, how's everything with you and Noah?"

"Everything is good. I can't complain. I love him so much and he's so good to me and Dallas," sang Sweetie with a smile on her face.

Nina beamed at her best friend. She was so happy that Sweetie found a good man in Noah. Allie and Chanel still had their reservations, however.

"So what you saying is that y'all just perfect?" quizzed Chanel. She hadn't learned the art of tongue biting yet and quite frankly, she didn't plan on it.

"It's not perfect, but it's as good as it gets," smiled Sweetie.

Nina looked at Chanel, wondering why she always had to be negative. Sweetie seemed extremely happy and she was elated for her.

Allie was the closest to Sweetie growing up so she could tell that Sweetie was hiding something, she just didn't know what. She decided to let it go and have some fun.

"Okay, enough with the sob stories, let's get you bitches pretty," squealed Allie. She loved giving the girls makeovers.

For the remainder of the night, the girls gossiped about reality TV, the injustices of the world, and everything else that came to mind. They even had a twerkin' contest, which Allie won much to Chanel's dismay.

Even with all the drama between them, the girls all went to bed that night thankful that they had each other.

CHAPTER 7

Allie was up at six a.m. Saturday morning prepared to go visit a few gyms to find a trainer that would fit her schedule and budget. After showering and brushing her teeth, Allie quickly fixed the kid's meal for the day and their breakfast. She made Spade a plate of leftovers and stuck a note on the refrigerator. She then took out two of both of her kid's favorite toys and sat them on the couch and she put both remotes on the end table. Once she was satisfied that she had done all she needed to do, she quickly ran out of the house, grabbing a banana on the way out.

She looked at the time: 6:20 a.m. She was getting faster and faster at getting her morning routine done. She pulled up to the first gym, Fitness Express, and walked in. A cheery young girl greeted her.

Allie instantly felt a good vibe from the place.

"Hi, I was actually looking to see if you had any trainers here today?" asked Allie politely.

"It's Saturday so they're all over the place. They're the guys with the highlighter yellow wristbands on."

Allie looked around and spotted a few trainers and thanked the receptionist before walking over to the one wearing the wedding band. She didn't need any of these men thinking she needed anything other than training.

"Hi, I'm Allie. I'm looking for a trainer who can train me five days a week for five weeks," Allie smiled.

"Wow, that's a lot. That's going to cost a pretty penny. I don't know if we even have anyone available that often," replied the old trainer guy.

"I have the money," she lied. "I just need somebody with dedication."

He let out a chuckle. "Okay, I got you." He looked around the gym for a few seconds before pointing to a light skin guy with a lot of tattoos. "He's new here and honestly, he's probably the only one that will commit to that schedule. He's good at what he does; he just doesn't have that clientele yet."

Allie really didn't have room to be picky so she walked over to the man, whose name she didn't even know.

"Hey, I was looking for a hardworking, dedicated, skilled trainer that can work with me for five days a week, five weeks straight. Word is you're the man that can get it done."

"Oh yeah?" he laughed, happy to know that he was being talked about already. Allie could see in his eyes that she had given him a major ego boost and he would likely say yes.

"What is it that you want to work on?"

"I'm doing this for a class so I don't know," she shrugged.

"I don't have a problem training you, but I need to know what you want out of this. I need something that's going to help motivate you."

Allie felt naked. She walked over there with the confidence of a queen, but now she felt like nothing more than a peasant. She didn't know what she wanted to work on because there was so much wrong with her. Allie tried to ignore it, but she knew she had let herself go. At one time, Allie was what all men wanted. Back when being a yella bone was in style Allie was at the top of the list with long pretty hair, nice legs, and an ass out of this world. All of Allie belonged to Spade, who had been her boyfriend since she was fifteen years old.

After having kids, going to school, and being in love, Allie had let herself go. The only time she got to eat was late at night while she was studying, then sleep afterward. Allie began gaining weight, she stopped getting her hair done, and she just stopped caring about her appearance overall unless she went out. By no means was Allie sloppy, she just didn't have the physique she should have at the age of twenty-three.

"I don't know. I guess I need to lose this baby fat and tone my legs," she answered.

"What is it that you don't like about your legs?" he asked.

Allie grew annoyed at his question. Why did it freakin' matter? "Umm, I don't know. I just would like them stronger."

"What *do* you like about your legs?"

Allie put her hand on her hips. "They're nice legs," she snapped.

"Who told you that you have nice legs?" he questioned with a smirk on his face.

Allie frowned her face. "Excuse me, I have some sexy legs under these sweatpants. My man loves my legs," she retorted in a matter of fact type of way.

The trainer began to laugh. "There it is, you want to tone your legs for your man. He can be your motivation."

Allie laughed at the way he pulled that out of her. "That was good, you got me."

He nodded his head and extended his hand. "Heem."

"Allie." She extended her hand to shake his. Allie recognized his dimple instantly and slid her hand away from him. She didn't want him to feel the sweat that had just accumulated. She was so hell bent on getting him to agree to train her that she didn't notice how fine he was.

Heem let out a small chuckle seeing how flustered Allie got. He looked at the young lady who was so hidden underneath big clothes and realized that she needed to fall in love with herself again.

"So, Heem, how much is this going to cost me and can I set up a payment plan?" asked Allie bluntly. She wasn't about to waste her time beating around the bush.

Heem took notice to the serious expression on her face. She thought she needed this for class, but she really needed it for herself.

"I'll tell you what, if you trust my judgment, give me one hundred percent dedication, and do as I say, it's on me," he offered.

Allie thought about his terms and felt a bit uneasy. "Do as you say?"

"Within reason," he smiled. "Nothing outlandish, but it may be things that will pull you out of your comfort zone. But that ties into trusting me and you giving your all."

"I won't feel comfortable not paying you anything. Will fifty dollars a week work?"

"Make it forty and we got a deal," smiled Heem. He saw a small smile creep onto her face as she nodded her head and walked away.

"I'll be here Monday at six," she called over her shoulder.

Heem watched her walked away knowing she was hiding a lot under them big ass pants she had on.

"We're going to Chick-Fil-A for lunch boss, you want something back?" asked Travis's receptionist Wendy.

Travis sat at his desk and rubbed his temples. Here he was on a Saturday working overtime to take Nina on this trip to Jamaica she'd been bugging him about and he couldn't even get a lunch. Normally, he would decline but given what happened the night before, he needed a break.

"You know what, Wendy? I will go," he agreed, standing up. Travis had just been given the manager position at the construction company where he worked and had been under a lot of stress. When he got home, all he wanted was a nice dinner, a shower, sex, and some peace and quiet but that's been impossible.

Travis didn't know what he was doing wrong but he felt his marriage was falling apart. He met up with Wendy and his co-worker Mike at the Chick-Fil-A around the corner from their job.

"What's the deal, boss man? You seem to be a little down lately," Wendy commented once they got their food.

"Man, we only have an hour for lunch. Don't get me started," sighed Travis shaking his head.

"They said mo' money, mo' problems," Mike added as he ate his chicken.

"Shit, ain't that the truth," Travis chuckled. He couldn't catch a break at work or at home. "I'm just under a lot of pressure so if I'm hard on y'all don't take it personal."

"Shit, I don't pay your ass no mind anyway," Mike replied, waving Travis off. "How's the wife?"

Travis let out a sigh. "Shit, I couldn't even tell you. Women are some complicated ass people."

"Excuse me!"exclaimed Wendy, putting up a hand. "I am sitting here, you know."

"I'm aware," laughed Travis. "I just can't figure women out."

"We're complex. But that's why men can't get enough of us," explained Wendy, looking seductively at her boss. Travis was very attractive in a rugged sort of way. He reminded her of

38

Michael Ealy in Barbershop. From what she knew, he was a stand-up guy and she didn't mind him standing up in her.

"Y'all crazy as hell, not complex," Travis fired back.

"Your wife seems so nice though," said Wendy.

Travis laughed. "She's nice alright. She just so fucking stubborn to the point where I don't know who wear the pants in that mother fucker."

Wendy sat back and took note. *So, he likes a woman who can submit*, she thought. "See, I believe in catering to my man: fixing his food, running his bath, giving him head. Those types of things. But men don't appreciate that."

"Shi-it,"belted Travis. If he had that type of woman, he would worship the very ground she walked on.

"You just ain't messing with the right type of men," offered Mike.

Wendy smiled. She liked the way the conversation was going. It wouldn't be long until her boss was between her legs making her call out his name.

"Yeah, but the good men are already taken. Usually by women who don't even appreciate them," flirted Wendy.

Travis ate his waffle fries and thought about what Wendy said. Did Nina appreciate him? It seemed more and more like the answer was no. Travis thought about his relationship with Nina and how it had been all about her.

She didn't want kids, so they haven't had any. She didn't want a beach wedding, she wanted to be married in a mansion, so Travis worked hard to afford to marry her in a mansion. Nina wanted the big townhome they stayed in, so he got it for her. But what was he getting? He hardly got sex or head and lately he couldn't even get a decent meal.

But her friends? They got her undivided attention. Travis hated to sound jealous but all he wanted was his wife back. Thinking of Nina caused him to lose his appetite.

"Sorry to cut this break short, I need to get back and handle some business," Travis apologized as he stood.

Wendy smiled to herself knowing their talk had prompted him to re-evaluate his relationship. She was taking Travis. St. Claire from his wife, it was her duty. He was polite, hardworking, loving, and fine as hell and obviously Nina didn't know how to treat him.

Travis walked to his car and called Nina. He always called her when he travelled from one place to the other, just to let her know he made it safely. He asked her to do the same but it rarely happened.

"Hey baby, what you doing?"

"Trying to finish up everything for the party tonight," said Nina who was frantically running around her house. She was having a party for the 4th of July in her backyard.

"Oh okay. I miss you," he flirted.

"Travis, I'm trying to get the house together, call me later."

Before he could object, the line went dead. Travis tried to keep his cool but he was slowly starting to wonder if there was something else out there. Obviously, the woman he married had better things to do than please her man.

CHAPTER 8

"Jaheim, why can't you come with me?" pouted Chanel. She was in the mirror fixing her makeup to go to Nina's pool party.

"I told you already, Chanel. My nephew's party is today. I'll try to make it later," he replied.

"Something is almost more important to me. This morning, it was the gym now it's your nephew," whined Chanel.

Jaheim laughed at his childish girlfriend. "I'm glad I did go to the gym today, I secured a new client."

"Oh, that's good." Chanel sounded uninterested. She was pissed that Jaheim wasn't coming to the party. What's the point in having a fine ass boyfriend if you could never show him off? Of all her friends, Jah only knew Travis and Nina, and that's because he grew up with Travis.

"You can't be mad at me Chanel, you told me about the party at the last minute," reasoned Jah.

"I thought I did tell you," lied Chanel. Truth is, Chanel wanted Eric to go but of course, he declined in the rudest way possible. Chanel liked Jaheim. He was nice, his sex was good, and he was good to look at but Eric still had her heart.

When they started their love affair, Chanel knew Eric was with Talia but he was supposed to leave her. He claimed to be so miserable and trapped, but as soon as Chanel got pregnant, he started singing a different tune. He told her he would never leave his wife, hoping she would abort their son. When that didn't happen, he became the asshole he is today.

"I'll be at the next event, I promise," Jah leaned in and kissed her neck softly. She stuck her tongue at him through the mirror.

"You better be or I'm going to start thinking you're ashamed of me," Chanel joked.

41

"Never that. You fine as hell and you know it," he jested, walking out of the bathroom.

"You damn right I do," Chanel replied with conviction.

Truth is, Chanel didn't feel beautiful at all. It had been something she was called many times as an adult but as a child, she was tormented for the color of her skin. Chanel was raised by her light skinned father, who married a white woman, who in turn had lighter skinned babies. They would always tease Chanel and tell her that her skin was dirty. Her father didn't make it any better. He would get so drunk sometimes that he would simply call her "the black one." Naturally, she grew up resenting what so many people tell her is beautiful. They see beauty; she sees pain. They see smooth skin; she can still feel the scars. They see a glow, but all Chanel sees is darkness.

So to hide the pain, she bought expensive hair, expensive clothes, and sucked on expensive dicks; whatever she could do to try to run far away from the girl that stared back at her every morning.

Chanel gazed in the mirror with a plastered smile on her face. She batted her lashes and poked out her lips as she posed for selfies to put out for the world to judge.

"Feeling fabulous," she muttered as she typed the caption then posted to her Instagram page. Chanel sighed and walked into the closet filled with material things. She thumbed through a few outfits trying to find something to wear.

She finally settled on a pair of denim shorts, a white crop top, and red Chuck Taylor sneakers. Fuck it, she thought, Why not be festive?

After she curled her hair to perfection, Chanel grabbed her purse, Chanel of course, and skipped to her Bentley. She threw on her shades and snapped back into diva mode.

"She's on her way to shut the party down," she giggled to herself, speaking in third person again.

42

Spade sat in the backyard smoking a sweet as he waited for Allie to get dressed. Her mother had picked up the kids earlier that day so it was just the two of them at the house. Normally, they would be sexing in every room, but this time was different.

They were so distant; it was almost unbearable to be in the same room together. Spade tried to figure out when it got to that point. He knew he was to blame for their problems, but it wasn't like Allie to let their issues go on so long. She normally would nip the shit in the bud immediately.

As he inhaled the smoke, Spade realized he might really lose Allie this time. His worst fear may have come true.

For much of Spade's life, he was praised for almost anything he did. Whether it was football, basketball, dressing, or pulling a bitch, he could do it all. And the rare instances where he did mess up, people made excuses for him.

Not Allie. He loved her so much because she kept him on his toes. All that fly talking didn't mean a thing to her. Spade fell in love with her instantly. Just like that, at sixteen, he knew who he wanted to spend the rest of his life with. He wasn't perfect because he was still young and had more than a few slip-ups but in the end, it was always Allie. Spade felt that it would always be Allie.

When she gave birth to his children, a boy and a girl like they wanted, he just knew they were on cloud nine. But shit start getting rough. They were arguing over the smallest things and Spade began to drink. He would occasionally smoke but usually a beer would do the trick. Over time, one beer no longer did it for him. Then he started smoking weed again after five years.

After that, things just began falling apart. They were getting behind on bills because Spade couldn't stop drinking his problems away. Ironically, he was selected for a random drug test and failed and was fired on the spot the day after he started back smoking.

Spade felt terrible about not being able to provide for his family how a man should do. He just hadn't gotten out of that slump to pick himself back up and start searching again.

Spade put out the sweet and walked into his house. He entered the restroom where Allie had on a sundress with the some sandals.

"You still have the nicest pair of legs I've ever seen," complimented Spade.

Allie spun around to see her soul mate leaning in the doorway with a smile on his face. She wasn't sure what had gotten into him but she was happy to see him smiling.

"Thank you, baby," she replied, walking over to give him a kiss.

Spade put his arm around her waist and squeezed her. "I love you Alyssa."

"I love you too Jeremy," Allie replied.

"I'm going to get my shit together, Allie. I can't lose my family," Spade told her seriously.

"I know it, baby. When everything and everyone is nowhere to be found, you will always have us."

"I believe that. I truly believe that," agreed Spade, nodding his head.

"Babe, guess what Jeremiah had Jerricka doing earlier?"

"What?"

"The Nae Nae," laughed Allie. "She was in here moving her arms and just dancing. It was funny..."

Allie kept rambling on about the kids when Spade noticed that the only time they really talk and laugh together was when it was concerning the kids. Once again, Spade felt like he was losing all control.

"Did you hear me, babe?" quizzed Allie.

"Yeah, I did." Spade's eyes shifted around the room. Allie just continued talking like it was nothing. Spade couldn't shake the feeling that he was losing everything he loved. This time last year, Allie would have never bought that lie.

Guess she was sick and tired of being sick and tired.

CHAPTER 9

Nina paced her backyard making sure everything was in order for the party she was hosting. She looked at the décor, which looked nice as always. Under the tent in her backyard, Nina had a long table sat out with a white table cover that looked much more expensive than it was. She had three centerpieces on the table, two blue and one red. She also had bows on the chairs, alternating from red white and blue.

"How does it look?" questioned Nina when she saw Travis walking over.

"It definitely looks like you love your country, babe," he laughed, walking closer to her.

Nina was so busy asking herself what was missing from the table that she didn't notice when Travis leaned in to give her a kiss.

"Napkins!" She remembered, snapping her fingers. "How could I forget napkins?"

Travis shook his head and walked over to the cooler to get himself a beer. Nina was slipping in so many ways and he just couldn't figure out why. As he sipped his beer, his mind couldn't help but wander back to his conversation with Wendy. Dinner, head, and a bath sounded great to him. He wondered what he had to do to get some of that treatment.

"Travis, why are you just standing there? Can you help me with something instead of just looking crazy? Make yourself useful," suggested Nina, with her hand on her hip.

"I made myself useful when I went to work this morning. All this shit you doing is on you," he replied, gulping the remainder of his beer and walking off.

Nina rolled her eyes at her husband who had been so bitchy lately. She didn't have time to cater to his ego; she had a house full of guests on the way.

"The queen has arrived!"

Nina turned around and watched Chanel walked towards her looking like a model. She envied Chanel's flawless skin and long legs.

They hugged and checked each other out.

"Bitch, you cute!" squealed Nina.

"Ain't I?" Chanel answered while flipping her hair. "You're looking good yourself, thickums."

Nina was dressed in an olive green jumper with tan wedges. Her hair was up in a high bun and her cheekbones were contoured for the Heavens. Chanel wished she had Nina's confidence. Even though she was the thickest of them all, Nina was bad to the bone. She wore her weight very well.

"Where's Jaheim?" Nina looked over Chanel's shoulder in search of her date.

"He had to go to his nephew's party," Chanel pouted. "Sooner or later, Allie and Sweetie are gonna think I'm making his ass up."

Nina laughed and walked arm and arm with Chanel into the house. Chanel looked around and noticed her friend's husband was absent. "Where's Travis?"

Nina threw her hand up. "Probably somewhere changing his tampon."

"Nina!" Chanel scolded. "That was out of line."

Nina shrugged. "Every time I look around, he's looking at me crazy. Like literally, staring at me in disgust. I don't know what his problem is."

47

Chanel furrowed her brow. "Have you tried talking to him?"

Nina pulled the ribs out of the oven and lied straight through her teeth. "Yeah. He don't wanna talk."

Truth is, Nina realized she hadn't been talking to Travis. She made up her mind that she would make it up to him that night. She and Chanel walked back outside to check on the rest of the food.

But what she didn't realize was that Travis had heard every word she said and was fuming on the inside. Nina had been a bit disrespectful in the past, but the way she just disrespected him to her friend was unacceptable.

Travis walked into the bedroom pacing back and forth trying to calm his nerves. He wanted to march outside and tell Nina a thing or two about herself but he would never want to cause his wife embarrassment. As hard as it was for him to act like everything was okay, Travis refused to ruin the party for everyone.

"Nina, where-" Sweetie stopped dead in her tracks when she saw Travis pacing. "I'm so sorry; Chanel said Nina was probably in here."

"It's fine," Travis fumed trying to compose himself.

"Is everything okay?" Sweetie asked with concern. She'd never seen Travis look so stressed.

"Yeah, just had a long week. But it's time to turn up," said Travis, clapping his hands.

Sweetie giggled and shook her head. "Turn up!"

Travis laughed hard because Sweetie was so shy and reserved that it was funny to hear those words from her. When they turned around the corner, Noah was standing there with a weird expression on his face.

"I was looking for you," he smiled at Sweetie. It wasn't a genuine smile though; it almost looked wicked.

"I was looking for Nina," she smiled back at him.

"Nina just walked outside. I don't know how you missed her," said Noah with a far off expression in his eyes.

Sweetie kind of stuttered before shrugging her shoulders. "I don't know either."

Travis felt awkward standing between them so he decided to make his exit. "Noah," he said nodding his head.

"Sorry about that, I was just looking for Jameka because our daughter called. How's it going, man?" asked Noah as he reached out to shake Travis's hand.

"Shit, I can't complain. Ready to let loose tonight," confessed Travis.

"You and me both," agreed Noah, nodding his head but still gazing at Sweetie.

There was a lot of commotion going on outside so Travis, Noah, and Sweetie all rushed to the backyard to see what the hell was happening.

Allie and Spade pulled up to Nina's house around six pm. As usual, they were the last ones to make it.

"Damn it, I thought we would beat Noah and Sweetie this time," Allie joked as they walked up and greeted their friends, who were standing in the front yard. The car ride to Nina's was mostly silent, just casual conversation here and there.

"That was you taking all day," laughed Spade.

49

"I was trying to perfect my bun, that's hard work." Allie patted her bun playfully.

Spade put his arm around Allie and pulled her close to him. "It paid off. You look beautiful."

He noticed a genuine smile sweep across Allie's face and he couldn't resist leaning in to kiss her.

"Aww, look at the lovebirds," beamed Nina as they approached her and Chanel.

"Pull through bun!" Yelped Chanel, hugging Allie. "I love your hair."

"Thank you, legs," countered Allie, checking Chanel out.

Spade rolled his eyes. "Hey bun, hey legs," he mocked. "What happened to just using people's names?"

"Whatever, hater," laughed Chanel. She and Spade had always gotten along fairly well despite her and Allie's constant bickering.

After speaking to Nina, Spade looked around. "Where's the fellas?"

"I think they're in the house," Nina replied. "Let me-"

"I'M GOING TO FUCK YOU UP!"

All of their heads turned in the same direction. An angry Eric was speed walking in their direction. He looked so angry, you could damn near see smoke shooting out of his head.

Allie quickly called out, "What the fuck?"

Eric stomped toward them, fuming. When he got close and reached into his pocket, Spade quickly pulled out his gun and pointed it in Eric's face.

The girls screamed in fear.

"Whoa!"Eric retreated, holding up his hands, with a hoop earring dangling from his fingers.

Noah, Travis, and Sweetie rushed outside with confused expressions. By the time they made it over to the where the madness was, Spade's gun was tucked away safely and Eric was going off on Chanel.

"You can't just walk up on people like that," warned Spade. He had changed a lot but he didn't take any chances these days.

Allie grabbed Spade's hand and gave it a squeeze to calm him down. He was still on edge about Eric just walking up on them so aggressively.

"What's going on?" Travis inquired.

"This bitch left her fucking earring in my bed for my wife to find, "Eric growled, glaring at Chanel. She stood there unbothered while Eric's eyes shot daggers at her.

"You said you checked the bed," shrugged Chanel, secretly loving the fact that he was in the doghouse with his wife.

"You keep trying to ruin my fucking family, I will beat your ass," growled Eric.

"Say, bruh. You not going to threaten this lady in front of me. It's bad enough you've already disrespected my partner's house," Spade yelled, yanking away from Allie.

"Relax, fellas," Travis offered, stopping Spade from walking up on Eric. "We can talk about this like adults."

"Ain't shit to talk about, he needs to fuckin leave," spat Nina.

"I'm going to leave and as a man, I apologize for the way I approached the situation but that bitch is sneaky," said Eric, pointing at Chanel.

"Whatever, nigga," Chanel responded dryly as she yawned, clearly bored with the conversation.

Allie and Nina pulled Chanel away from the drama, while Sweetie was holding on to Noah.

"I'm really sorry, fellas. That bitch is just trying to ruin my marriage," complained Eric. He rarely got out of character but he knew Chanel left her earring on purpose. Granted he was wrong for sleeping with Chanel in the bed he shared with his wife, but she was always on his side of the bed so the fact that Talia found the earring under her pillow showed him that Chanel knew exactly what the hell she was doing.

"You're ruining your own marriage, E," reasoned Travis.

"Especially bringing her to the house. You take your thots to a hotel room," Noah replied absent-mindedly.

Spade, Travis, and Eric all looked at Noah in shock, seeing as how Sweetie was standing right next to him.

Noah noticed the look his boys were giving him but couldn't figure out what he said wrong. Sweetie eased Noah's arm from around her shoulder and walked over to where the girls were standing. She was just going to pretend Noah didn't just go there.

"You tripping man," laughed Travis looking at Noah.

"What happened? What I do?"Noah's shoulders were hunched as he tried to figure out what he did wrong.

They all laughed at how clueless he was. "Don't even worry about it," Travis dismissed.

"My bad for pulling out my pistol. I just don't like that hoe ass domestic violence shit," admitted Spade, still a little pissed off.

"I wouldn't put my hands on her. The shit just set me off." Eric was still burning up on the inside despite his efforts to calm down.

Spade nodded but didn't say anything else. He didn't have respect for Eric for trying to be a tough guy knowing he was in the wrong. If he wasn't cheating on his woman, he wouldn't be in that position.

After a few more awkward moments of silence, Eric said, "Well, I'll holla at you boys another time."

When Eric walked away, Travis looked at Spade shaking his head."You good, bro?"

"I'm straight, I just don't like that shit. Big ass niggas trying to intimidate these females. Any nigga that gotta be that aggressive is a bitch deep down," Spade observed. He'd experienced domestic violence first hand with his mother and he didn't go for that shit. He hardly ever even raised his voice at Allie.

Noah looked on in silence not knowing what to say seeing as how he didn't know Eric well. He hardly knew Travis and Spade but he dealt with them on account of his wife.

Meanwhile, Chanel was reading the text message Eric sent her about how he was through with her and blah blah. She'd be in his bed again in no time so she wasn't concerned.

"Chanel, are you listening to me?" Sweetie questioned as she snapped her fingers.

Chanel looked at her friend. "What?"

Sweetie shook her head. "You need to leave him alone. He's married and clearly in love, so just stop."

"He can't be that much in love if he still sleeping with me," Chanel countered.

"That's not true. Sometimes men are just stupid," said Sweetie adamantly.

Chanel raised one eyebrow. She decided to just let it go. Sweetie was married so Chanel could understand why she had such a problem with what she was doing.

"It's always some drama, all I wanted was to have a good time," complained Nina, shaking her head.

"Well damn, my bad. I didn't think he would come here starting shit," replied Chanel walking away. "I'm going to get a drink."

Chanel walked away from her friend's judgmental stares. As she was getting her drink, she saw Noah whispering on the phone to somebody. She pretended to mind her business as she eavesdropped on his conversation.

"I'm busy now, I'll handle it later.... I know.... I'll make Jameka do it, no worries... I'll see you later tonight... Love you too Brandi."

Chanel quickly grabbed a wine cooler and walked away, wondering who the hell Brandi was and what was Noah going to *make* Sweetie do.

CHAPTER 10

"Okay, okay it's Allie's turn," slurred a drunken Nina. They had been laughing, drinking, and partying for hours and almost everyone was wasted. They were currently playing a game of truth or dare.

Sweetie picked a card out of the truth bowl. "Allie, if you were a homosexual, who in this room would you hit on?"

Travis erupted with laughter. "The fuck kind of question is that?"

Allie scanned the room before answering. "I would take a tall glass of Chanel."

The ladies began screaming and laughing. "Really?" squealed Nina.

"Yes, y'all know I love me some chocolate," Allie leaned over and kissed Spade's lips.

"All that screaming y'all doing is out of control," laughed Spade.

"That's all I heard last night. Screaming and giggling," added Travis, shaking his head. "Makeup and wine night needs to be at one of y'all house next time." He pointed his finger back and forth between Spade and Noah.

"It's Mascara and Moscato," Sweetie corrected.

"Close enough," joked Spade. He was truly enjoying himself and happy that Allie was having a good time.

"Allie, pick someone to go next."

"Spade," she said quickly, smiling at her man. She loved seeing him full of life. That's the man she fell in love with. "Truth or dare bae?"

"Dare."

55

She pulled out a card and giggled. "It says to breathe on my lips for a minute without kissing me."

Spade laughed and put his lips to Allie's. They didn't last ten seconds before they were tonguing each other down.

"Alright, alright!"Chanel groaned, mad that Jah still couldn't make it. "Sweetie, you're next. Truth or dare?"

Sweetie decided to go against her normal answer. "Dare."

A plethora of gasps spread throughout the room before laughter. Sweetie never picked dare so everyone was surprised. She gave every person that was snickering the middle finger and her best mad face.

Spade reached in the dare bowl and pulled out a card. "Challenge someone in here to a twerk-off."

Sweetie looked around the room. "Allie's ass is way too big, that's not fair. Chanel stays in the clubs, so I guess it's on Nina."

Nina stood up and laughed. Allie pressed play on her phone. "Ten seconds, go!"

"Throw that ass in a circle, throw that ass in a circle."

Nina and Sweetie tried their best attempt at twerking before falling on the ground overcome with laughter.

They played a few more round before everyone got tired. "Y'all can crash here tonight if y'all don't want to drive," offered Travis.

"Cool, I call the guestroom." Spade stood up and stretched, ready to call it a night.

"I'll take the couch," Chanel said casually.

"Noah and Sweetie, y'all can crash in the man cave," offered Travis.

"Ok thanks" Sweetie shrugged her shoulders. She didn't care where they slept, she was just ready to lay down.

"Actually, we won't be staying," revealed Noah, looking at Sweetie.

"Oh, okay. Well I guess not." Sweetie became fidgety and almost child-like as she mumbled the words.

"You sure man? It's no problem. It's not safe out there around this time," said Travis. It was nearly one in the morning. They were all pretty wasted, and he was concerned.

"Nah, man we have something to do in the morning," replied Noah casually. "Thank you for inviting us, though."

They said their goodbyes and Noah and Sweetie were out the door.

"Chanel you want to sleep in the bed with Allie? I can crash on the couch," Spade offered. He couldn't let a woman sleep on the couch while he rested comfortably in a bed.

"I don't know, your wife might try to take my booty while I'm sleep," joked Chanel. "She just admitted she wanted a tall glass of me."

Allie laughed. "Thank you for being such a gentleman, babe."

"I'm cool on the couch, Spade. Thank you, though," replied Chanel.

"Bet, goodnight y'all. You don't have to tell me twice," muttered Spade as he retreated up the stairs.

Noah drove silently to their three-bedroom home. Sweetie gazed out of the window intensely, not knowing why Noah seemed so uptight.

Once they made it home, Sweetie walked into the restroom to turn on the shower.

Noah walked behind Sweetie as she wrapped her hair in the mirror. "Did you have fun bae? I really-"

WHAP!!

Before Sweetie could finish her sentence, Noah had hit her across her head. The force from the blow of her angry husband caused Sweetie to cry out in pain. Her ears began to ring as she gazed at him through the mirror.

"What-What did I do?" She trembled. Noah's hits were becoming harder and harder and soon, it would be impossible to hide the bruises.

"Didn't you tell me that Travis wasn't going to be at the house, huh?" he asked. His face was in a tight scowl and his eyes were full of rage.

"I didn't know he was there," Sweetie said with desperation in her voice. "He never came downstairs, I swear."

Noah reached back and sent a powerful blow to Sweetie's mouth. The bitter taste of blood seeped on Sweetie's tongue as she whimpered in pain. She had learned that the louder she was, the madder he became so she stayed as quiet as she possibly could.

"You lil lying ass bitch," growled Noah as he grabbed Sweetie by her hair and swung her onto the ground. "I saw the way y'all was laughing and joking. You think I'm stupid, huh?"

Sweetie curled into the fetal position on the ground. "Noah, please!" She cried. She wasn't sure what hurt most, the fact that his fists were so violently pounding her flesh or the fact that he promised her it would never happen again.

Noah ignored the pleas of his wife as he punched her everywhere besides her face. When he was satisfied that she had learned her lesson, he stood up and kicked her. "Stupid bitch."

Sweetie lay helplessly on the floor, praying that God spared her life. Noah could get so upset sometimes that he completely blacked out and didn't realize the pain that he was causing her. At least, that's what she told herself.

"Tell me you're sorry and it will never happen again," Noah snarled as he towered over her like a monster.

Sweetie shuddered and fought to make her words audible through her sobs and chattering teeth. "I-I'm sorry. It won't happen again," repented Sweetie.

Noah looked at his pitiful wife and got pissed off again. "Lying bitch."

Sweetie frowned her face. "Noah, I didn't know he was there. I promise."

"But you knew what you were doing when you were shaking your ass for all them niggas to see, didn't you?"

Noah didn't wait for Sweetie's answer. He was pissed all over again. He grabbed her by her hair and tossed her on the bed. "You know what, bitch. Get back on the floor."

"Please stop, Noah." Sweetie begged her husband and pleaded with her eyes, but he was too hell bent on beating her ass to care.

"NOW!"

Sweetie quickly slid back on the floor and cried silently. She couldn't understand what made him so angry; she thought she was on her best behavior. Noah quickly dropped his pants.

"You want to be a slut, I'm going treat you just like one."

"Noah, please don't."

"Shut up and take this dick," he growled as he forcefully turned her over and entered her.

Sweetie grimaced in pain. She had fibroids so sex was normally painful for her even when Noah tried to be gentle.

Today, he had no mercy. He rammed into her while pulling her hair tightly. She chewed on her lip, which was already busted and prayed that he would finish soon. Sweetie closed her eyes and counted to seventy-five, trying her hardest to fight the pain that she felt throughout her entire body.

"Don't you ever shake your ass in the presence of another man? You hear me?" he growled in her ear.

"Yes," Sweetie whispered.

"Yes, what BITCH?" Noah spat before punching the back of her head.

"Yes, sir," Sweetie whimpered.

When Noah felt himself about to climax, he pulled out of Sweetie and released himself on her back.

"Clean yourself up," he demanded as he stood and pulled his pants up. He walked over to shower and opened the glass door, motioning for Sweetie to get in.

Sweetie used all of her strength to pull herself up and walk into the shower. Each step she took was more painful than the first but she didn't want to make Noah more upset so she quickly did as she was told.

"Ahhhh!" she screamed and jumped out the shower as soon as the water touched her skin. The water was so hot it felt like it was boiling.

"Get in now before I put your ass in here," threatened Noah.

Sweetie reluctantly stepped into the scalding hot water. The water burned her skin but the hurt cutting her soul was one she couldn't ignore.

Once he was satisfied that she was in the shower, Noah walked away.

Sweetie couldn't understand why the man she loved so much, the man who promised to love her forever, would hurt her so badly. Sweetie knew Noah shouldn't have drunk as much as he did. She was so busy with her friends that she allowed him to fall into that dark place.

Sweetie vowed that she would be a better wife to him. She was wrong for twerking in a room full of men; she didn't know what she was thinking. Sweetie stepped out of the shower and looked at her lip in the mirror. She then looked at her bruised naked body.

Sweetie's caramel complexion had so many spots of purple; they looked like they belonged there. She looked at her rustled hair and tired eyes and sobbed. She didn't know who she was anymore, but what she did know was if she tried to leave Noah Hartsford, he would kill her, their daughter, and then himself.

He told her that on many occasions, and she believed every word he'd said.

Meanwhile, back at Nina's house, Nina was in the restroom getting sexy for her man. She slipped into some lingerie after she showered; planning to show Travis how sorry she was for the way she had been acting lately.

Travis showered before she did, which was perfect because she wanted to catch him completely by surprise. Nina sprayed on a dab of Ralph Lauren Romance and checked herself out in the mirror. She had the BBW game on lock.

She pranced out of the restroom and stood in the doorway. Travis didn't flinch.

Nina cleared her throat. Travis looked over at her with a bored expression on his face. "You good?"

Nina tried her best to keep calm. "Sometimes. But tonight I wanna be bad." Nina crawled seductively into bed with him. Travis watched his wife but didn't feel moved by anything she was doing. Nina smiled seductively as she inched her fingers up his leg until she got to his penis, which was still soft.

She frowned her face. "What's wrong with you?"

"It's that time of the month, maybe I should go change my tampon," he sarcastically replied.

Nina looked into his hazel eyes and saw a flicker of pain. "Travis."

"You know what Nina, you're disrespectful. I would never speak that way about you, especially to my friends. The minute I start disrespecting you, they're going to feel like it's okay for them to do the same. You were out of line for that shit."

"I'm sorry you overheard that. I was just frustrated," Nina explained as she tried to grab his hand.

He quickly snatched away from her. "You're not sorry that you said it, you're sorry I overheard it." Travis shook his head and stood up. "Well, I'm not sorry that you have to hear that you've been acting like a selfish bitch lately and I'm tired of it!" he yelled.

"Travis, be quiet. We have guests."

"Don't tell me to be quiet in my fucking house! Pay a bill or two around here, then you can start making rules!" he fumed.

Nina looked at him with wide eyes. "Where is all this anger coming from?"

Travis let out a small laugh to keep himself from going all the way off. "I don't know Nina, maybe I don't eat enough, maybe I don't have enough sex; maybe I'm just not fucking happy!"

Nina sat on her bed, looking sexy as hell but she felt so lost and confused. "Are you really not happy Travis?"

Travis stared at his wife with intense eyes. "No, I'm not." He walked out of the room and went downstairs quietly, trying not to wake anybody. He slowly slid the backdoor open, noticing that it was unlocked. He figured he forgot to lock it earlier.

He walked over to the swing that sat in front of the small lake that was in his backyard and was stunned to see another figure sitting there.

"Did I scare you?"

Travis took a closer look and noticed Chanel smoking what looked like a cigarette, but he was all too familiar with the smell of what was being put in the air.

"Nah" Travis replied, sitting down next to Chanel.

"It's so peaceful back here." Chanel passed the sweet to Travis, who gladly took it from her.

After a few moments of gazing off in the distance, Travis finally spoke up. "I don't know how much longer I can do this."

Chanel wasn't shocked at his statement. She could tell by the way Travis and Nina interacted with one another that some things weren't right.

"You gotta fight, Trav."

"Nobody wants to have to fight alone, Chanel," Travis's voice was full of sadness and desperation.

"She loves you so much Travis."

"Why can't I see it? Why can't I feel the love that she has? Cus all I got is leftover Nina. When she's done over extending herself to everybody, I get what's left of her when I give her all of me," said Travis.

Chanel sighed, wishing she had the answer. Travis was really a good man and Nina did take advantage of it to some extent. "You have to understand, Nina's been hurt badly before."

"So have I, Chanel. I've been hurt, I've been lied to, and I've been cheated on. But I've done more than prove myself to Nina. If she wanted to protect her heart, she shouldn't have married me. I'd do anything in the world for that woman and all I want is a little love and affection."

"Nina works because she wants to," continued Travis. "She doesn't pay a single bill in this house. Every dime she makes, she keeps and I don't complain. All I ask is that she fix me a decent meal, offer me a massage after a long day, or break me off with a lil sumthin' sumthin'. Hell, I'll even take one out of three. But I can't even get a conversation out of her."

Chanel sat there speechless not knowing what to say. She loved Nina to pieces, but she was dead wrong.

"I'll talk to her, Travis. I'll let her know where you're coming from," said Chanel, forgetting she had the sweet.

She tried to pass it to Travis, who declined. She felt so bad for him sitting there.

"I don't want my marriage to fall apart, Chanel. Tell me what I'm doing wrong," he pleaded.

Chanel patted Travis' shoulder as they sat rocking back and forth on the swing. Nina had better get her shit together, thought Chanel. She wished she had a man that loved her as much as Travis obviously loved her friend.

She vowed to call Nina on her shit, she wouldn't be a friend if she just sat back and watched them self-destruct.

CHAPTER 11

Allie woke up and looked at the time. 6:00 AM. She was so used to waking up early with her kids that her body didn't know what sleeping in meant. She looked over at Spade who was still sleeping peacefully and kissed his cheek.

His eyes fluttered a little but he didn't wake up. Allie decided to cook breakfast for the house since she was already up. She crept down the stairs and saw Chanel still asleep on the couch. She was surprised to see that Nina was sitting at the bar in the kitchen having coffee.

"Morning beautiful," greeted Nina when she saw Allie walk into the kitchen.

"Morning love," she replied, walking over the refrigerator. She scanned Nina's food collection and decided to make biscuits, eggs, grits and cheese, bacon, fried sausage, and a few pancakes.

"You have all this food in here and you hardly cook," Allie noted as she put the ingredients on the counter.

"Travis buys all that food," replied Nina. She thought about their argument last night and decided to talk to Allie about it. "He thinks I neglect him."

Allie looked at Nina with a face that said "Duh."

"You think so too?"Nina was shocked that Travis wasn't the only one who felt that way.

"Nina, really? I can't speak for y'all everyday life but yes, you do. Yesterday, Sweetie and I both fixed our men's plate and you just sat there."

"Travis is very capable of fixing his own plate," Nina countered.

"They all are! But as a woman, it's important to make your man feel like the king of his castle," Allie explained.

"But Travis knows that he is the king" retorted Nina.

"Knowing and feeling are two different things. You know he loves you but you still expect him to show you, right?"

Nina nodded her head. "You're right."

"Just put your pride to the side. Let him lead you, Nina. That's all he wants."

Nina decided she was going to take Allie's advice. Although she wasn't married, she was able to keep a man happy for nine years so she obviously knew a thing or two.

As Allie effortlessly maneuvered through the kitchen, Nina imagined herself in that position and she didn't like the thought of it. She couldn't picture herself being happy living that life. She looked at Allie, who was a great mother and spouse, but she had so little time for herself. Everything was about the kids or Spade.

"It's about time y'all shut y'all rude asses up," yelled Chanel from the couch.

"Shut up, you old grouch," snapped Allie as she put the biscuits in the oven. "Nina, watch the biscuits please I need to go brush my teeth. Thank you for the toothbrushes, you're always on it."

Nina smiled, happy to know that her friends appreciate her kindness and dedication to them. "Anything for my girls."

Nina picked up her phone to call Sweetie, but decided to text her instead. It was still pretty early and she didn't want to interrupt anyone's sleep.

Nina: **Just making sure you made it home safely. Text me when you wake up.**

Sweetie: **srry. 4got 2 text u. hubby and I were all over each other (wink)**

Nina laughed at Sweetie's reply. She must have still been half asleep because she never texted that way.

"Well, Sweetie had a good night," announced Nina.

Allie and Chanel were now both sitting down on the couch. "Her and Noah didn't seem a little off to y'all?" Allie tilted her head, recalling how weird Sweetie seemed.

"You know what? They sure did." Chanel snapped her fingers. "They were so clingy almost."

"And secretive," responded Allie.

Nina looked at both of her messy friends in shock. "Are y'all serious? They seemed perfectly normal to me."

"That's cause you don't read between the lines, Nina," replied Chanel, slightly annoyed with how naive Nina was.

"That's because there are no lines to read in between." Nina was growing frustrated with the conversation.

"I don't know what the issue is, but they are not as good as it gets," mocked Allie referring to Sweetie's statement about her marriage.

"He was on the phone with somebody named Brittany or some name that starts with a B. Anyways, he told the girl that he loved her and that he was going to MAKE Sweetie do something," Chanel revealed.

"Bitch, what?" Allie's mouth dropped.

Chanel had the tendency to be over the top so Nina was sure she had put her own spin on what really took place. "I talk to Sweetie all the time. They are better than ever."

"When did you and Sweetie start talking so much?"Questioned Allie, curious to know when they became so buddy-buddy because for the last few months, she couldn't get hold of Sweetie to save her life.

"I don't know. When they moved, she reached out to me a few times for advice and we've kept in touch a lot since then."

Allie nodded her head. She made a mental note talk to Sweetie about why she rarely returned her phone calls while she was away but reached out Nina on several occasions.

"Well, I know Sweetie and she was acting weird all day up until truth or dare," shrugged Allie.

"So what exactly are y'all trying to say?"Nina asked, folding her arms and rolling her neck.

"We ain't trying to say nothing, Nina," replied Chanel waving her arms dismissively. She knew that Nina would go on and on about the subject and frankly, Chanel didn't care that much about the situation. She loved Sweetie but she had problems of her own and until Sweetie opened up to them, Chanel would act like she was clueless.

Allie got up and walked upstairs to check on her man. She was over Nina's bullshit. She could believe everything was all well and good with Sweetie, but Allie knew better.

She peeked in the room and saw Spade with her phone in his hand. He looked like he was focused on whatever he was looking at.

"Morning babe."

"Hey, what nigga you supposed to be seeing tomorrow?" asked Spade.

Allie looked at him, confused. "What are you talking about?"

"Think real carefully before you lie to me Allie," warned Spade, getting more and more pissed by the second. He looked at Allie sternly as he waited for her reply.

"I'm not going to see anyone tomorrow," Allie replied, trying to figure out where the hell all this bullshit was coming from.

Spade stared at her with a blank expression on his face, which caused Allie to wonder what the hell was really going on.

"Seriously? I'm not going anywhere but to the- oh! I'm starting with my new trainer tomorrow, but that's it," she replied.

"Oh okay," said Spade, tossing her phone on the bed.

Allie walked over and snatched her phone. She read the message that Spade was reading.

ARE WE STILL ON FOR TOMORROW?

"This must be the trainer. He must have gotten my number off the forms I filled out," she explained.

Spade nodded his head and stood up to stretch. "A'ight." He believed Allie; he just wanted to make sure that she would be honest with him.

"Do you not trust me or something?" Allie glared at Spade, impatiently waiting on his response.

"I trust you, Allie. I just so happened to look at your phone for the time and saw the message. That's all."

Allie didn't know whether she believed Spade or not. She had so many mixed feelings about them and their future. Allie wanted to be with Spade but she truly needed to find herself again.

"Okay, well breakfast is ready" Allie walked over and gave him a hug.

His embrace resembled one of a friendship hug, their kiss was so empty that Allie couldn't help but wonder if they'd lost their spark. Allie walked out the room hand-in-hand with her man but she'd never felt so far away from him in her life.

CHAPTER 12

Breakfast was unusually awkward. Because of their little spat, Nina wasn't really speaking to the girls and Travis wasn't speaking to her. Besides asking for the jelly or the syrup, the only sound in the room was the forks scraping against the plates.

Chanel was the first one to be over the bullshit. She ate quickly, washed her plate out and said her goodbyes. She wasn't one to kiss anyone's ass, so Nina could take her attitude and shove it for all she cared.

Once she made it to her apartment, Chanel took a nice long shower and lay naked across her bed. All she wanted to do was rest until her cousin brought EJ back home. When she heard her door open and close about an hour later, she knew her relaxation had come to an end.

She drug herself out of bed and threw on a robe. She walked into the living room and was shocked to see Eric in her kitchen.

"What the hell are you doing here?" asked Chanel, putting her hands on her hips.

When Eric licked his lips at her, Chanel realized that her robe wasn't tied. She sucked her teeth and repeated her question.

"I didn't think you would be here, you've been at your little boyfriend's house lately," said Eric as he eyed Chanel. He knew she was nothing but trouble but she was fine as hell.

"So when you got this place for me, you kept a spare key?" asked Chanel.

"Of course," replied Eric, searching her pantry for snacks.

"You can't just be popping up over here. What if my man was here?"

"I know to keep driving when I see the candy red Buick," replied Eric as he chewed on a honey bun.

Chanel was shocked and turned on at the same time. Eric had his own way of showing her how much he really loved her. She quickly regained her composure and cleared her throat. "Why are you here?"

"Because it's my favorite place to be. Aside from being inside you," he lusted.

Despite her pussy throbbing, Chanel rolled her eyes at Eric. "Tiff and EJ will be here any minute now so you should leave."

Eric walked over to where she was standing, looking like a chocolate goddess. "I'm sorry about what happened yesterday."

"You're good," Chanel said, finally tying her robe. She really wasn't in the mood to deal with Eric or his lies.

"Come give daddy a hug, Chanel," said Eric as he reached for Chanel.

She took a few steps backward. "Seriously, Eric. You need to leave."

Eric was shocked that Chanel was being so combative towards him. "What's your problem?"

"Nothing is wrong with me. You're not my man so I don't owe you shit, just like you always tell me. I don't want to fuck you today, that's all."

Chanel loved the confused look on Eric's face. She smirked at Eric before turning to walk away. Maybe he would learn to start appreciating her.

"Let yourself out, please and get that damn honey bun wrapper off my counter."

Chanel walked into her room and heard her cell phone ringing. She jumped on the bed and answered her cousin's call.

"Hey Tiff! You on the way?"

"No, the kids just got invited to a party so I'm going to keep EJ until tomorrow," answered Tiffany.

"That's fine," said Chanel, wondering what she could get into since she was kid-free again.

"Alright, see you then."

Chanel got up and walked into her living room only to find Eric still there. "I asked you to leave, Eric."

"I don't have nowhere to go. Talia trippin' right now so I need to crash on your couch," confessed Eric.

"Go to one of your friends houses!"

"I'm not going nowhere, Chanel," said Eric as he stretched out on the couch. Chanel let out a sigh and stomped back to her room and slammed the door.

She hadn't heard from Jaheim since he left her yesterday so she decided to do a pop up at his house. She refused to sit at home while Eric was laid up like he was *that nigga.*

Chanel grabbed her keys and walked out the house, not acknowledging Eric. It took her less than ten minutes to get to Jaheim's house. She called his phone to see if he would answer, but it went straight to voicemail, something it had been doing since last night.

Chanel walked up and knocked on the door. She could hear the television playing so she knew Jah was in there. After a few seconds, Chanel began knocking on the door at a rapid pace.

Moments later, Jah swung the door open. "What is wrong with you?

"What is wrong with you? Why the fuck haven't you been answering my calls?" Chanel asked as she brushed past him and searched for any signs of another bitch.

She walked into his bedroom and noticed his bed was neatly made. "Why is your bed made?"

Jaheim laughed at Chanel. He was confused and slightly amused at this outburst she was having. "My nephew threw my phone in the pool yesterday so I'm out of a phone and my bed is made because I was taught to make my bed when I get out of it."

Chanel couldn't argue with him because she never really paid attention to things like that. She wasn't sure if it was insecurity or her guilty conscience weighing her down. She decided it was both.

"I'm sorry, Jah," said Chanel, sitting on the edge of the bed. "I have trust issues and sometimes I over react."

"I know this already. Just give me a fair chance, okay? I'm a good guy and I really like your psychotic ass," said Jaheim.

Chanel looked up at him and smiled. It felt nice to be wanted and as hard as it would be, Chanel knew she had to leave Eric alone for good.

CHAPTER 13

Nina woke up at 5 am and made Travis a few breakfast burritos. She didn't have time to make him a lunch but she hoped he would take her efforts in consideration. She really did want to keep her marriage intact but she honestly felt that Travis was much too needy.

As she got dressed to head out to work, she shook Travis gently. "Babe, I'm on the way to work. I made you breakfast," she whispered.

Travis groaned and turned over, not really hearing what Nina said. Nina sighed and got dressed to head to work for the day.

Once in the car, Nina called Sweetie, who didn't answer the phone. She then thought about calling Chanel to see why she abruptly left breakfast the day before.

She dialed Chanel's number and waited patiently for her to answer the phone.

"Hello?" Chanel answered groggily.

"Chanel, what's the problem? Why did you just leave like that?"

"What time is it?" asked Chanel as she looked at the time. "Bitch, you did not call me at six in the morning about some bullshit."

"It's not bullshit; I want to know what the issue is with us. It seems like we've been at odds over petty shit."

"Nina, we're friends. We're going to argue, it's just what we do. I still love you the same. What you need to be doing is talking to your husband," replied Chanel.

75

Nina scoffed. "You worry about the two men you're sleeping with and I'll worry about my husband because we're good."

Chanel didn't even let Nina's words affect her. She simply sighed and replied, "Of course, I forgot you and Sweetie live the perfect lives with the perfect marriages."

"I didn't call you to argue, so if all you're going to do is snap at me then we can end this conversation now," said Nina.

The phone went silent much to Nina's annoyance. "Hello?" She looked at her phone only to find her home screen pulled up. *No this bitch didn't hang up on me*, thought Nina.

She was about to call Chanel back when Travis called her.

"Hey babe!" She answered cheerfully.

"Thank you for the breakfast beautiful," said Travis.

"You're welcome. Let me call you back though. Chanel just hung up in my face, she got me fucked up."

"Nina, is it that serious? I wanted to talk to you before I went in to work. We still have some things we need to discuss about our marriage," replied Travis.

"Can this wait until later? I don't want to go to work with that kind of drama on my mind," said Nina.

Travis looked at his phone in disbelief. His wife had just told him she and her friend were arguing, yet *he* was the one putting drama on her mind?

Travis followed Chanel's lead and hung up in Nina's face too. He was tired of fighting for a position in his wife's life.

Nina was too busy trying to send Chanel a nasty text that she didn't even notice the stop sign in front of her. By the time she heard the horns blaring, there wasn't anything she could do. Her body jerked forward as her face slammed into the airbag. Before she could comprehend what was happening, Nina had blacked completely out.

Sweetie rummaged through her drawers desperately looking for her phone. Since the Fourth of July party, Noah had been holding her phone hostage. She was sure her family and friends were trying to get in touch with her but she had no idea where Noah put it.

After searching all over the house, Sweetie walked into the kitchen and pulled out a carton of ice cream. She hated when she was on punishment. Noah didn't allow her to go to work or talk on the phone. She just felt trapped. She knew better than to complain, though. That was the life she'd chosen to live.

Sweetie sat at her dining room table and dug into the Butter Pecan ice cream in front of her. She had about two more hours before Noah got home so she chose to relax for a while before she started to clean the house.

The sound of the door opening caused Sweetie to jump from her seat. She quickly ran and put the ice cream away and turned on the water in the sink pretending she was busy.

Noah walked into the kitchen carrying his briefcase. Sweetie smiled at him. "Hey, babe. You're home early."

"Yeah, today was a slow day. Besides, I had to get Brandi. She's moving in today. Now I know you two haven't always gotten along but y'all are both very important to me so y'all need to respect each other."

Sweetie nodded her head and rolled her eyes when she heard him walk away. She knew that Brandi would be moving with them until she had her baby but Sweetie didn't like the damn girl. Family or not, she just wasn't Sweetie's cup of tea.

"Jameka!"

Sweetie jumped when Noah called her name. She quickly dried her hands and walked down the hallway to her room. "Yes, babe?"

Noah stood by their drawers looking confused. "What were you looking for?"

Sweetie cursed herself for forgetting to straighten them back up. She didn't expect him to be home for another few hours. "I was looking for my pink bra. This one was feeling a little tight."

Noah pointed at his drawer, which was partially open. "You thought it might have been in my drawer?"

Noah knew damn well all the drawers were closed when he left because that's a pet peeve of his. He hated doors, cabinets, drawers or anything of that nature to be left open.

He quickly lunged at Sweetie and grabbed her by the neck. "Why the fuck you always lying to me, huh?"

Sweetie stared at him, trembling. "I'm sorry; all I wanted was my phone to check on Dallas." Their daughter was with Noah's parents. That was also a part of her punishment; she couldn't see her daughter.

"All you had to do was ask," said Noah as he released his grip around her neck. He then kissed the red marks that were caused by his fingers.

He reached into his pocket and handed Sweetie her phone. "Call my mom."

Sweetie grabbed her phone and looked at him sadly. "Now?"

"Yes, now. You want to talk to Dallas, call her now."

Sweetie trembled as she dialed her mother in law's number. "Sweetie, are you okay?" asked Ruthie when she answered the phone.

Ruthie knew that her son was abusing Sweetie and she'd encouraged her plenty of times to leave him. She loved her son to death but the military did something to his mind. It caused him to become a completely different person and she feared for Sweetie's life a lot.

"I'm fine, Mama. How's Dallas?" said Sweetie, trying to sound as normal as possible.

"She's fine, child. She running around outside with Kelly and the kids," replied Ruthie. She loved keeping Dallas because she was such a good child. Additionally, she wanted to keep her far away from the madness that was going on in the Hartsford household.

"That's good. Have her call me when she comes in. I miss her a lot but I know you want her to stay for a few more days, so I'll let y'all enjoy the time you have together," replied Sweetie.

Ruthie could tell that Noah was somewhere close to Sweetie by the guarded way she was talking. Her first mind was to call him and tell him about himself but she knew it would be no use. She just hoped and prayed that Sweetie got out before it was too late.

"Alright, sugar. You take care of yourself, now. Call me if you need me," she said sadly. Her heart broke for that poor girl but it broke more for her grandchild. She feared that Dallas would end up with a dead mother and an incarcerated father.

As soon as the line disconnected, Noah snatched the phone away from her. "Your friends keep blowing your phone up. They are really bad influences on you Jameka"

Sweetie ignored Noah's comments as she stood In front of him, twiddling her thumbs. She didn't know how to react toward him anymore.

"You don't have to be afraid of me, Sweetie. I never try to hurt you. You just need to grow up and the only way that will happen is if you're punished when you make mistakes. You understand that, don't you?" Noah lifted Sweetie's chin and searched her eyes for an answer.

She nodded her head while she stared blankly back into his eyes.

"Good, now let's go get Brandi and make her feel comfortable," said Noah as he walked out of the room, smiling and humming to himself.

Sweetie let out a deep breath and promised herself she would find away to get herself out of that situation.

Allie walked into the gym dressed in a pair of basketball shorts and a white t-shirt. For some reason, she was extremely nervous about her first day of training.

She spotted Heem in the corner of the gym doing push-ups effortlessly. The way his skin was glistening with sweat caused Allie to feel things in places where she shouldn't have felt them.

She casually walked over to where he was and took a seat on the bleachers. It wasn't long before he noticed her sitting there.

"Alyssa, hey!" Greeted Heem. "I wasn't sure if you were going to make it or not, you didn't reply to my text."

"Sorry about that, I forgot," said Allie, remembering the trouble he almost caused by sending that text.

"It's no problem. Alright, let's get the assessment out the way first," said Heem, standing up and motioning for Allie to follow him.

"And call me Allie, please," she said following behind Heem, watching the sweat particles drip down his back.

"Cool," he replied, leading Allie into what looked to be a storage room.

Allie looked around the small room, wondering what the hell was going on. Noticing the expression on Allie's face, Heem laughed.

"It's not much, but it's mine," He shrugged his shoulders and grabbed his clipboard.

"What exactly is it?" asked Allie.

"It's my office," he answered. He pointed over to a wooden table. "There's my desk." He then pointed a stack of clear bins. "Those are my filing cabinets."

Allie laughed aloud. "Well, we all gotta start somewhere."

Heem shared the laugh with Allie before getting down to business. "Alright, first things first, let's get your height, weight, and measurements."

Allie shifted her weight to one side of her body. She wasn't comfortable with that. "Do we have to?"

"We do. How else will we be able to track your progress?" asked Heem, patiently. He could tell there were a lot of insecurities within Allie but he didn't know why. She was drop dead gorgeous in his eyes.

Allie still felt slightly uncomfortable but she didn't know what she'd expected; of course, she would have to step on the scale. "Okay."

Jaheim stood up and walked over to the scale and asked Allie to remove her shoes and step on. When he read her weight, he nodded his head and wrote the figure down on a piece of paper.

Allie squealed as she stepped off the scale. "How much?"

"I'm not telling you. I don't want you to get caught up in a number so unless you weigh yourself at home, it's a secret. I will weigh you each week and give you updates about your progress. The goal is for you to feel better and not be focused on a number dropping. At the end of your five weeks, if you want your results I will give them to you then. Deal?"

"Deal," said Allie, nodding her head. She liked the way he operated.

"Okay, now let me get your measurements," Heem said as he walked over to her. "Stand straight up," he instructed.

As he put the tape around her body, Allie realized that no man had ever been that close to her but Spade. Heem was being very respectful as he measured her body so she tried to relax a little.

Allie shifted her weight, which caused Jaheim to drop the measurer. He tried to catch it before it hit the ground, causing him to hit Allie's ass in the process.

"I'm so sorry," said Heem, embarrassed.

"You're good," replied Allie, smiling to herself. She knew he hadn't done it on purpose but she could only imagine how awkward he felt.

After jotting down her measurements, 36-29-42, Heem checked Allie out and noticed that she was doing herself a complete injustice by wearing all those baggy clothes.

"I'll be back," said Heem as he hurried out of the small space he called his office.

Allie sat for a while debating whether or not she wanted to see the numbers that Heem had written down. He left the clipboard within arms-reach but Allie decided against it.

When he returned, Jaheim was carrying a bag in his hand. "This may not be within your comfort zone but this is what I need you to wear in training."

Allie eyed the bag as he handed it to her. She pulled out the outfits and stared at her trainer. "What the hell is this?" She held up the sports bra in one hand and the shorts in the other.

"Listen, Allie. I need you to trust me. Follow me," he instructed. He led Allie to the workout area where he would be training her. The workout area had mirrors all over the place, a trait that Jaheim loved.

"This is where you'll be working out. Since you don't have access to your numbers, this is an opportunity for you to look at yourself and see the changes in your body and attitude over the course of the class. You'll go from seeing pain in your face to noticing how relaxed you are over time. You'll see the places that jiggle start to tone up. Trust me; it's for your own good."

Allie heard everything he said but she was unsure of herself. She wasn't that fine young cheerleader anymore. Allie had two kids and tons of problems and every stretch mark on her stomach and dimple on her ass was proof of that. Allie had no choice but to go along with the plan. Aside from needing the class in order to graduate, Allie really wanted to lose a few pounds.

"Okay, okay. I'll be back."

Allie walked to the dressing room and changed into her workout attire. She looked at herself in the mirror and grimaced. She wasn't happy with what she saw. Maybe that's why Spade seemed so distant; maybe Allie just didn't do it for him anymore.

She walked back into the training area feeling self-conscious. Jaheim took one look at her and saw the discomfort written all over her face. "I hope I don't offend you in saying this, but you are beautiful. A lot of women wish they had a body like yours."

Allie tried to play it cool but she could feel her face turning red. Every woman loved compliments and Allie was no different. "Thank you."

"Let's get to work," smiled Jaheim, happy that he could get Allie comfortable in her own skin once again.

CHAPTER 14

Travis was at work when he got the phone call that no husband wants to hear. The second he heard Nina had been involved in an accident, he left work immediately to be by his wife's side.

Once he arrived at the hospital and got checked in, he walked into Nina's room holding a bouquet of sunflowers because he knew they were her favorite. He was elated to hear that she wasn't seriously injured.

Nina's face lit up when she saw her husband walk through the door. Travis rushed to her side and kissed her softly.

"You scared me," he whispered as he stared into her eyes and brushed a few loose strands of hair off her face.

Nina didn't speak out of fear she would break down crying. She could have lost her life in the blink of an eye and the reality of that was so overwhelming. She reached her arms out and pulled Travis into a loving embrace.

"I love you so much, Trav."

"I love you, too baby," he replied, rubbing her back slowly while taking in her scent. Despite her flaws, Travis couldn't live without his wife.

There were a few soft knocks on the door before Nina's nurse walked in. "Hey, Miss Nina. How you feeling?"

"Better now that my husband is here," Nina smiled and grabbed Travis's hand, giving it a gentle squeeze.

"Good, good. I was just reminding you to call Chanel back. When she didn't answer earlier, you told me to remind you in an hour, so it's about that time," she said as she looked at her watch.

Nina nodded her head at her nurse and thanked her. She turned back to Travis with loving eyes only to find him glaring at her.

Travis looked at his phone to make sure he wasn't tripping. "Did she say an hour ago?"

Nina shrugged her shoulders. "Yeah, why?"

"Because I got the call twenty minutes ago," he said, standing up. "You called Chanel an hour ago but you called me, your husband, forty minutes later to let him know that you're laying in the fucking hospital?"

"Travis, I was going to call you to let you know that I was okay but I was calling Chanel because she was texting me-"

"I don't give a damn. I'm supposed to be the first person that crosses your mind when shit like this happens. You know what? I'm glad you're okay, Nina. I'm done with this shit."

Travis threw his hands in the air and walked out of Nina's room. He hated to be so harsh but that was his last straw. She called her friends first but them bitches still ain't here, he thought. He was sick and tired of coming second to Nina's friends. If she wanted to over extend herself to them, she was going to be single doing it.

Travis walked out of the hospital and called Jah. "Ay, what's up bro?"

"Nothing, chillin' about to leave the gym, what's up?"

"I'm leaving Nina." Travis winced as he spoke the words aloud for the first time.

"Nigga what?" asked Jah through the phone. Travis's whole world revolved around Nina so this news was a complete shock to him.

"She don't appreciate me so I'ma let her hang herself. She wants to be an independent woman so damn bad that she just lost a good man. I'm done, man."

Although the thought of leaving Nina hurt Travis, he knew what he had to do. He was done being walked over and stepped on. It was time for him to live his life. He was only twenty-six years old and there was a whole world waiting on him. If Nina didn't get her shit together, they would be divorced before the end of the year.

"Shit, meet me at the crib so we can go shoot pool and chop it up," suggested Jah.

"Bet. I'm headed your way now."

Travis and Jah headed to a local bar to have a few drinks and unwind. Nina called Travis a whopping one time since he left the hospital three hours earlier.

"Talk to me, bruh. What's going on?" asked Jah once he was tired of ignoring the elephant in the room.

Travis let out a deep sigh. "I don't know what I'm not doing right, Jah. I do everything in my power to make Nina happy but when it comes to making me happy, she drops the ball each time. I can't deal with that shit man. She got into a car accident, guess who she called before she thought to call me?"

"Her mama?" asked Jah.

"Wrong. She called Chanel. No offense, I know that's your girl but Chanel of all people?" asked Travis as he downed his fourth beer.

"Damn," said Jah, shaking his head. "I don't even know what to tell you, bruh. I just know that you take your marriage seriously so think about those vows you took before making any rash decisions."

"That's the thing, Jah. It's not rash at all. I've been feeling like this for about six months and now I'm at my breaking point. I fight temptation every fucking day trying to be a good man, a good husband but all that gets overlooked. If I stop coming home at night, maybe she'll get the fucking picture."

Jah sat silently shaking his head. He'd always thought that Nina was a stuck up bitch but his friend loved her to death so he always stayed in his place.

"So, what's your next move?" Jah asked. He took a shot of Hennessy and waited patiently as Travis thought about his answer.

"I wish I knew," he finally said. "I don't want to walk out on my wife but a nigga gotta get his message across someway."

"And leaving is the best thing you can do? You've tried everything else?" Questioned Jah. He just wanted to make sure his boy wasn't doing something he would later regret.

"I've tried all I know how to try and it's gotten me nowhere, so now I gotta put my foot down and make a change. And so do you, cus I'ma need that spare bedroom at your place, bruh."

A waitress walked over to their table and sat down two drinks before turning to walk away.

"Excuse me, we didn't order any more drinks," said Travis with a confused expression on his face.

The waitress smiled. "That nice lady over there did," she replied, motioning her head towards a lady sitting at the end of the bar with her back turned.

Jah and Travis looked at each other amused as the waitress walked off to tend to other patrons.

"Who you think she wanna fuck? Me or you?" asked Jah.

"Definitely me; bitches love married men," he joked, holding up his hand showing his ring. It didn't take long before the lady walked over to where they were seated.

"Hope I got your drinks of choice right," she said, smiling. She was a very attractive woman who Jah wouldn't mind sleeping with. Travis on the other hand wasn't interested although he did find her attractive.

"We appreciate that," answered Travis politely. He avoided eye contact with the woman though she tried her hardest to hold his gaze.

"Carla," she replied, holding out her hand. "And you are?"

"Travis."

"Nice to meet you, Travis. Hope to see you again soon," she answered before walking away.

Jah and Travis looked at each other as she walked away. "The fuck was that about?" asked Travis shaking his head.

"Beats the hell out of me. She acted like I wasn't even sitting here."

Travis laughed as he got up and walked over to the pool table. "It's the ring, brother; it's the ring."

Carla scurried away to the ladies room and called her friend, Gabi. "Bitch you were right. That's him, his said his name was Travis."

"Good. I'll make my debut soon."

CHAPTER 15

Allie was leaving the gym when she got the phone call letting her know that Nina was involved in a car accident. As soon as she finished talking to Chanel, who'd heard the news from her boyfriend, Allie's day got a lot worse when she received the text message that her daughter was on the way to the hospital.

Frantically, Allie rushed to the hospital where her daughter was. She didn't want to think the worst, but Allie couldn't stop the tears that were cascading down her cheeks. Panic set in immediately and Allie prayed all the way to the hospital that her baby girl was okay.

"Please God, don't let anything happen to my daughter. I know I'm not living right but please spare my child," Allie prayed silently. She tried calling Spade again but he wasn't answering his phone, which was pissing her off more and more. The fact that she didn't know what happened to her baby made the situation so much worse.

When Allie made it to the hospital, she rushed to the front desk. "Hello, my name is Alyssa Spencer. My daughter Jerricka Marquez was admitted here."

"Here, sign this paperwork please," said the bored receptionist as she slid a clipboard toward Allie.

Allie tried her best to be professional because the woman was only doing her job, but this was an urgent matter and she didn't have time to fill out no damn paperwork.

"Why am I filling out paperwork, lady? Take my fucking I.D and tell me where the fuck my child is!" yelled Allie.

"Ma'am, you need to calm down," said the receptionist with more attitude than Allie appreciated.

"The only thing I need to do is see my child. Now either you can allow me to do that or I can walk my ass back there and face whatever repercussions that follow. I'm trying my best not to jump over this counter and slap the shit out of you, lady so it's best you stay on my good side," said Allie sternly as she slid her ID to the woman.

Allie had just left the gym so her hair was all over her head and her chest was heaving up and down at a rapid pace. The receptionist must have known that Allie wasn't bull shitting because she quickly got herself together and gave Allie a Visitor's pass. "She's in room 5262."

"Allie!"

Allie heard Spade's voice and immediately got angry as she rushed toward him. "What happened to my baby?"

Spade looked at Allie, who looked like she just escaped from prison, and tried to give her a hug. She stepped back and repeated her question.

"What's wrong with my baby, Spade?" She asked through gritted teeth, preparing herself for the worst. She looked at Spade and couldn't tell if his rugged appearance and bloodshot was the result of him crying or drinking.

"She had an accident. She fell and hit her head on the table," he replied, somberly.

"The glass table?" shrieked Allie as she started to cry again.

"Relax, baby. She's okay. I just brought her here to be safe," replied Spade, trying his best to console Allie. He took her hand and led her to the room where their daughter was resting while her nurse was checking her vitals.

Allie's heart almost jumped out of her chest when she saw her daughter lying in the hospital bed. "Where's Jeremiah?"

"Ms. Hallie is watching him," he answered, referring to their next-door neighbor.

Allie walked over to her sleeping daughter and planted kisses all over her face while fighting back tears. She wouldn't know what to do if she lost her baby.

"I'm sorry, I'm Allie, Jerricka's mom," said Allie as she introduced herself to the nurse.

"Nice to meet you, I'm Nurse Carrie. I'll be leaving in a few; I'm just checking her vitals."

Allie nodded her head as she stroked Jerricka's hair. "How is she?"

"She's fine. Everything is normal. We performed an X-Ray and there is no swelling around the brain. There may be a small bump where she hit her head, but nothing to be too concerned about." Nurse Carrie looked at Jerricka and smiled. "She's just worn out from consoling daddy. He cried more than she did coming in."

Allie looked over and Spade and gave him a small smile. He was such a good father to his children but lately he had become so irresponsible.

"I'm glad to hear that she's okay. I would go crazy without my baby," said Allie so low that it almost seemed she was talking to herself.

"Why don't you two go grab lunch? I can watch her," suggested the nurse.

Allie shook her head. "No, it's fine. I don't have an appetite plus I want to be here when she wakes up."

"You need to eat something, babe," Spade told her.

After much hesitation, Allie kissed Jerricka and agreed to go have a bite to eat. She was a little settled knowing Jerricka was okay, but she and Spade needed to have a serious talk.

Allie fixed her hair in the mirror before walking behind Spade to find the cafeteria. Allie hugged herself tightly, shuddering because of how cold the hospital was. Or maybe she was shuddering because her worst fear was so close to coming true.

Spade noticed Allie's unusually quiet demeanor and braced himself for the talk that was destined to come. Allie was only that quiet when she had a lot on her mind and even more to get off her chest. They spotted a McDonalds and decided to eat there. Surprisingly, it was fairly empty.

"Yeah, can I get a number three and a double cheeseburger, no pickle, add mac sauce; with a medium fry and a drink," ordered Spade as he reached into his wallet to pull out some cash to pay for their food.

Once they sat down, Allie didn't waste any time. "You didn't even ask me what I wanted."

Spade shrugged. "You always order the same thing."

Allie rolled her eyes. "Maybe I wanted something different this time."

Spade looked at Allie and was shocked when he saw a serious expression on her face. "Okay, why didn't you say that before I paid?"

When Allie failed to answer, Spade instantly got pissed off. "When did we start beating around the bush with each other?"

"What happened today, Spade? How did my daughter end up in the hospital?" asked Allie, coldly.

Spade paused mid-bite and sat his burger on the tray in front of him. "OUR daughter had an accident while she was playing with her brother."

93

"Why did you let them play by that table, Spade?"

Spade frowned his face. "I walked into the kitchen to get something to drink, I heard a BOOM, she cried for ten fucking seconds then she was back to playing. I brought her here to be on the safe side."

"Spade, you were drunk. I can smell the liquor on your breath," spat Allie.

Spade couldn't believe they were even having this discussion. "What does that have to do with anything? Wait. You mean to tell me you think I was too drunk to watch my kids?"

"Well, were you?" Allie leaned back in the booth and waited for his response.

Spade laughed in disbelief. "Word?" he nodded his head and stood up, not uttering a word. He wanted to take his burger and throw it at her face for being so fucking stupid.

Allie didn't budge as she stared at him with dark, serious eyes. Spade nodded his head. "You got it, Allie. But that's fucked up for you to even think something like that."

Spade had lost his appetite so he got up and left Allie sitting alone. He walked around the hospital trying his best to calm down. "She got me fucked up," he said aloud. "I love the hell out of my kids."

Allie stared at the food sitting in front of her and fought the urge to throw up. She felt bad for accusing Spade of being anything less than an amazing father. She knew that he would lay down his life for all of them but she needed someone to blame. She had been so angry lately and she had no idea why.

She looked around the food court and noticed an older homeless man. Allie looked down at her food, which hadn't been touched. She walked over to him.

"Hello, I just bought this food but I don't have the appetite to eat it. Would you like it?"

The older man looked at Allie and smiled. "Thank you, sugar." he reached out his hand and Allie handed him the food but not before noticing that his hands were so worn out and dirty.

She reached into her purse and pulled out her hand sanitizer and a twenty-dollar bill and handed them both to him. "Here you go, have a good day."

The old man smiled another toothless grin. "God bless you, darling. Go talk to your man. He needs it right now. It's hard enough being a black man in America. He's got everybody else beating him down, he don't need you doing it too. He needs you more than you know right now. Just tell him you love him."

Tears instantly filled Allie's eyes. She nodded her head. "Thank you so much. I will." Allie walked away feeling awful for treating Spade the way she did.

When she walked back into Jerricka's room, she saw Spade lying on the bed. Jerricka was lying on his chest with her arms wrapped tightly around his neck. Allie silently walked over and sat on the edge of the bed. She looked at Spade with tear filled eyes.

She didn't get the chance to apologize because she broke down crying as soon as she felt Spade grab her hand and squeeze. Spade knew Allie was under a load of pressure dealing with him, the kids, and school and she never complained. She deserved to flip out every now and then.

Allie laid her head in Spade's lap and before she knew it, she was knocked out. Spade watched both of his girls as they slept and felt so low. He wasn't in the position to give either of them the life they deserved because he couldn't stop getting high and he couldn't put down the bottle.

"I need a fucking blunt," he muttered, hating that he couldn't cope with real life when he was sober. He tried his best to get comfortable, which was almost impossible but he was in dreamland shortly after.

Nurse Carrie walked into the room a few hours later and saw them all lying in the bed and smiled. Allie must have felt her presence because her eyes shot open.

"I'm sorry, you all just looked so peaceful," Nurse Carrie apologized.

"No worries. I'm sorry, I know we're supposed to be on the couch," said Allie as she stretched and sat up.

"You're fine. I was just coming to let you know that you can take her home. There was no trauma or signs of a concussion so she's good to go."

After Allie thanked her, she woke up her two sleeping babies and told them they were set to go. They both stared at her with blank expressions on their faces. Just like Spade, it took Jerricka a few minutes to adjust to the world after a nap. She was her father's child through and through. They both had smooth chocolate skin, with dark curly hair. They laughed, smiled, and even slept the same as well.

Once they were checked out, Spade picked Jerricka up and held Allie's hand as they walked out of the hospital.

"Mommy, me have a doohickey on my head!" Announced Jerricka.

Allie burst into laughter. "What is that?"

Jerricka laughed too and shrugged her shoulders. Allie immediately looked at Spade. She knew he was responsible for their daughter's newfound word.

"Y'all didn't call knots or bumps 'doohickeys' growing up?" he asked incredulously.

Allie laughed harder. "No, we called them bumps and knots."

"Y'all missed out on life," laughed Spade.

Allie smiled at his sense of humor. As they exited the hospital doors, Allie spotted the homeless man from earlier. He saw her too and winked his eye and gave her a thumb up. She was beaming from ear to ear. Despite their many flaws, Allie knew she and Spade had something special. She just hoped that he realized it soon because she wasn't trying to be a "girlfriend" forever.

CHAPTER 16

Nina sat at her desk and tried her best to focus but 5 pm wasn't coming fast enough. It was Friday, which meant two things: Payday and Mascara & Moscato night. This last week was so hard for her. Between being in an accident and having a leak in her roof at home, Nina was in desperate need of a girl's night.

Chanel was hosting the event at her apartment so Nina decided to go straight there after work.

"Miss Nina, what you over here daydreaming about?" asked Rashaun. He was Nina's very flamboyant best friend at work.

"Just ready to get the hell out of here," she sighed as she rocked back and forth in her chair.

"Well, bitch before you do, I have a bone to pick with your ass," he said with much attitude.

"Why? What did I do?"

"Nothing! Your ass ain't did nothing all day," he pointed out.

"I've done some work," Nina replied defensively.

"Bitch, where?" he asked quoting the popular saying that's been floating around social media.

"Rashaun, give me a break, okay?" Sighed Nina. She knew she had been working at a slower pace than normal but she normally gave it her all so why couldn't she get a pass?

"Alright, I'll break my foot up in your ass, how about that? Did you forget the VP was here today? You talking about moving up but you sit on your ass and daydream all day the one day he is here?"

Nina gasped. "Oh my God! I forgot," she said as she sat straight up.

Rashaun rolled his eyes at her. "You better get it together Miss Nina because it's always somebody willing to take your spot."

With that and a flip of his non-existent hair, Rashaun sashayed away. Nina cursed herself for forgetting this was the week to prove herself. She looked at the papers on her desk and instantly got overwhelmed.

"I'm gone for the day, guys," she announced as she stood up and grabbed her purse. She saw Rashaun shaking his head but she didn't give a damn. She needed a drink and she needed it fast.

Once she was out of the office, Nina made it to Chanel's house in less than fifteen minutes.

"You're early," said Chanel as she opened the door to let Nina in. Nina walked past her and flopped down on the couch. She was still mad at Chanel, who never apologized to her for storming out of her house a few weeks ago.

Chanel rolled her eyes and went back into her bedroom. Moments later, she reappeared with Eric following behind her carrying EJ.

"Hey, Nina," Eric spoke as he left the apartment. Nina continued to play with her phone as if she didn't hear him.

Once Chanel kissed her son goodbye, she walked back into the house and slammed her door. "What the hell is your problem? This is my house and it's bad enough you didn't speak to me but to think you're going to be rude to my guest who did nothing to you, you've lost your damn mind."

"The man came to my house and disrespected me, did you forget?" Nina snapped.

Chanel put her hand on her hip. "I remember, but this is not your house or his, so please respect my shit."

"Why is he even here? You have a man but you're steady running back to this nigga."

"He came to get his son so I could have the girl's night here tonight," Chanel replied.

Nina folded her arms and crossed her legs on Chanel's tan couch. "I guess."

"Bitch, you really-"

The doorbell rang and interrupted Chanel's rant. "Saved by the motherfucking bell," she muttered. She opened the door to find a smiling Allie.

"Bitch, why you so happy?" she asked.

"Why you so mad, hoe?" Countered Allie as she hugged Chanel. Allie walked in the house to see a bothered Nina sitting on the couch like she had an attitude.

"Hey Nina-Bina," said Allie as she tried to hug Nina. When Nina stuck out her arm to stop the hug, Allie snapped. "What the fuck is your issue?"

"She's been tripping since she got here," said Chanel, frowning at Nina.

"Anyway, where is Sweetie?" asked Allie, looking around. Sweetie was normally on time.

"She text me today and said she couldn't make it. She had to take Dallas somewhere," replied Nina, dryly. She kept her eyes glued to her phone.

"Did she lose our number?" asked Chanel, looking at Allie.

"She must have," shrugged Allie becoming annoyed with Sweetie. "When did she become such an avid texter anyway?"

"Why don't y'all give her a break, damn?" snapped Nina as she stood up and walked toward the kitchen. "Where's the food?"

"It should be here any minute now," replied Chanel.

Nina raised one eyebrow. "You ordered food?"

Chanel walked in the kitchen behind her and grabbed some wine glasses. She took the Moscato out of the ice bucket and poured them each a glass. "Yes, I did. Problem?"

"Why didn't you ask me to cook?" asked Nina.

"Because, I didn't need you to cook," shrugged Chanel.

"What is it? Chinese?" asked Allie, not caring one way or the other what they ate. It was free so she was all for It.

"Pizza," Chanel replied. "Why?"

"Pizza?" exclaimed Nina.

Chanel paused from pouring the wine. "Yes, pizza and if that's an issue, you don't have to eat."

"I'm just saying. I'm in the kitchen for hours cooking for y'all when it's at my house, but I get pizza when I come to yours," said Nina, folding her arms.

"Not everybody has a rich husband who worships the ground they walk on. I live off child support and random hair appointments so excuse me if I'm not making steak and lobsters for a person that I'm not fucking. You can leave if it's such an issue because I'm tired of your ass already," said Chanel, fuming.

"Nina, what's up? Your attitude has been on ten all damn day," interjected Allie.

"I was in the hospital and neither of you came by to see me. I'm always there for the both of you but the minute Nina needs help, no one is there," yelled Nina.

"Whoa, wait one minute. I texted you and told you what happened with Jerricka. My child will always come first," said Allie with conviction.

Nina turned to look at Chanel. "And your excuse?"

"I don't have one. They said you weren't hurt so I didn't see a need to go," shrugged Chanel. She gulped down her glass of wine and wished she had some shots to take. Nina was working her last nerve and her patience was running very thin.

"You don't know the first thing about being a friend, Chanel," said Nina, shaking her head. She was irritated with her friends. She didn't understand why they couldn't return her same loyalty.

"Excuse me?" Chanel asked, walking towards Nina.

"Come on, not today," groaned Allie. She really just wanted to have a good time with her girls.

"No, let's take it to the sandbox," insisted Chanel. Anytime a girl took it to the sandbox, it meant they would be completely honest with each other, no matter how harsh and intense it may be. Once the conversation was done and they left the sandbox, they wouldn't mention the situation again.

Allie rolled her eyes and let out an exaggerated sigh. Since Sweetie wasn't there, she would have to mediate the situation herself.

"What's the real issue?" asked Chanel, staring at Nina.

"I just really don't understand why you weren't there for me, since it was your fault that I was in the hospital," said Nina.

"My fault, how the hell was it my fault?"

"Don't even worry about it," said Nina, throwing her hand dismissively.

"Nope, talk it out," said Allie. "You're so quick to run away. Just talk."

"You were being a bitch while I was trying to diffuse the situation. I was so caught up in trying to make peace with you," Nina continued.

"That's your problem, Nina. You always so worried about the wrong thing, that's why your marriage is crumbling," spat Chanel, fed up. She was tired of sparing Nina's feelings.

Nina put up her hand. "Don't fucking go there." Her face was hard as stone as she glared at Chanel angrily.

"No, let's go there. You're so quick to judge someone else's relationship but your shit ain't even together."

"Trust me, my husband and I are good," stated Nina adamantly.

"Then why is he sleeping on my man's couch?" asked Chanel, folding her arms.

Nina shot a glance at Allie, who looked at Nina with curious eyes. Nina looked at the couch and grabbed her purse. "I don't have to deal with this bull shit. I'm out. I knew I shouldn't have come to this low budget ass shit."

"Bye!" said Chanel, waving her hand. She wasn't kissing Nina's ass anymore. "And them shoes you wearing are low budget, bitch!"

Nina stormed toward the door. "Go to hell, Chanel."

"Nina, come on. Talk it out. We're your friends," said Allie, trying her best to stop Nina from leaving.

"I can't tell," she replied as she exited Chanel's apartment.

Allie looked at Chanel pleading with her to try and stop Nina but to no avail. Chanel was tired of Nina acting holier than thou.

"Fuck that. We had girl's night here because she didn't want us to know that Travis hasn't been home. She's always so quick to judge me when her house ain't in order," said Chanel pacing back and forth.

Allie walked out of the house. "Nina, come on! Stop!"

Nina kept walking as if she didn't hear Allie calling her name. She had too much going on to argue with these women. They were the reason her marriage was falling apart. She just needed a break from everything and everybody.

"Allie, just let me go. I need to get myself together and y'all are nothing more than distractions."

Allie stopped in her tracks. "Wow. Over ten years of friendship and we're distractions?" She nodded her head before replying. "You got it, Nina."

She turned around and walked into Chanel's house, slamming the door behind her. "She done pissed me the hell off."

Chanel sipped her wine and shook her head. "I don't know what's wrong with her. It's like she is blaming us for her marriage falling apart."

Allie nodded her head. "She's always done that though. She always finds a way to blame her issues on someone else."

"Well, it's just us tonight, I guess. And I don't really like you like that," joked Chanel.

"Fuck you, bitch. I'm all yours for the night," replied Allie.

"Well, once the pizza comes we can watch movies and talk shit all night," shrugged Chanel.

"Fuck the mascara tonight, long as I got my Moscato," said Allie, raising her glass.

Nina walked into her big empty house and felt so small. She had spent so much time decorating the place but her crystal chandelier didn't shine as bright as Travis's smile. The original paintings that were strategically placed on her walls were not worth half as much as the love she had for her husband.

It was hard for her to accept the fact that she is the sole reason for being alone. It was hard for her to feel like she was losing all control. Nina slowly undressed and stepped in the shower. She cried her eyes out as she scrubbed her skin trying to scrub away the toughness that prevented her from being vulnerable. Being a bigger girl, Nina learned a long time ago that she had to have thick skin if she wanted to survive in this world.

She was always teased about her weight and the braces that she wore so Nina built a wall so that no one could get close enough to hurt her. Then one day, she met a man who claimed he loved every part of her. And he did, until his friends came around. He would act as though he was ashamed of her and even went as far as to call her names in public. But in private, he couldn't get enough of her.

Nina suffered through his verbal abuse for three years before walking away; but not before he humiliated her in front of all their friends and family. She thought he was going to propose to her on her birthday, but he had other plans. "Look at me, then look at you," he said. "What do I look like marrying you?" Nina couldn't believe someone could be so cold, so in turn she built a tough exterior to avoid being hurt again.

Travis came right in and swept Nina off her feet and Lord knows she fell hard. He loved to show her off every chance he got. He brought her flowers at least once a week, he constantly told her she was beautiful, and he loved every stretch mark and roll on her 180 pound body. He loved her so much that it almost scared her and though Nina loved him back, she couldn't let that wall down. She was afraid to be vulnerable again so she clung to her friends who have always loved her despite her flaws. They looked up to her, saw her strength, and kept her going.

Yet, she was even being awful to them. Nina cried for what felt like hours. She stepped out of the shower and was nearly crippled by the silence in her home. She put on her nightgown and crawled into her King size bed, which felt so uncomfortable. What's the point of a king size bed when your king is nowhere to be found, she wondered.

Nina cried herself to sleep that night, missing Travis's presence but not once did she pick up the phone to call her husband.

Meanwhile, Travis was sitting on the couch with his phone in his hands silently praying it would ring. As much as he wanted to go home to his wife, Nina had to learn to appreciate him. She needed to understand that he only wanted the best for her. He loved Nina with everything breath in his body but even love had a limit. He wanted respect. He wanted to affection.

"Stop sulking like a lil bitch and come take a shot," said Spade, interrupting Travis from his thoughts. He was seated on the couch while Jah and Spade were playing dominoes in the dining area. This was actually their first time meeting each other and they got along pretty well.

Spade and Jah tried their best to cheer Travis up but he couldn't find it within himself to be happy without his wife. He stood and reluctantly walked over to his boys. The least he could do is take a few shots with them since they did take time out of their days to cheer him up.

One shot turned into five but Travis still couldn't shake the pain. He did everything he thought he was supposed to do as a man. He loved his wife, he honored her, he wined and dined her, he tried his best to make her feel safe and secure, yet it wasn't enough.

Travis stood 6'3, but somehow Nina still made him feel small. She acted as though he was just an extra in her life instead of her leading man. He looked at Spade, who was on the phone with Allie and felt a twinge of jealousy. He had so much respect for Allie, who did everything she could to make Spade feel like the man of the house even when he'd fallen on hard times.

Yet, Travis worked sixty hours a week to keep all the bills paid, be able to give Nina whatever she wanted, and put money in a trust fund for their future children. Travis grew up in a broken household with a mother who so desperately needed to be loved. At the age of seven when his father left, Travis tried his best to love the hurt from his mother's eyes but it wasn't enough. She didn't know her own strength. She felt she could never teach him how to be a man not knowing that seeing her cry every night was all the motivation Travis needed to become a man of honor.

Before Nina, Travis thought he loved a woman who only wanted him for what he could give. She played with his heart and even made him believe she was carrying his child. When the truth came crashing that she was cheating on him for two out of their three-year relationship, Travis was devastated but he didn't give up on love.

When he met Nina, he felt like he had hit the jackpot. She was so strong, confident, and funny that he knew he had to make her his wife. Six months into their relationship, he proposed and she accepted. He knew in his heart that he had finally got it right. As always in the beginning, things were great. The sex, the passion, the love was all there. She had always had a strong devotion to her friends but her devotion to him was stronger.

Now, it felt like the flame of their love had burned out. It seemed like Travis kept trying to light it, only for Nina to blow it out in his face.

"I'm still fucked up about this situation. I know y'all trying to cheer me up, but this shit just doesn't feel right," confessed Travis.

"I feel you, bro. Just go home to your wife, man," suggested Jah.

"I can't be the one to always give in," said Travis. "I gotta stand my ground, man."

"Let me ask you something, man. Is being right more important than your marriage?" asked Spade.

Travis was caught off guard by the question and stood back to think about his answer. "Not at all."

"Then it shouldn't matter who gives in first. What matters the most is that y'all love each other enough to put y'all pride to the side and make it work," said Spade.

"Damn, my nigga. That was a lil' deep," Travis replied, taking in his words.

"Hell yeah. Who you got that from?" asked Jah, laughing.

"Just like a nigga to think I got it from somebody," laughed Spade. "Man, life taught me that. I've been with Allie nine years. It's been plenty of times that I had to swallow my pride to keep my woman. I ain't ashamed. I know she's the one for me so I'd do anything I can to keep her."

Travis asked a question he'd always wanted to know. "After all this time, why haven't you married her? You know you want to spend the rest of your life with her, right?"

"I'm *going* to spend the rest of my life with her. But I won't make her my wife until I'm able to be a husband and that's all I'm going to say."

The room got silent while Jah and Travis processed what he'd just said. Travis wondered if Nina moved too fast with him.

He was sure about her, but what if she wasn't so sure about him? He didn't want to think that deep so he took a few more shots with the fellas and they talked sports until they all passed out.

CHAPTER 17

Two weeks had passed and besides a few texts being exchanged, Allie hadn't really talked to her friends. Mainly Nina. She tried to call but was sent to voicemail so she gave up. One thing about Allie was she didn't kiss nobody's ass. If Nina wanted to be a bitch, then so could she. She was a Leo and could be as stubborn as they came so she wouldn't back down until Nina apologized.

Allie walked into the gym and received a text from Chanel telling her to call her. She replied she would after her training session. Surprisingly, Chanel had become very close to Allie in the last two weeks. Being two strong-minded people and both being Leos, they tended to go at it a lot but they were also very similar.

Before Allie got changed into her work attire, she called Spade. They had been going at it a lot lately because he was drinking much more than usual. Allie was pissed that she had to pay a baby sitter to watch their kids because all Spade wanted to do was lay around.

Allie loved Spade to death but he wasn't the man she fell in love with. Her Spade was an over achiever. He loved to be out and about, he loved to win so Allie couldn't understand why he had let himself go. It had been a little over two months since he'd lost his job and Allie couldn't say that he was even trying to find another one. It frustrated her so much that he was just wasting away his potential.

Spade was very intelligent. He used to teach her new words all the time and could tell you who wrote any book or quote. He had so much drive and ambition and Allie loved that about him. Over the years, she noticed that he'd lost his passion for a lot of things but he made sure he took care of his family. He wasn't the richest man in the world, but he would make sure they never wanted for anything. His family was his main priority and Allie respected that.

Now, he was like a child. He was so moody and never seemed to be satisfied. One-minute things would be fine, and then the next minute, he would snap. She desperately wished she could figure out how to get through to him.

Allie dialed his number and waited for him to pick up.

"Hello?" He slurred. There was a lot of noise in the background and Allie wondered where the hell he was.

"Where are you?" She asked, holding one of her ears to hear him over the ruckus in the background.

"At this lil' spot, why what's up?" he answered.

"What you mean what's up? What happened to you going job hunting today?" She asked angrily. Not only was Allie paying out of pocket for her trainer, she had so many bills to pay and their only income was her makeup gig, which wasn't guaranteed money. She didn't care if he took a job at Wal-Mart. She needed help.

"Ahh, I'll do it tomorrow. I needed to get out the house. Yeah, let me get a crown and coke," said Spade to the bartender.

"Spade, where did you get money to be spending at a fucking bar? We are already low on money," Allie cried.

"I took the money that was behind our picture, but I'ma put it back when I get it," he replied nonchalantly.

Allie froze in place. "Spade, what the fuck? That was the money for Jeremiah's school clothes!"

"I said I'd put it back, Allie damn!"

Allie fought the urge to cry. She was beyond pissed. "How Spade?" Before he could answer, she took a deep breath. "How much of it is left?"

"Bout twenty bucks," he said.

"TWENTY DOLLARS? Jeremy you've got to be kidding me! It was $150 behind that picture!" yelled Allie.

"Look, you tripping right now and it's killing my buzz. Call me when you calm down," he slurred before hanging up.

Spade downed his drink hoping to drown in his sorrows. Truth is, he went to several places to interview and they told him he was "over-qualified." The fuck kind of shit is that?

He looked at the remaining twenty dollars in his hand and decided to call a cab. Then, he remembered he had a few homies that would be willing to pick him up.

"Bartender, give me two more," he slurred as he slid his last twenty to the bartender, who in turn, slid him two shots.

Spade liked sitting at the bar; he didn't feel judged. He imagined the bartenders were used to seeing lost souls foolishly trying to drink their problems away. Spade knew they wouldn't disappear, but the liquor did ease the pain.

He thought about Allie and their Mascara and Moscato night. He finally understood why they needed it so much; why they needed each other so much. Love is a powerful feeling, he thought, but resentment is so much stronger. He thought about how much Allie must have resented him for leaving her hanging after all the shit he's put her through.

Spade looked at the bottom of his empty glass and saw the sad eyes of man who was on a destructive past to loneliness. Spade looked at Allie's debit card that was attached to their joint account and tried hard to put it back in his wallet, but the alcohol was calling his name so loud he couldn't help but answer.

When Allie got off the phone with Spade, she had so much anger burning inside her. She couldn't believe how selfish he was being.

She walked into the private training area in her sports bra and shorts and immediately got on the treadmill before Heem even got the chance to tell her to do so.

"Okay, somebody's motivated today," nodded Heem as he smiled at his new favorite client.

Normally Allie would joke back but today just wasn't her day. She just stared at herself in the mirror and ran. She looked at her sad eyes and felt sorry for herself. She was only twenty-three and already felt old. She didn't have the careless, free-spirited attitude as most girls her age. She was too focused on her next move; thinking of giving her kids a life that she could only dream of. She wanted a house of her own, not one that government assistance provided for her. Her kids deserved a playground in the backyard. They deserved to see how tall they'd grown over the years.

Allie didn't even realize she was crying until Heem stopped her machine and asked her if she was okay. Allie nodded her head but couldn't stop the tears.

"Come here," said Heem as he pulled her into his arms. He held her tightly as she cried into his chest. He rubbed her back slowly as he whispered in her ear to let it out.

After she was no longer heaving, Heem asked her to sit with him on a mat. "Talk to me, what's wrong?"

"A lot. My boyfriend and I are having issues. I don't think he loves me anymore. I think I'm failing my kids. I'm letting them down. My son wanted a toy from Wal-Mart and it broke my heart that I couldn't afford it because I had a water bill to pay."

"Some kids don't even have the luxury of having water. You're blessed and your children know they have a great mom. I'm sure he didn't even think about that toy after y'all left the store. Stop being so hard on yourself," said Heem sincerely.

"It's just hard, you know?" she asked rhetorically. Heem leaned forward and wiped some of her tears away.

"Life is hard, but you're strong. I watch you come here every day and give me one hundred percent each time. You're like superwoman or some shit. Give yourself some credit," he replied, looking her in her eyes.

"I try but it seems like I just can't catch a break. I'm just so tired," said Allie, feeling like she was on the verge of having a nervous breakdown.

"I'm going to tell you like my mama told me; there is always a light at the end of the tunnel. You just gotta push through it no matter how dark it gets. That way, when you finally get out, you'll appreciate the sun so much more."

Allie nodded her head; still feeling lost and beat down. Heem sensed her sadness and felt so bad for her.

"You're an amazing woman, Allie. You're beautiful; you're smart and caring. Your jokes be a little corny, but overall you a'ight with me," joked Heem.

Allie laughed and leaned over to push him. He wasn't prepared for the push so he fell backwards pulling Allie on top of him. Allie's first mind told her to quickly get up but for some reason she stayed there. She looked into Heem's eyes and saw a man that cared about her.

When she felt his hand pulling her head towards him for a kiss, Allie would have normally pulled back but she didn't resist. She was too drained to do any more fighting. When their lips touched, Allie felt a shot of electricity jolting through her whole body.

Allie let out a moan and opened Pandora's Box. Heem wrapped his arms around Allie's waist as he hungrily kissed her. When he felt her grinding on him, he knew it was on. He caressed her ass checks as their tongues did the tango.

Heem grabbed Allie and gently flipped her over so that she was lying flat on the mat. He alternated between sucking and nibbling on her neck as he grinded on her. Allie ran her hands over Heem's muscles and became so wet she almost thought she came.

Heem's hands were making their selves familiar with every part of Allie's body. After teasing her nipples, Heem stuck his hand in Allie's panties and rubbed her clit. Allie's back arched and Heem knew that it had probably been a while since she was fucked properly. He wondered who her man was and how could he be so damn stupid.

Allie lifted her butt off of the mat to make it easier for Heem to get her shorts down. When he tried to get her bra off of her, Allie tensed up. She still wasn't comfortable with being completely naked. She always kept her bra and shirt on when she had sex with Spade.

"What's wrong?" Heem asked, feeling her legs give his waist a small squeeze.

"I'm just-I don't know. I don't really..." Allie's voice trailed off.

"Allie, you're beautiful. Have you looked at your naked body in the mirror lately?" asked Heem.

Allie shook her head no. He thought for a few seconds. "You trust me?" he asked.

Allie's eyebrows shot up. "It depends."

"Take your bra off, trust me," he said looking into her eyes.

Allie took a deep breath and did as she was told. Heem stood up and got completely undressed. "Come on."

"What? Where?" Allie asked, confused. She was starting to think twice about what she'd gotten herself into.

"Trust me, Alyssa," said Heem sternly. He didn't wait for her to answer; he just grabbed her hand and led her to his sanctuary.

Allie walked into the room with all the mirrors. Allie's first instinct was to wrap her arms around her body but Heem gently pushed her hands down.

"Look at yourself, you look great," replied Heem looking at her through the mirror. He saw significant changes in her and it had only been about a month.

Allie stared at her naked body and was pleasantly surprised. Her love handles were gone and her waist appeared to be slimmer. Her thunder thighs looked more toned, which made her ass, sit perfectly. Allie smiled at her reflection; she was too busy dealing with life to even notice the changes in her own body.

Heem walked behind Allie and kissed her neck. He wrapped his arms around her and cupped her breasts while using his index finger to tickle her nipples. Heem looked at Allie who was biting her lip with her eyes closed. "Open your eyes; look at yourself."

Allie opened her eyes and became wetter than a rainforest. The sight before her turned her on in so many ways. Heem's fingers found their way into her wetness and Allie loved how sexy she looked while standing there, eyes full of lust.

"Come on," said Heem as he walked to the center of the room and laid out a large mat. Allie pranced over to him, while looking into the mirror to her right. She almost felt like she was in high school again judging by the way her ass was looking. Heem and Allie kissed and groped on each other all the way to the ground. Allie lay on her back, pulling Heem in between her legs.

Heem could feel the moisture between her legs and he wanted badly to dive in. But first, he needed to accomplish his goal. Allie needed to fully feel beautiful and sexy again. "Prop yourself on your elbows," he instructed.

Allie did as she was told. In a swift motion, Allie's right leg was over Heem's shoulder while his face was buried in between her legs. Allie's head immediately fell back as she closed her eyes and moaned. As soon as she opened them, she was greeted by another mirror on the ceiling. She watched herself squirm and wiggle as Heem made her cum over and over again. She began playing with her titties as she watched a personal porno starring her and Heem.

She pulled Heem up by the shoulders. "I'm ready to feel you."

Heem opened Allie's legs wide and rubbed his head up and down her lips, teasing her before he slowly entered her so that she could adjust to his size. When she let out a gasp, Heem knew he was just what she needed. He plunged deep inside her quickly causing to her to let out a loud moan. The pleasure and pain that Allie felt caused Allie to come all over Heem's monster.

For the next hour, Heem and Allie tried as many positions as they could. Allie came at least five times but Heem was still going hard. Allie looked in the mirror and admired the way her ass jiggled each time Heem stroked her from behind. She looked at his face and smiled. His eyes were low and his mouth was in the shape of an O.

Allie bounced her ass on his dick, hoping to make him come; instead, she was the one screaming and shaking. "Ooooohhhhhhhhhhhh," moaned Allie as waves of pleasure shot through her body. Her orgasm was so intense; she could hardly hold herself up. When she rested her head on the mat, Heem knew he had worn her ass out.

"You tired?"

"I'm okay," she panted.

Heem rubbed Allie's ass and gave her a few more deep strokes and forced himself to ease out of her. Allie looked at him through the mirror. "What's wrong?"

"Nothing, I'm good. I just know you're tired," said Heem.

"But you didn't get your nut," said Allie, looking confused.

"I just wanted to make you feel better. I'm good. The sex was great but I only have an hour 'til my next training session and I need to do some cleaning," he laughed looking around the room.

Allie turned to face him. She wrapped her arms around his neck and kissed him. "Thank you for everything."

"Truly my pleasure," smiled Heem as he rubbed her ass.

"You think it will be awkward between us now?" asked Allie as she stood up and stretched. She glanced in the mirror and did a slight twerk.

Heem laughed to his self. Allie wouldn't even look in the mirror at first, now she couldn't stop checking herself out.

"Nah, not if we don't make it awkward. We're grown," replied Heem.

Allie drove home that day in silence. She felt bad about what she'd done but she didn't regret it. She definitely didn't want to make it a habit, but Allie needed to feel good about herself again. For two hours, she was a new woman. One with no fears, doubts, or inhibitions.

She took a deep breath as she pulled into her driveway noticing that Spade was still gone, which meant her kids were still with the neighbors. Any orgasmic bliss that was still dwindling quickly faded as Allie slowly walked back to her reality.

CHAPTER 18

Two weeks had passed and Nina still hadn't contacted Travis. She missed him so much but he walked away from her, which she didn't respect. They both had their flaws but as a married couple, they were supposed to work through all their issues not run away from them.

She couldn't deny the fact that she missed her husband so much but she refused to give in. Nina walked downstairs and noticed that the leak in her living room had gotten worse. She decided to put her pride aside and call Travis.

As the phone rang, Nina got butterflies in her stomach.

"Hello?" Nina's heart began to race the second she heard Travis's baritone.

"Hey. I was just calling because this leak in the living room has gotten worse, I need you to come look at it when you can."

"Alright. I'll be through there later," replied Travis.

"Cool, see you then. Bye."

Travis looked at the phone once the call was disconnected. With each day that passed, he was becoming less and less hopeful about the future of his marriage. Nina knew she was wrong so he couldn't understand why she wouldn't just apologize and get it over with. He was tired of staying with Jah; he was ready to go home.

Nina took a deep breath after she hung up with Travis. She wanted to tell him to come back home for good but she refused to beg any man to be with her. If he wanted to sleep on another's man couch, then so be it. She slept very comfortably on her Egyptian cotton sheets every night. At least, that's what she told herself.

Nina decided to call Sweetie. Besides a few texts here and there, she hadn't spoken to Sweetie in weeks. She needed to vent to someone who wouldn't judge her so Sweetie was just what the doctor ordered. Besides, she still wasn't speaking to Allie or Chanel. When Sweetie didn't answer, Nina decided to leave her a message.

"Hey Sweetie, I know y'all are probably still settling in. I miss you; call me back as soon as possible."

Somehow, Nina made it through her shift. She just didn't feel like herself lately and it showed in her work performance. She wasn't her usual cheery self, instead she was quiet and standoffish and she moved at a much slower pace than normal. Once 5 o'clock hit, Nina ran out of the office and headed home.

She wanted to make it home and get dressed for when Travis got there. She wanted to look her best so he could see what he was missing out on. When she pulled in her driveway, she was surprised to see that Travis was already there. She looked at herself in the mirror and quickly fixed her hair and powdered her face. She applied lip gloss to her lips and walked into her home.

Travis was standing in the living room shirtless talking on his cell phone when Nina walked in. He glanced at her as she walked in but didn't speak. Nina didn't even make eye contact with him as she headed to the bedroom where they used to make sweet love.

Travis knocked on the bedroom door before walking in. Nina was in the process of changing clothes when Travis appeared. "Hey, I was just letting you know that I patched up the roof so that it will stop dripping, but I'll get a contractor to come in and do a full repair."

Nina nodded her head, avoiding eye contact. "Okay."

Travis turned around and started to walk away. Before he left out of the room, he turned back around to face Nina. "Is this how you want us to be?"

"You're the one who left so you tell me," she snapped, folding her arms.

"I left because I didn't feel appreciated, why can't you understand that?" asked Travis.

"You sound like a woman, Travis. I don't feel appreciated," she mocked.

Travis clenched his jaw and balled his fists at his side. He was tired of Nina and her blatant disrespect. "You know what, Nina? Fuck you!"

Nina looked at Travis with a shocked expression on her face. He'd never spoken to her that way before.

"You want to be an independent woman so fucking bad so you got it. I'm done with this shit. You don't want to show your appreciation for me, fine! Fuck it. But I don't bust my ass getting overtime every week to be disrespected in a house that I pay for so you can get your shit and leave," he said.

Nina shook her head. Clearly, she misunderstood what just came out of Travis's mouth. "Excuse me?"

"You heard what the fuck I said, Nina. This shit has gotten out of hand and I'm tired of the shit," Travis yelled.

Nina stood speechless. This was the last thing she expected to happen but it was too late to turn back. "Fine, I'll be out by Friday."

"Good, because the locks will be changed Saturday," Travis replied coldly before walking out the house. He didn't plan on really changing the locks, nor did he expect Nina to leave but he was tired of being the nice guy.

Nina watched the love of her life walk out on her as she stood in her bedroom fighting back tears. She didn't know where she would go if Travis was serious about her leaving. She never had a backup plan; she planned on being married to Travis forever.

Travis reappeared in the doorway minutes later. "So, just like that? You're willing to throw our entire life away instead of just changing your attitude. Are you that prideful?"

"You want me to leave so I will," shrugged Nina. She turned around and pretended she was looking for something in her drawers so Travis wouldn't see her tears. Nina wanted a man who was going to fight for her. She never stopped to realize that she wasn't fighting back.

"If my name was Chanel or Sweetie, you would have tried to work it out. I love you to death Nina but I feel like I'm in love by my damn self."

"Travis, I can't control how you feel. I'm sorry that you feel unappreciated, I'm sorry that you feel I don't love you but I do. I don't give you this hard of a time."

"Because I don't give you a reason to," reasoned Travis.

"Sorry that you're so perfect and I'm so fucking flawed!" Exclaimed Nina as she threw her hands in the air.

Travis shook his head feeling like he was talking to a brick wall. "I'm not perfect but I do what I'm supposed to do as a husband. I go to work every day, I keep the bills paid, I support everything you do, I spoil you and I show my love for you every chance I get. What do you do as a wife?"

Nina hated to be put on the spot so she didn't have an answer for his question. "Obviously, nothing."

"When was the last time we had sex, Nina?"

Nina shrugged her shoulders. "I don't know."

"You don't see an issue with that?" he questioned, growing impatient.

"Travis, does it matter? You left already, now you're kicking me out so what's left to talk about?" asked Nina. She walked over to her closet and began stuffing her clothes in a duffel bag.

Travis gave up. "Keep the house, Nina. Fuck it, I don't want any reminders of your ass," he said as he stormed out the house.

"Stupid ass girl," muttered Travis on the way to his car. He walked to his car feeling hurt that his wife refused to fight for him and their marriage; but he got her message loud and clear.

Travis left his former home and drove over to an apartment complex that he had applied to a few weeks earlier. He walked in, paid his deposit, and signed all the paperwork so that he could move into his own place. He hated that it came to this but if Nina was willing to let their marriage go down the drain, then he was ready to turn on the garbage disposal. After picking up his key, Travis drove to his office to handle a little business to keep his mind off of Nina.

He was sitting at his desk filing paperwork when Wendy knocked on his door. "Hey boss man," she said peeking her head in. "Can I come in?"

Travis motioned for Wendy to enter. He noticed that the shirt she wore exposed her cleavage while her pants hugged every curve on her body. Travis wondered if she always dressed that way because he never really paid attention.

Wendy sat down across from him. "Is everything okay? You're here late."

Travis rubbed his temples. "Yeah, just a little stressed out."

Wendy nodded her head and noticed how worn out he looked. "Work problems?"

Travis leaned back in his chair and stretched. "Woman issues."

Wendy smiled on the inside but her facial expression was full of concern. "I'm sorry to hear that. I'm sure you two will work it out."

"I don't think so. Not this time," replied Travis. His voice was full of sadness as he spoke those words. For the first time, he really believed that he and Nina wouldn't bounce back from this.

Wendy fought her hardest to not stand on his desk and start twerking. He was right where she wanted him. She planned on providing Travis with a shoulder he could cry on so in return he could give her a dick to ride on. Wendy noticed a lease sitting on his desk and decided to make her move on him. If he was moving out, he and Nina were probably over for real.

"I'm really sorry to hear that but you deserve a woman who understands how great of a man you are. If she can't understand that, then that's her loss."

Travis nodded his head but he really didn't want to talk about Nina anymore.

Wendy sighed. "Have you eaten?"

"Nah, I'm probably going to grab a burger when I leave here," said Travis.

Wendy stood up. "Nonsense. I'll be back." Wendy sashayed out of Travis's office and returned a few minutes later carrying a container. She walked over and sat it in front of Travis, removing the top.

Travis stomached growled as soon as he saw the food sitting in front of him. There was meatloaf, mashed potatoes, candied yams, mac & cheese, and a roll. Travis couldn't remember the last time he had a meal so hearty.

"Damn, you made this?" he asked, rubbing his hands together preparing to dive in.

"Yeah, I always cook these large meals and they go to waste every time so I decided to start bringing the food here for all you hungry men to eat," said Wendy.

"Thank you. I'm about to tear this food up," marveled Travis. "Meatloaf is my favorite dish."

"You thirsty?" asked Wendy. Cus I am, she thought.

"Yeah, but I'll go get it in a minute," he said, diving into the food.

"Boy, eat! I'll go get it," said Wendy as she stood up. She noticed that Travis had on basketball shorts, which was perfect for the plan she concocted. She walked into the break room and poured Travis a big cup of sweet tea, which she knew was his favorite.

She walked back into his office and noticed that he had eaten nearly all the food. "Whoa, somebody was hungry today."

"I can't tell you the last time I tasted something so good. You put your foot in this food, girl. Thank you so much."

"Oh, no problem. I got you some tea," she said, handing him the cup. She purposely let the cup go early so that it fell and wasted in his lap.

"Whoa!" he exclaimed, quickly standing up to shake the ice off of his lap.

Wendy pretended to be mortified. "I'm so sorry!" She shrieked as she grabbed a few napkins and dabbed around his crotch area.

"You're good. I got it," he replied. Travis didn't know what happened but the next thing he knew, Wendy had pulled his pants down and his dick was in her mouth.

"Wait, what are you-"

"Shh," whispered Wendy as she bobbed her head up and down on his dick. She knew she was taking a huge chance by doing this, but she knew men. Travis was already vulnerable, he was full, and he was sexually deprived.

Travis resisted for a few seconds but Wendy was a beast at what she did. Travis rested his hands on Wendy's head as she continued to deep throat him. Travis wanted to tell her to stop but he couldn't remember the last time he got head: good head at that. Nina had never shown as much enthusiasm as Wendy did when she went down on him.

He let out a groan and thrust his hips forward as she matched his rhythm. Wendy hummed, licked, and slurped like her life depended on it. Once Travis started grinding in her mouth, she knew her mission was accomplished. Suddenly she stopped and covered her face. She quickly stood up and pretended to be embarrassed. "I'm so sorry. I don't know what got into me, I'm so ashamed."

Travis was still in shock but he quickly put his penis away and pulled up his shorts. "I don't know what just happened but no need to be ashamed. You're good."

Travis didn't know how he went from eating a meal to receiving head all in a matter of fifteen minutes, but it was much needed. He just wished it came from the woman he married, not one of his employees. Wendy and Travis stood awkwardly for a few seconds before Travis finally broke the ice.

"Thank you, though. I appreciate it," he said sincerely.

Wendy wasn't sure if he was thanking her for the food or the head but she didn't care. Once she saw how he reacted to what she did, she knew that he would be her man soon. Wendy smiled at him as she picked up the empty container that Travis ate out of. "See you tomorrow, boss."

Travis watched Wendy as she walked out of his office. He stood for a few minutes waiting for his dick to soften before he sat down and rested his head on his desk. Although there was no penetration, he couldn't help but feel like he had just cheated on his wife. Granted she hasn't been on her job, but she should have been the only woman with his dick in her mouth.

"Fuck!" he said, banging his fist down on his desk. Travis' emotions were all over the place, especially since he wanted to call Wendy back in to finish what she started.

CHAPTER 19

Allie and Chanel met up to have a few drinks since Mascara & Moscato was clearly on hold. Neither of the girls had spoken to Nina although Chanel attempted to reach out to her a few times.

Allie arrived at the restaurant and immediately ordered a margarita. Her and Spade had been constantly arguing and it was stressing Allie the hell out. She was sick of feeling like a prisoner in her own home. She constantly felt the need to tip toe around Spade trying not to irritate him but after him spending their son's money and her rendezvous with Heem, Allie was fed up.

She knew she deserved more and she planned on demanding more. She loved Spade to death but she started to feel like he was holding her back. She was growing more confident by the day, thanks to Heem, and she was ready to move forward with her life.

The thought of Heem made Allie smile. She hadn't slept with him since their first time together because she didn't want to become a habitual cheater but they definitely flirted a lot. Allie was with Spade so long, she'd forgotten what it felt like to flirt and be intrigued by somebody.

"What you smiling about?" asked Chanel as she walked up to the table where Allie was seated.

"I didn't even realize I was smiling," replied Allie, standing up to hug Chanel.

"Girl, look at you! You look awesome!" Exclaimed Chanel, looking Allie over. She was casually dressed in a black fitted shirt that showed her midriff, paired with some distressed blue jeans with sandals. "Spin around, let me see you!"

Allie did a confident twirl letting Chanel see her new and improved body.

"Look at that ass, girl. All you need is some pom-poms and you'll be high school Allie again," gushed Chanel. She truly thought Allie looked amazing. Over the last few weeks, they've become closer than they'd been since they met way back in middle school.

After they ordered their food, Allie and Chanel caught each other up on what had been going on in their lives. Allie skipped the part about how she slept with her trainer. She and Chanel were cool, but that was something Allie would take to her grave. After next week, she and Heem would probably never see each other again because Allie planned on getting a membership at a gym closer to her house.

"So has he replaced the money he took," asked Chanel, referring to Spade taking Jeremiah's school money.

Allie poked her lips out and tilted her head. "Now you know damn well he hasn't. That's why we've been walking around the house not talking."

Chanel shook her head as she ate her pasta. "That's a damn shame. So, what are you going to do?"

"Oh, Jeremiah will be good, trust me. One of these bills is just going to have to wait," shrugged Allie, picking at her salad. "Spade's phone is at the top of the list."

"You're going to cut his phone off?" laughed Chanel.

"Yeah, he don't need it. It ain't like he waiting on no calls for work," Allie said becoming irritated.

"I commend you, girl. You're such a strong woman," admitted Chanel.

Allie smiled. "Thank you. What's going with you and Jah the Ghost?" Allie joked, referring to Chanel's boyfriend, whom she's never met.

"Oh, you tried it!" said Chanel, mimicking Tamar Braxton. "We're good. You will meet him very soon. "

"What about Eric? And how's EJ?"

"Girl EJ is good; he is with Eric this weekend. His wife finally let him back home, especially when she found out he was staying at my house," said Chanel with a smirk on her face.

"You need to leave that girl alone," laughed Allie.

"I will once she leaves my man alone," laughed Chanel. She knew Eric would never leave Talia but she also knew he would never leave her alone.

Allie laughed but didn't respond. She didn't agree with the fact that Chanel was sleeping with a married man but who was she to judge? She had unprotected sex with her trainer, a man she barely knew. Her only regret was being so caught up that she didn't make him protect himself, but Allie went and got tested and came out clean.

"So, have you talked to Nina?" asked Allie.

"I called the heifer twice and she sent me straight to voicemail," said Chanel, rolling her eyes.

"Maybe Travis is back and she's giving him all of her time."

"Girl lies! Travis moved out completely, bitch. He has a whole apartment," said Chanel.

"That's tea! Are you serious?" asked Allie in shock.

Chanel nodded her head as she sipped her margarita.

"I feel bad now," said Allie. She was pissed at Nina but she had no idea that Travis had moved out. "We need to go check on her. And Sweetie."

"Yes! I haven't heard from her in forever. And I find it odd that she only contacts Nina," Chanel pointed out.

"Via text, at that." Allie stressed. "Sweetie has never been big on text messaging." Something was definitely up with Sweetie and she needed to figure out what it was. "Let's pop up at her house after we pay."

Allie waived over the waitress so they could pay for their meals and then show up to Sweetie's house. By popping up on her unannounced, Sweetie wouldn't have time to make up some fake story about why she was acting so distant.

The waitress came back and walked over to Allie. "I'm sorry, the card was declined."

Allie frowned her face in confusion. "Are you sure?" The waitress confirmed that she was.

"There must be something going on with my bank because I have money on this card," said Allie.

Chanel looked at Allie, who was turning red. She picked up her wallet and pulled out two twenty-dollar bills. "Here; keep the change."

Allie was still confused. She knew damn well she had money in the bank. She wasn't rich but she had more than enough to cover a thirty-dollar ticket. "I'll pay you back for that. Their machine must be broke or something."

"Girl, please. Next time, lunch is on you," said Chanel trying to make light of the situation. She could tell that Allie was extremely embarrassed. "Now, let's pay Miss Sweetie a visit."

Allie decided she would call her bank after she left Sweetie's since she lived only ten minutes away. Allie pulled up behind Chanel and parked on the side of the street. Noah's car was gone but Sweetie's car along with another car was parked in the driveway.

Allie and Chanel rang the doorbell and waited for Sweetie to answer. They could hear some noise inside the house but no one came to the door. Chanel stepped off the porch and took out her phone to call Sweetie but the phone went straight to voicemail.

Allie rang the doorbell again and knocked harder. Seconds later, the door swung open and a heavyset girl appeared wearing a large t-shirt and an even larger scowl on her face. "Who are you?" She asked looking directly at Allie.

Chanel looked her up and down. "Who the hell are you?"

"I'm a friend of Sweetie's," replied Allie. She decided to be polite and not petty because she was a guest at her friend's home.

The girl rolled her eyes and walked away. "Jameka, you have visitors."

Allie and Chanel looked at each other before stepping inside the house and closing the door. Allie hadn't been to Sweetie's house since she moved back so she felt weird standing there. Chanel was trying to figure out who the bitch with the attitude was.

"What, who?" asked Sweetie as she peeked around the corner. "Oh shit," she said and disappeared.

"What the fuck is going on?" Muttered Chanel. Allie shrugged, asking herself the same thing.

Seconds later, Sweetie reappeared, wearing a wavy brown wig. She didn't have enough time to put makeup on the bruises that were plastered on her neck. She was so surprised to see Allie and Chanel standing in her foyer. She tried to calm down and act as normal as possible but she wasn't allowed to have company so she needed them gone as soon as possible.

"Hey ladies," said Sweetie, walking towards her friends with open arms and a big, fake smile.

After they exchanged hugs, Allie gave Sweetie a once over. "I love the wig! I don't even want to know what your hair looks like underneath there. You ran and grabbed that wig so fast!"

Sweetie laughed and turned around and led the ladies into her living room. She didn't want to seem suspicious by not letting them further into the house.

"Screw all that, who's the bitch with the attitude?" asked Chanel, wondering where she had disappeared to.

"Y'all have to excuse her, that's Noah's sister," replied Sweetie, nonchalantly.

"Noah's sister needs an attitude adjustment," replied Chanel, annoyed.

Allie took a seat on the couch next to Chanel while Sweetie busied herself in the kitchen.

"So, why haven't you returned our calls?' Allie cut straight to the chase.

"I'm sorry y'all, I've just been constantly on the move. I haven't had time to talk to anyone," said Sweetie bringing the girls bottles of water before walking over to her dining table and taking a seat.

"You text Nina quite often," Allie shot back. She could have sworn she saw Sweetie's eyes widen before she replied.

"Y'all know how Nina is. She wouldn't have stopped calling if I didn't. I have been so busy so I just send her a text for assurance," lied Sweetie. "You know Nina can be a bit annoying."

"You're right about that!" Chanel agreed. "We haven't talked to her either."

"What, why?" asked Sweetie. She then remembered that Noah could be home any minute. "You know what; we can talk about it over lunch tomorrow." Sweetie knew damn well she couldn't go to lunch with them but she would worry about that later.

"That sounds good," said Allie, looking at Sweetie. Her face seemed swollen and she wondered if Sweetie was pregnant and hiding it.

"I'm about to go pick up Dallas," said Sweetie, standing. Chanel and Allie followed suit.

"Can I use your restroom before I go?" asked Chanel, who did not want to hold her bladder until she got home. Chanel was leery about using other people's restrooms, but Sweetie was her girl and super clean.

"Sure, first door to the right," replied Sweetie.

Chanel quickly scurried to the restroom. After she handled her business and washed her hands, Chanel went to reach for a napkin when she saw a hospital band. She read Sweetie's name and noticed the date. Sweetie was admitted into the hospital over a week ago.

Chanel dried her hands and walked to the living room. She didn't see Allie or Sweetie so she walked outside and saw them talking in the driveway. She walked over and interrupted their conversation.

"Why didn't you tell us you were in the hospital? And don't say you weren't because I saw the arm band in the restroom." Chanel stood with her arms folded waiting on Sweetie to answer.

"I wasn't feeling good so Noah insisted that I go to the ER to be safe. I came home the same day, it was just dehydration." Sweetie was becoming such a good liar and she hated it.

Chanel breathed a sigh of relief. "What is it with you heifers and hospitals lately?" Chanel said a quick prayer that her or her son wouldn't end up in the hospital at the rate they were going.

Noah's headlights interrupted their conversation. Shit, Sweetie thought. Noah was going to lose his mind over the fact that her friends were there. She watched as he pulled in the driveway and parked. He stepped out of the car with a smile on his face. He walked over to Sweetie and gave her a hug and kissed her on her forehead. He looked at Allie and Chanel and smiled. "Hey ladies, why are y'all standing in this heat, come inside."

"Oh, we're leaving but thank you," said Allie. She watched Noah whisper something in Sweetie's ear before walking in the house. Sweetie said her goodbyes and walked into the house.

Chanel and Allie walked to their cars and hugged. "Did she seem a little weird to you?"

"I think she's pregnant. Think about it! She hasn't been feeling good; this hospital visit, her face was a little swollen. She's pregnant," concluded Allie.

Chanel agreed with Allie; it made sense. "One down, one to go," she said.

"Yes, we'll pay Nina a visit tomorrow," said Allie. Chanel and Allie said their goodbyes and went their separate ways.

Sweetie stood in the window watching her friends in her driveway, wishing they would hurry and leave. Noah towered over her silently, which caused Nina to shudder.

"Why were they here?" he asked as he gazed out of the window.

"They came to check on me. I told you they would get suspicious about all the texts," replied Sweetie.

"What did you tell them?" he asked.

"Nothing. I told them that I was dehydrated," replied Sweetie. She wanted to scream and let them know that he'd almost choked her to death but she knew better. Noah was a powerful man in their community so the chances of him being reprimanded were slim to none. He expressed to her many times that he would always come back for her. The only way out was in a box.

"Did they come in the house? You know you're not allowed to have company, don't you?" he asked, running his hand through the wig Sweetie wore.

"Brandi let them in," Sweetie tried to explain.

"You're behaving like a child. Being a little tattletale. They're your friends, not Brandi's. I told you not to have company, not Brandi. You deserve to be punished you know that, right?"

"Noah, please. I'm in enough pain as it is."

Noah reached out to grab her and Sweetie jumped. She was terrified of Noah because she never knew when his mood would switch.

"Please, please," she said on the brink of tears. "Don't hit me."

Noah reached out and softly rubbed her cheek. "I'm not going to hit you, darling. Don't worry." When Noah turned around and walked into their closet, Sweetie breathed a sigh of relief. She was on her way to the kitchen when she heard a loud pop and felt stinging on her neck and shoulders.

Sweetie spun around and saw Noah standing with a leather belt in his hands. "I'm not going to hit you today because my knuckles are still sore, but you will get your ass beat for disrespecting me."

Before she could move, the thick leather ate into her skin causing her to fall backwards. She held her burning cheek and became dizzy. The pain swept through her head as she tried her best to stay awake and focused. The next whip landed on her arms. Sweetie feared for her life as she bit down on her lip to avoid making him angrier by screaming. Noah usually only hit her in places that weren't visible, such as her stomach and back. She knew he was livid since he hit her in the face.

He hit her at least five more times before she finally shrieked. "STOP!"

Noah ignored her pleas as he mercilessly raised his hand and struck her with the belt at least ten more times before Brandi came in and yelled for him to stop.

Sweetie laid helpless as she cried in agony, her entire body trembling. She saw Brandi give her a look of pity before pulling Noah away. Noah, on the other hand, had a face full of rage as he walked away. He shot her a look that said it wasn't over. For the first time, Sweetie just wished he would go ahead and kill her.

She looked up and saw a picture of her daughter Dallas and cried so hard for her. She refused to let him harm her daughter so she took all the abuse instead. At first, Noah made it easy for her to cover the fact that she was being beat and raped on a consistent basis. Now, he just didn't care which let Sweetie know that the end was coming for them both.

CHAPTER 20

Allie left Sweetie's house feeling a lot better about their relationship. Once she was settled in, she called her debit card to check the balance. She knew good and damn well she had money on her card.

"Your balance is eight hundred seventy six dollars and twenty two cents."

The balance was actually more than Allie expected but she didn't question it. She was just satisfied knowing that it was indeed the restaurant's mistake about her card being declined. No sooner than Allie hung up her phone, Spade walked through the door.

"Where are the kids?" asked Allie.

"With your mama," he replied.

"Why?" Allie was confused.

Spade ignored her question as he approached her. He opened Allie's hand and placed two hundred dollars into her palm. "I've been doing a lot of thinking and I have a lot of making up to do. You put up with so much from me and I just wanted to use this weekend to show you how much I truly appreciate you."

Spade looked deep into Allie's eyes as they filled with tears. He wrapped his around her waist, which had gotten slimmer, and squeezed her tight. He buried his head in her neck and caressed her back. He held her so tightly because he could feel her slipping away. Spade made a promise to himself that he would get his self together before he lost his family.

Allie cried as Spade held her because all she wanted was for him to get it together. She didn't want to start over with someone new. She wanted to build her life and career with the person who had been there from the very beginning.

"I love you," she whispered.

"I love you too, baby," he replied, not wanting to let her go. When Spade finally released her from his grip, he stared at Allie and fell in love with her all over again. Something about her had changed in the last few weeks but he couldn't quite put his finger on it. He knew Allie was making some lifestyle changes; he just hoped he wasn't one of them.

"Get dressed; I'm taking you somewhere real special tonight," he said excitedly.

Allie was enthused by Spade's excitement but she also had her reservations. "Baby, we can't really afford to do much of anything right now."

Spade smiled from ear to ear confusing the hell out of Allie. What the hell was so funny about being broke, she thought.

"We can afford a lot right now," said Spade, still smiling. "Come here." Allie followed Spade wondering what the hell he had up his sleeve. He led Allie into their walk-in closet and pulled out a royal blue dress.

"I know blue is your favorite color and since this weekend is all about you, I figured you would like it. It's cool if you don't, I ain't no fashion expert or nothing but I thought this would look good on you."

Allie giggled like a child. It's been a while since she bought herself something new. She grabbed the dress and ran into the bathroom to try it on. She held the dress out and looked at it before stepping into it. Her eyes stopped on the price tag.

"Two hundred dollars?" Allie wouldn't dare spend that much on one article of clothing and neither would Spade, especially since they were in a hole financially.

Allie stepped into the dress and walked back into her bedroom so that Spade could zip up the back. Allie looked at herself in the mirror and gasped. She couldn't believe how perfect it looked on her. The color of the dress was bold and commanded attention. Her new figure filled out the dress in all the right places causing Allie to feel so sexy.

"Wow" whispered Spade, looking at Allie in awe. The way her body looked in that dress, you would think it was made exclusively for her. He licked his lips as he stared at her cleavage, which was classily exposed due to the plunging neckline of the dress. Her hips seemed to be fuller and rounder since her waist was becoming almost non-existing. His eyes dropped to her ass and his dick immediately began to jump.

"You look beautiful, Allie," he said as he kissed her neck softly. She smiled at their reflection in the mirror and knew that they would be okay. "Let's shower and get ready. We need to be out the house in an hour and a half to meet our reservation."

"Reservation?" She asked, stepping out of the dress so that she could freshen up before dinner.

Spade smiled. "I'm going all out for you because that's what you deserve."

Allie tried her best not to kill the mood but she just had to know one thing. "How are you paying for all of this, Spade?"

"Well, I didn't want to say nothing because I wasn't sure how everything would pan out, but I filed a wrongful termination suit against my old job. My nigga Sam in HR told me that my drug test results came back inconclusive, not negative, so I was supposed to be given the opportunity to re-test. Instead, they fired me so I filed the suit three weeks ago. Sam paid for everything because he knew I would win."

Allie's eyes got big. "So, what happened?"

"Shit, they knew they were wrong so they offered me some bread to settle out of court. Money was deposited today," he said proudly.

Allie wanted to jump up and down but she kept her composure until she heard the amount. Spade was desperate so there's no telling how much he would have accepted just to have some money. "How much?"

"Fifty racks," he said as he began to dance around the room.

"WHAT?" yelled Allie. She couldn't believe her ears.

"You heard me right. 50 G's!" he said proudly. As soon as the money hit, he paid Allie back, with interest although she still wasn't aware that he'd overdraft her account at the bar.

Allie screamed and jumped into Spade's arms. Their kiss was so passionate it almost felt as though their tongues were fighting.

"I have ten G's aside for you. I will put the kids some money aside, so you do whatever you want with your portion. It's yours. Let's get caught up on the bills and work towards buying us a house. I'ma give you everything I promised I would," he said sincerely. Truth is, the settlement was 75K, but he had other plans for that money that Allie didn't need to know about.

After they showered and got ready, Allie and Spade walked out of their home feeling like Jay-Z and Beyoncé. Allie's face was beat down and her hair was pulled into a tight bun. As much face as she was giving, she didn't need to hide behind hair. Spade looked so sharp wearing a fitted gray blazer, a pair of straight leg blue jeans, paired with some casual denim shoes. To top it all, he had on a royal blue bowtie, which matched perfectly with Allie's dress.

Spade made dinner reservations for two at Ruth's Chris Steakhouse. They laughed and talked the entire night with no distractions since they agreed to turn their phones off for the night. They made plans to go into business together. Spade would open a barbershop, while she would own the salon and spa. She still planned on becoming a nurse; she would just also be a business owner. They agreed they would buy a house in a nice neighborhood and possibly have another kid in five years.

Allie listened to Spade tell her all his plans for their future and couldn't help but notice he didn't mention the topic of marriage at all. Allie's mama always told her never to question a man about marriage. She said it was the quickest way to run them off so Allie never asked when he would marry her. She often talked about how she wanted her wedding to look while Spade pretended to listen.

Spade noticed a weird expression on Allie's face. "You okay, babe?"

Allie snapped out of her thoughts and tried her best not to ruin their night. "I'm fine baby. I'm just so ready for what's ahead of us."

After dinner, Spade took Allie on a horse and carriage ride through downtown Houston. She was overwhelmed by the power of love as she rested her head on his shoulders. The bright lights and car horns had Allie in a trance. She didn't smoke but she imagined it felt like being high and for a moment, she understood why Spade constantly craved that feeling.

Allie had loved Spade for ten years. They grew up together and fought through the toughest times so she would always love Spade. But that night, Allie fell in love with him again. She remembered why she fell in love with him in the first place. Spade loved the hell out of Allie and would do anything for her and their children. He was nowhere near perfect but he was a damn good man.

Although Allie enjoyed her time with Heem, she knew that she was wrong and would never let it happen again. But she needed it. She needed to feel desirable and confident again; she needed to love herself again. She knew that Spade loved every inch of her so he didn't mind that she was gaining weight. He also didn't notice what it did to her confidence so she was glad she met Heem.

But Spade was the only man for her. She'd wanted to walk away plenty of times but she knew that she would always go back. They planned their lives out a long time ago and they stood together every time their plans didn't work out.

"I know I don't really talk about the subject too much but I just want you to know that I'm going to marry you, Allie," said Spade with a serious expression on his face.

"I know baby, I'll wait forever if I have to," replied Allie.

For some reason, that statement bothered Spade. Allie deserved much better than him but he believed that she really would wait forever for him. But why should she have to? Spade started to wonder if he was holding Allie back. She had the potential to be great but she had to constantly slow her pace so he could keep up. Sure, they were blessed with a lump sum of money but that was his salary for the year. What was he going to do after that?

All that money only meant one thing: more expensive weed and bottles. Spade wasn't strong enough to fight temptation so he knew somehow, someway he would find a way to fuck everything up. His mood instantly changed and he was drifting to a darker place. Allie took his hand and rubbed it as if she was telling him everything would be okay; it was funny how they could communicate with one another without ever saying a word.

Allie was his soul mate. Spade believed God created her especially for him. That's why it hurt so bad to have to leave her. Spade quickly blocked out all negative thoughts and focused on enjoying his night with Allie.

Spade checked them into their suite at Hotel ZaZa. Allie looked around the hotel in shock. She'd never seen anything like it. The Marriott was fancy to her so she was obsessed with this upscale hotel. Spade opened the door and let Allie walked in first.

Allie lost her breath for a second. She not soon as she stepped in the room, which smelled like lavender and vanilla, her favorite scents. The walkway was dimly lit and lined with white votive candles. White rose petals lead the way to the master bedroom, which was closed. Allie looked back at Spade who was smiling at her.

"You really outdid yourself, babe," she said.

"Open the door," he instructed. Allie nervously pushed open the door and was caught by surprise. The room was filled with several bouquets of blue and white roses.

She looked at Spade with tears in her eyes. It was the most beautiful thing he'd ever done for her.

"Nine bouquets for every year we've been together. Each bouquet contains twelve flowers for every month that I didn't buy you flowers these last nine years," he said. He reached into his back pocket and pulled out a little blue box. "And this is a thank you gift. For everything."

Allie opened the box and was greeted with a sparkling platinum diamond necklace. Although it was gorgeous, Allie hoped that it would be a ring inside the box. Nonetheless, she was having the night of her life.

She thanked Spade the entire night, almost everywhere in the hotel room. As they made love, Allie was on cloud nine and hoped that she would never have to come down.

CHAPTER 21

A loud noise caused Nina to shoot up. She looked at the time and noticed that it almost noon. Nina couldn't remember the last time she'd slept in so late but it had been awhile since she had been depressed. Not talking to her friends and Travis was really weighing in on her. She listened for the noise again but when she didn't hear anything, she figured she might have had a bad dream.

Nina lay back down and tried to go back to sleep. She tossed and turned for a few minutes before she heard her bedroom door open. Nina's heart began to pound as she looked around her room for some sort of weapon. When her door opened slowly and she saw Allie's head peek through, she breathed a sigh of relief. How could she have forgotten they each had an emergency key? Allie and Chanel walked in carrying doughnuts and orange juice and Nina couldn't help but smile.

They sat on her bed and ate silently as Allie put Maury on TV. Nina knew she needed to apologize to her friends despite her ego. "I know I've been a bitch lately and I apologize. I was wrong for taking my problems out on you guys."

Allie waved her hand dismissively. "It's fine; we understand."

Chanel nodded her head knowing Nina was going through a tough period in her life. "Nina, we're not the ones that deserve an apology, Travis is."

Nina rolled her eyes and let out a groan. "Chanel, stop."

"What type of friend would I be if I sat back and watched you throw away your marriage?" asked Chanel as she stared at her best friend waiting for an answer.

"I'm not throwing away anything, Chanel. We're in a fight, and he's sleeping on his friend's couch. It's no big deal," shrugged Nina.

Chanel flipped her hair but remained silent. She didn't want to stir up more issues. Allie avoided eye contact as she chewed her doughnut.

"I love you girls, but seriously, my marriage is fine. I'm sure Travis will be home any day now," said Nina confidently.

Chanel was tired of biting her tongue so she finally told Nina the truth. "Travis is living in his own apartment, Nina. He really feels unappreciated and lost."

Nina suddenly lost her appetite. She tried her best not to regurgitate the doughnuts she's just consumed. She looked at Allie, who still refused to look at her.

Chanel gave her a look of sympathy. "I'm only trying to help you before you lose a good man, Nina."

Nina couldn't believe her ears. Travis got his own place? Was he seriously done with her? Nina had to get her shit together fast because she refused to lose her husband over bullshit.

"Enough about my marriage, what's been up with you ladies?" Nina asked with a smile.

"Nina, talk to us. Stop pretending that you're okay when you're not," said Allie.

"What do y'all want me to say? Yes, I'm hurt, okay? I'm miserable but Travis left so that's on him. I'm not chasing him. I just don't want to lose him and you two," replied Nina, sadly.

Allie scooted next to Nina and hugged her. "We will always be here, Nina. And so will Travis if you just let him love you." Chanel joined in on the group hug as Nina finally broke down and cried.

"My life is spiraling out of control and I don't know what to do to stop it," cried Nina as the hot tears burned her cheeks. She couldn't remember the last time she had actually just let her guard down and released all the emotions she had bottled up.

Her friends hugged her and comforted her the entire thirty minutes of her bawling her eyes out. Nina knew she had to make some changes if she planned on keeping her husband.

"Let's get dolled up and go have drinks. You need to get out of this house. Later on, you need to call Trav, okay?" said Chanel.

Nina nodded her head as she got dressed in a graphic tee and a pair of skinny jeans. She threw on a pair of sandals and was ready to go. Although all the girls were dressed casually, they were still sure to be the baddest in any setting.

The girls decided to go to Buffalo Wild Wings to drink and catch up. They tried to call Sweetie but she didn't answer, as usual. She texted Nina and told her that she and Noah were taking some quality time for themselves so Nina understood. She wished she would have done that with Travis and maybe he would still be home with her.

Once the girls sat down and ordered drinks, they began to catch up on each other's lives.

"Well, I have good news!" Announced Allie. "Not only will I be walking the stage this fall, Spade and I are doing so good y'all."

Chanel and Nina smiled at Allie noticing how happy she looked. "I forgot to tell you that you are looking fabulous these days, girl," said Nina. "And I'm so glad to hear about you and Spade. Is he working again?"

Allie shook her head. "Not yet, but his job did an out of court settlement with him and he got a nice amount of money. Apparently his drug test was inconclusive so they had no right to fire him."

"Won't He do it," said Chanel jerking her body like she caught the Holy Ghost.

"I'm so happy. I feel like we can finally start our lives together the right way," said Allie, still smiling. "He took me on the most romantic date ever last night."

Allie explained every detail of what Spade had done for her. It had been a while since she was able to brag about her man so she was excited to tell her story, not missing one thing. Chanel and Nina listened intently, genuinely happy for Allie. Lord knows Spade had put her through enough so she deserved all that was coming her way.

"Maybe, we'll hear some wedding bells soon," said Nina, sipping her Strawberry Margarita.

Allie shrugged her shoulders bashfully. "Maybe." Allie was truly on cloud nine so she believed anything was possible.

"I'm so happy for you, girl," said Chanel, reaching out to hold Allie's hand. "You're one hell of a woman."

"Is this seat taken?"

All three heads turned simultaneously as Eric's wife Talia stood there with a smug expression on her face. Talia wasn't an ugly woman by far, but nothing about her stood out. She was cute in a Plain Jane sort of way.

Chanel looked her up and down before answering. "No, it's not but you're not welcome to sit."

Talia smirked before firing back. "That's fine. I have no problem standing to say what I have to say."

"What you have to say can wait, as you can see I'm busy talking to my friends," replied Chanel, getting annoyed with this bitch. She had some nerve approaching them like she was some kind of boss bitch.

Nina and Allie watched in silence. Chanel could hold her own when it came to talking but it would only take one wrong move for them to be on her ass like white on rice.

"Woman to woman, I'm asking to speak with you. You can either continue to be a child or you can woman up and at least have a conversation with me. After all, you are fucking my husband. Now, would you like for this to be one on one or should it be a group discussion since I'm sure they know about your whorish ways," said Talia, calmly.

"Girl, watch yourself before you get clowned. No need for the name-calling. The only whore in this situation is your husband, who can't keep his dick out of me. Have a seat, if that's how you feel," said Chanel dryly.

Talia sat next to Allie and stared Chanel down before speaking. "It's obvious that you and my husband are still sleeping with each other. Why you would continue to sleep with a man who doesn't respect you is beyond me."

"You think he respects you, Talia? Fucking me in your bed?" asked Chanel. She was slightly amused by the situation at hand.

Nina didn't like the way this conversation was going and wanted to intervene, instead she sat silently watching the mess unfold.

Talia let out a small laugh. "You think that's cute don't you, Chanel? Understand this, I can change those sheets and wash away any trace of you. But you? You have to lie in a bed that will never be yours. Getting fucked by a man that will never go to sleep and wake up to you every day. Fucking in my bed hurts you more than you know. That's why you left your earring under my pillow. You wanted to prove a point that has already been proven. He's a dog. But guess what? I have papers on that man and that earring only solidifies the fact that when I walk, I leave with half of all that."

Chanel let Talia's words go in one ear and out the other. "Who gives a fuck? EJ will always be good; it only takes one trip to the attorney general. None of that matters because Eric is always going to want my pretty little pussy because it's the best he's ever had. So, run along boo because I don't care about your marriage one way or the other. I'll be glad when your dusty ass is out of the picture."

Talia suddenly became angry. "Then what? Huh, Chanel? He'll be with you? Hell no! You're not the only boo. So don't feel special. You're just the most convenient. So after you take that trip to the attorney general, take another to the clinic and pray he didn't give that pretty little pussy the same herpes he gave me, bitch."

Allie and Nina's mouths dropped. They were so much in shock that they had no clue how Talia's hair ended up in Chanel's hand. Chanel had her hair gripped so tight it looked like she was trying to pull the girl clear across the table. Talia grabbed Chanel's drink and threw it in her face, causing Chanel to stumble backward.

Allie, who was sitting next to Talia, pushed her out of instinct. Talia fell out of her chair and onto the floor where Chanel sat on top of her and began hitting her in the face. Nina let Chanel hit her a few times before breaking the fight up.

By that time, the staff was surrounding them and all the customers were looking at them like they'd lost their damn minds. Chanel was cursing and telling Talia she was going to kill her. One of the waiters helped Talia up. Her hair was covering her face, so Nina gasped when she saw the blood covering her mouth and nose. Allie pulled five twenties out her purse and threw it on the table. She tapped their server to let him know that the money was there. She grabbed Chanel and started to push her out of the restaurant.

"I will beat your ass every time I see you, bitch!" yelled Chanel.

Talia licked her bloody mouth before laughing. "Why, bitch? Because the truth hurts?" Talia knew she deserved that ass whooping but it was worth it. The look on Chanel's face was priceless and she loved watching her fall off that white horse. Talia hated Eric's ass! She wanted nothing more than to leave him, but having herpes caused her to stay; she couldn't live the rest of her life without dick and she damn sure didn't want to infect anyone else. Talia sighed as she got in her car. She knew she should have left his ass when he got Chanel pregnant; she just wanted to prove that she won. Joke was clearly on her.

Allie and Nina tried their best to calm Chanel down but she was still fuming. "Bitch come in there and say some foul shit like that in front of the whole restaurant. Lying and shit!"

Nina didn't want to be the bad guy in this situation but she loved her friend too much to not say anything. "What if she wasn't lying, Chanel?"

Allie grimaced when Nina asked that question but honestly, she wondered the same thing. Chanel looked at Nina like she lost her mind. "Because I ain't no dirty ass bitch, I don't have herpes!"

"It has nothing to do with you being dirty, Chanel," said Allie as she rubbed Chanel's arm. They were sitting in the backseat of Nina's car.

"How would he have caught it though?" asked Chanel, clearly shocked or in denial. Hell, maybe she was both.

Nina looked at Chanel through the rearview mirror and her heart broke. Chanel looked beyond hurt. "I mean, Talia did say he was sleeping with other people."

Chanel fought back the tears that had been trying to fall since Talia spat that news at her. She didn't want to believe that she had that disease and she just wanted her friends to drop it. Chanel instantly regretted a lot of the decisions she made in life. Most of them to be spiteful.

On the outside, Chanel tried her hardest to be tough but inside she was just a scared little girl. The same girl that got bullied for being tall, black, and skinny. She never learned to love herself so she took whatever she could get when it came to men. All she needed was to feel wanted and though Eric treated her awful, he made her feel wanted. When they met, she never intended to have an affair with him.

She was working as his receptionist and he told her all the time how much he needed her because she made his job easier. Soon, he began to tell her that he wanted her and she would make his life easier. Chanel fell in love with his lies because for once she felt good about herself. Soon she would realize that he was no different than the rest but instead of admitting that she failed, she accepted what she could get from him. Some love was better than no love in her eyes. Here she was dark chocolate Chanel sleeping with the husband of a light skinned girl. It may sound crazy, but that made Chanel happy given the way she grew up.

She stared out the window as Allie held her silently. Chanel flipped her hair and looked at her nails. "Did I look cute when I was fighting? I think I saw a few cameras."

Allie and Nina knew that Chanel was probably embarrassed so they allowed her to change the subject.

"You know you never miss a beat," said Nina, who planned on letting the situation go for now. But she would make damn sure Chanel took her ass down to the clinic to get tested.

When they made it back to Nina's house, Allie had to leave to grocery shop so Nina offered to take Chanel home.

The car ride to Chanel's was mostly silent. Chanel was lost in her thoughts and preparing herself for the worst. At least it's not AIDS, Chanel thought. She shuddered as soon as the thought crossed her mind. She didn't know why she thought Eric was only sleeping with her. She should have known better.

"You have to tell Jah," said Nina, snapping Chanel out her trance.

Shit, she thought, I didn't even think about Jah. "Tell him for what? Talia is a bitter bitch and she's an uppity bitch. Do you really think if she had herpes, she would tell me of all people?"

Nina didn't care whether she was telling the truth or not, Chanel needed to get tested. "Better to be safe than sorry. And it's only fair to Jah, you have to tell him."

"No! I'm not telling him anything because I don't have anything!"

"Okay, so there shouldn't be a problem with us all going to get tested together. Just to make sure we're all good," insisted Nina.

Nina was like a hangnail. Just annoying and painful. Chanel groaned, knowing there was no winning or escaping this conversation. "I'll get tested Nina. And when I come back clean, there will be no reason to tell Jaheim anything."

Nina shrugged her shoulders, satisfied with the deal. "And I hope you don't plan on fucking Eric again," said Nina as she pulled up to Chanel's apartment building.

Chanel shot Nina an annoyed look as she stepped out of the car. "Bye, Nina St. Claire, don't forget to call Travis."

Nina watched as Chanel sashayed up the stairs to her apartment. She flipped the middle finger at Nina before walking into her apartment. Nina laughed as pulled off but she couldn't help but feel bad for her friend. Chanel had a good heart; she was just a mess. But Nina was a firm believer in karma, who was a bigger and badder bitch than Chanel could ever be. They tried to tell her nothing good would come to a woman who was sleeping with a married man.

CHAPTER 22

Chanel walked into her house and closed the door. The minute it was locked, she slid on the floor and screamed. She let out the loudest wail that her body could muster up. She just couldn't get it right. She hated that she wasn't strong enough to walk away, she hated that she was so weak. Jaheim was the best man she could ask for, but like a fool, she was stuck on man who treated her lower than life. Chanel was so used to being lost that she didn't know how it felt to be found.

She pulled her knees to her chest and rested her head on her arms and cried. She felt a hand on hers, which caused her to jump. Her heart nearly jumped out her chest when she saw Jaheim staring at her with concerned eyes.

She had been so zoned out that she didn't even notice his car outside on her way in. She was surprised to see him in her place because he never went there while she was gone.

"Are you okay, babe?" he asked, embracing Chanel. He had never in his life heard a scream so gut wrenching and piercing.

"What-what are you doing here," she said into his chest.

"I used my key but I thought you were in here sleep. I saw your car parked out there," he explained.

Chanel forgot Allie picked her up this morning to go to Nina's. She had no clue Jah was there, otherwise she wouldn't have been screaming like a lunatic.

"Talk to me baby, what's wrong?" asked Jaheim as caressed her back. He had a tight grip on Chanel, who was nearly shaking.

Chanel had to think fast because there was no way in hell she was telling him the truth. She took a deep breath and started to

154

talk slowly. "My friend came over today and we were talking and drinking and all of a sudden, I get these cramps so I go to the restroom and I feel pressure like maybe I have to do number two. I push and I feel myself peeing. But, it's not pee; it's blood, some of it coming out in clots. Then I see a gummy bear looking thing in the toilet and freak out. So, Allie runs in and tell me that I'm miscarrying. She drove me to the hospital, which is why my car is still here and they cleaned the rest of it out. Because I didn't take a picture, there was no way to know how far along I was but that's why I'm so distraught. I know how much you wanted a baby," said Chanel as she broke down again, surprising her damn self. She didn't know if that's how miscarriages really went down but men don't pay that much attention to detail so she was sure he would buy it.

Jaheim looked at Chanel in shock. He felt really bad for her but since he never knew she was pregnant, he didn't have a connection with the baby to feel the devastation. His heart went out to his girl, who was clearly shaken up. "It's going to be okay. We'll get through this."

"I just feel so bad because I didn't know! I've been drinking and smoking; it's all my fault."

"Shh...shh... Don't say that. God is in control, you want to say a prayer?" asked Jah.

For the first time, Chanel hated that Jah was a good man. She couldn't let him pray for her over a lie. "I just want to sleep, baby. Let's pray later when I have the energy to do it with you."

Jaheim nodded his head and stood up. He leaned down and scooped Chanel up and carried her to her room. He laid her down on her bed and took her shirt off. He wasn't surprised to see that she wasn't wearing a bra.

Chanel tried her best not to ask him what the fuck he was doing. She knew damn well he wasn't trying to have sex after she told him she had a miscarriage. She claimed to be too tired to pray so that meant she had to be too tired to talk shit too. Chanel started to panic thinking he really didn't buy her miscarriage story until he turned her on her stomach and began rubbing her back. She couldn't help but moan and tried her hardest not to jump his bones; that man was amazing with his hands.

As Jaheim massaged Chanel's tense back, he wondered why Chanel didn't call him. "Bae, why didn't you call me? I would have come to the hospital."

"I didn't know what to say. I wanted to tell you in person, plus I had to be strong for my friend who was freaking out more than me," said Chanel, wishing he would drop it. One more suspicious question and she was going to start snoring.

Jaheim thought about the story Chanel told him earlier. "Which friend was that again?" His heart started to beat as he started to put a few things together in his mind.

"Allie. You haven't met her yet but she'll be at my dinner next weekend," said Chanel, making a mental note to let Allie know what was going on so she wouldn't fuck up this lie Chanel worked so hard to create.

Jaheim began to think about a few things. Allie wasn't that common of a name so he started to wonder if he had sex with his girl's friend. Travis introduced him to Spade, who he remembered was in a relationship for almost ten years; Allie told him she was with her man for nine.

Jaheim shook his head as he tried to figure out how the fuck to clean this mess up.

"Babe, that's too rough," whined Chanel. Jaheim hadn't even noticed that he was taking his frustrations out on Chanel's back.

"Sorry, babe," he said, cursing himself out. He saw with his own eyes how much Spade loved Allie so it fucked him up to know that he had some real competition. It would be much harder to be with Allie knowing that both Chanel and Spade were in the way, but he was determined.

Jah was a master manipulator who always got what he wanted. And what he wanted was Alyssa Spencer.

CHAPTER 23

Travis invited Jah, Spade, and Noah over to his new apartment to watch ESPN and drink beer. It was a beautiful Sunday to relax and chill with boys. Travis still missed Nina but he was becoming used to not hearing from her so it started to bother him less and less. That is, until it was time to go to sleep. There was no better feeling than wrapping his arms around Nina as she softly grinded her round against his pelvis. His dick almost got hard just thinking about it.

"Nigga, is you smoking or what?" asked Jah as she nudged him. "I been trying to pass you the blunt for like ten minutes."

"You ain't been doing nothing for ten minutes nigga," Travis replied as he snatched the blunt and brought it to his lips. He took two long puffs and passed it to Spade. He refused.

"I ain't fucking with it. I ain't even drinking," said Spade, holding his hands up.

"That's what's up bro. I didn't know, I wouldn't have had you around this shit if I knew," said Travis feeling bad. Temptation was a motherfucker and he didn't want to be the one to throw him off track.

"Nah, you good man. Ain't nothing going to stop me from getting clean. Shit been looking good in my life lately. I gotta stay focused. I'm ready to give my girl the wedding of her dreams," said Spade. Travis was proud of Spade. He had that look in his eye that said he was serious about getting his self together.

"Much respect to you my dude. Congrats on admitting your problem and working towards a solution," said Travis as Noah agreed.

"So, you are going to marry her? You ready now?" said Jaheim in a joking manner.

"Almost. Once I do this rehab for these three months, I'll be ready."

"Wow, rehab?" asked Noah, shocked.

Travis frowned his face. He knew Spade liked to drink but he didn't know it was that bad to where he needed rehab.

"It's a voluntary rehab. I check myself in and out. I gotta conquer this demon before it takes everything from me. But y'all can't tell y'all girls because I don't want Allie to know," said Spade. He looked around the room and saw a bunch of confused motherfuckers.

"Look, with Allie pushing me and rooting for me, I can do anything because I'm not going to want to let her down. But I need to know that I can do this for me. I gotta fight this battle alone that way I'll know I really wanted it," explained Spade. Although he and Allie had a beautiful night together, he learned he was closer to losing her than he thought.

"So how are you going to do this without Allie knowing?" asked Noah, still not fully comprehending what he meant.

"I'm leaving her," Spade replied solemnly.

"Nigga, what?" Travis thought Spade had lost his damn mind. He needed that blunt more than he thought he did. "That's the dumbest thing I've ever heard."

Jaheim stayed quiet. It was actually a brilliant idea. Three months was more than enough time for him to make Allie fall for him. She already trusted him so it would be a piece of cake with Spade being out of the picture.

Noah shook his head in disbelief. He didn't care one way or the other; he was just entertained by the conversation. "So, let me get this right. You're going to leave your girl to secretly go to rehab for three months and then what? You expect her to be there when you get back?"

Spade answered with no hesitation. "I know my woman and she's going to wait for me. And when I get back, I'ma give her everything she deserve and more."

"Why are you doing this again?" asked Travis.

Spade thought long and hard about whether he wanted to reveal something so personal. Fuck it, he thought. "Allie cheated on me."

Jaheim shot his head up and looked around hoping no one noticed. "Why would you think that?"

"Nah, not Allie." Travis dismissed his statement with no second thought. Allie was one of the most loyal women he knew. Spade was tripping.

"I've been with Allie since I was fourteen. That's my soul mate, I know her. The other night when he had sex, she was loose and free and so fucking freaky. I loved it but that wasn't my Allie, bro."

"Maybe she was just extra excited," reasoned Noah.

"Somebody fucked my girl," said Spade. "I know what she feels like. I know her, man. She's given birth to two of my kids. So twice, I had to wait six weeks so I know what she's supposed to feel like if we haven't fucked in seven weeks."

Travis sat speechless as he looked at his boy. Spade looked like he was real fucked up about the situation.

Spade shrugged. "But I ain't even mad at her. I haven't been on my job. She been taking care of both my kids and me; she ain't never complained once. Another nigga did what my pride wouldn't let me do. The nigga made her feel appreciated. So, I deserved that but I ain't losing my girl without a fight. If I know Allie like I think I know her, she gon' hold me down.

"And if she don't?" asked Jah.

"Then I lost a good woman and I'll have to live with that forever," answered Spade.

The men got quiet for a few moments but luckily, the doorbell put the end to the deafening silence that had fallen across the room.

Noah was closest to the door so he answered it to find an attractive woman standing in front of him holding a pot.

"You gonna stare all day or let me in?" she asked impatiently.

Noah moved to the side, allowing the woman to walk into the house. Travis turned around to see who was at the door.

"Hey, Wendy," he said as she walked into the kitchen.

"It's more food in the car. Can you nice fellas go get it?" asked Wendy sweetly as she sat the pot of meatballs on the stove. She looked in his cabinet and pulled out a pack of napkins and set them on the bar. She wanted his friends to see that she had been there enough to know her way around the kitchen.

Although she spent a lot of time at Travis's cooking and cleaning, he had yet to give her the dick. Hell, she hadn't even seen the dick. She didn't want to cross the line and be pushy but she was growing very impatient. She needed to fuck his brains out if she ever wanted to make sure Travis never went back to his wife.

Spade broke his silence first as they walked to Wendy's car. "Who the hell is that?"

All eyes were on him as Travis looked at each of his boys. "It's nothing like that, fellas. Wendy works with me. She always cooking like she's feeding a village so she brings me food from

161

time to time to make sure her boss eats," explained Travis. He wasn't a square; he knew Wendy was feigning for a piece of his dick.

"She trying to get to your dick through your stomach, nigga. Be careful," warned Spade.

"I got this fellas, don't worry. I'm still a married man," said Travis as they each grabbed a pot and walked back toward his apartment.

"Long as you know it," said Jah.

Noah was silent as usual but he was glad he decided to go hang out with them. He learned a lot today, which was helping him with his plan of breaking that entire circle apart. That way, he could finally have Sweetie all to himself. They got her in way too much trouble; he really didn't understand why she liked them so much.

After the food was delivered to the kitchen, Spade was ready to bounce. He didn't want any parts in even getting to know Wendy because she gave him such a bad vibe walking around that kitchen like it was hers. "I'll fuck with you later; I'm about to skate," said Spade, dabbing Travis up.

"Shit, me too," said Jah, remembering to check on Chanel.

Noah followed suit and decided he would go home too. He needed to let Sweetie know how much of a whore her dearest Allie is. He tried to control his anger as he wondered whether or not Sweetie already knew of the infidelity and hid it from him.

"A'ight, I'll holler at y'all later," said Travis as he shut the door. Wendy walked out the restroom only to find an empty room.

"They left?" asked Wendy as she secretly jumped for joy on the inside. She thought she would have to wait all night for them to leave.

"Yep!"Travis replied, flopping down on the couch.

"You hungry?" She asked as she walked to the kitchen.

"Not right now!" he yelled.

Wendy got a little frustrated. She would just have to wait a little longer to seduce him. She made him a special bowl of mashed potatoes. The ingredients included sour cream, cheese, and bacon bits, with a few crushed ecstasy pills. She wasn't sure whether that plan would have worked but she damn sure was willing to try.

Travis was too good of a man to let slip away so if Nina wouldn't give him a baby, she sure would.

"Well, what about a drink? You still have this Jack Daniel's," she yelled.

"Yeah, go ahead and pour me one," he said.

Jackpot! She had been going to Travis's house often and studying him very closely. She noticed that Jack Daniels caused him to doze off after a couple glasses. She also noticed that his dick got hard when he was sleep, which made her plan so much easier. If she didn't know any better, she would have thought Travis wanted it just as bad as she did.

She took out her bag of X pills and crushed two in his drink. He would be good and horny by the time he realized what was happening and she would be riding him too good for him to stop. After she stirred his drink, she walked over and sat next to him on the couch. She handed him his drink and sipped her cup of sprite.

"What you drinking?" asked Travis, looking at Wendy's glass.

"Vodka and sprite," she answered with a smile. Wendy got comfortable on the couch and leaned her body towards him.

Travis felt bad for leading Wendy on. She was an amazing woman, but she no match for his wife. "Wendy, I really appreciate all that you've been doing for me. You're a great woman, too great of a woman to be any body's side chick. No offense, but that's all that will come from this. I love the hell out of my wife and it will take a much more serious situation than this to make me leave her."

Wendy was glad that Travis was behind her so he couldn't see the rage in her eyes. "That's good to know, boss but I was really just being nice. Even the head was a favor because you looked so pitiful," she laughed as she playfully hit him. "I don't want your ass."

Travis face burned with embarrassment. He could have sworn she was throwing the ass at him but then again, he was glad they were on the same page. Travis phone rang in his pocket. He pulled it out and his eyes lit up. "It's Nina."

Wendy wanted to gag as he damn near flew off the couch and went into his bedroom. She glanced at his untouched drink and got pissed off. She needed to get rid of Nina's ass.

Travis shut his door and answered the phone. "Hello?"

"Hey, are you busy?" asked Nina. She couldn't believe that she was so nervous to talk to her own husband.

"Nah, I'm chilling. What's up?" asked Travis as calmly as he could.

"Well, I just wanted to tell you that I miss you. A lot. This place just feels so empty without you here," said Nina. "I'm sorry for the way that I acted towards you and I understand that you may still want your own space, but I just want to see you so bad."

Travis smiled when he heard those words. He knew it took a lot for Nina to be the first to give in which let him know that she really wanted to fight for their marriage. "Of course. I miss you and want to see you too. And hold you and kiss you."

Nina blushed and couldn't help but giggle. "I can't remember the last time I blushed." Nina got silent after that statement. "I guess I never realized how much your compliments meant until I stopped hearing them."

Travis smile was so big, he was sure all 32 of his teeth were showing. "There's plenty more to come."

"Can I treat you to a date Wednesday night?" asked Nina.

Shit, why wait until then? Travis thought. He didn't want to seem too eager; he still needed to show Nina a different side of him. "That sounds good," he replied.

"Great, I'll see you then. Text me your address," she said realizing how silly she sounded. How did she manage to let her husband get a new address?

"I love you, Nina," said Travis before hanging up.

"I love you too, baby," she replied before disconnecting the call. Travis starting doing the dougie as he walked back to the living room to share his good news with Wendy.

"We gon be a'ight," he boasted. "My marriage is on its way to being back on track."

Wendy shot him a fake smile as she clapped her hands. "Yes! Let's take a shot to celebrate!" She picked up his glass and handed it to him. "To Nina and Travis," she said raising her glass to his.

"To Nina and Travis and this bomb ass makeup sex we bout to have," he joked as gulped down the entire drink.

Wendy swallowed her sprite as she watched Travis demolish his drink. "I have to use the restroom," she said as she excused herself. She walked into the bathroom and locked the door behind her. She reached into her bra and pulled out her bag of coke along with her credit card. She quickly sniffed two lines and let out a sigh. She ran the water for a few minutes. She was killing time so that Travis would get bored and start to dose off.

About ten minutes later, she walked out of the restroom feeling good as hell. "Sorry, boss I blew your bathroom up," she said as she sprayed air freshener. She looked at Travis on the couch in a daze. Her eyes landed on the bulge in his pants and she immediately undressed.

She walked over to him and immediately pulled his penis out and started stroking it. She watched as his veins pulsated as she slowly took him into her mouth.

Travis tried to open his eyes but they were way too heavy. His head felt light as he rested it on the couch. Out of nowhere, he felt a jolt of pleasure shoot through his body. He wasn't sure when he fell asleep, but this was one hell of a dream.

He heard moans from a woman, which caused him to thrust his hips. "Nina?"

Wendy bobbed her head a few more times before quickly sitting on his dick. She leaned forward so that if he happened to open his eyes, all he'd see was titties. "Yeah baby, it's Nina," she whispered, as she rode his dick slowly. She looked at his face and saw that he was out cold. Wendy smiled knowing she was getting pregnant that night.

Wendy opened her eyes and noticed that she was in her car. She looked at the time on her phone. It was 4:12 am. She tried to stretch but her entire body was sore including her pussy, which meant she had a good night. She wondered how her she ended up in her car as she sat up and turned on the light. She saw Travis's basketball shorts in the backseat and smiled. What a wild night we must have had, she thought. She looked at herself in the mirror and saw a host of hickies on her neck.

Wendy reminded herself to tip her dealer extra next time. She must have been really high to not remember what happened but the way her pussy ached let her know that she and Travis went at it all night. She thought about going in and asking for another round, but that was pushing it.

Wendy started her car and headed home hoping like hell that this time next month she would be telling Travis that she was pregnant with his child.

CHAPTER 24

When Nina got off from work Monday, she decided to be spontaneous and pop up at Travis's new place. Truth is, she couldn't wait all the way until Wednesday to see him. They had been apart for too long already.

Nina used her GPS to navigate to her to the place her husband had been calling home for the last few weeks. She was impressed with what she saw but she knew he had to be paying a pretty penny to stay somewhere so nice.

As she parked, she tried her best to calm her nerves. She followed the apartment numbers looking for the one that Travis was occupying. Nina walked past someone's bedroom window and heard moaning coming from a woman. "I'm trying to get like you girl," she mumbled.

She was confused when she realized she was in front of Travis's door. She began to loudly knock on the door as her blood started to boil. She was going to jail if Travis had another bitch in there. Nina waited impatiently and started to bang on the door again, but she realized that she never asked Travis if he had a roommate.

Travis opened the door, looking flustered. "Hey, baby." he opened his hands for a hug but Nina brushed past him.

"Where that bitch at?" She asked storming into the apartment looking around suspiciously. She began sniffing around trying to see if she could smell the scent of another woman.

"What bitch?" asked Travis trying to process what was going on.

"I heard the moans from way outside Travis. Where the fuck she at?" said Nina, fuming as she walked into the bedroom and opened the closet. "Where is she, Trav? Huh?"

Travis laughed finally realizing what was going on. He picked up his remote and turned on the TV and the moans resumed. "I didn't know it was that loud."

Nina felt so stupid as she watched the porn video for a few seconds. "Were you jacking off?" She asked laughing.

"I had to get these quickies out the way so I could be ready for you Wednesday. Cus I definitely planned on hitting that ass."

Nina walked over to Travis as she unbuttoned her shirt. "No need to wait for Wednesday." Travis watched his wife's every move as she slowly undressed for him. He quickly undressed himself and sat on the edge of the bed. Nina stood in front of him as he ran his hands up and down her ass. Travis grabbed her right leg and threw it over his shoulder, as he tasted Nina for the first time in months.

She let out a moan the second Travis's warm lips touched her pearl. He gently nibbled her sweet spot as she slowly grinded against his mouth. "Lay down," he whispered.

Nina followed her husband's instruction as she lay backwards on the bed. After planting kisses all over her body, Travis lips found comfort between her thighs. As he played with her clit, his tongue explored her walls causing her body to shake. Travis two fingers inside of her and moved them in a "come here" motion as he tongue flickered against her clit at the speed of lightning. As soon as he felt her walls tightening around his fingers, he spread her legs as wide as he could then entered her slowly.

As soon as Travis entered Nina, they both shuddered. Nina instantly came on his dick, which caused Travis to pick up his pace.

"I missed you so much baby," said Nina as Travis hit every one of her spots.

169

"Missed you too baby," he grunted, not slowing his speed. Nina started to match his rhythm and Travis could feel himself about to climax.

"Let me ride it," growled Nina, eyes full of lust. Travis laughed as he lay down and watched Nina straddle him. As soon as she sat on his dick, Travis felt pure ecstasy. He kissed and caressed every curve on her body as she rocked back and forth on his wood.

He used both hands to grab Nina's waist, helping her bounce on his shaft. "Fuck, baby. Yea, ride this dick girl."

Nina loved hearing Travis's words of encouragement so she bounced harder causing Travis eyes to roll to the back of his head. When his legs tensed up, Nina bounced a few more times before getting up in enough time to let him finish in her mouth. She was happy to have Travis back, but she still didn't want kids yet.

Travis laid back in pure bliss, staring at the ceiling. He quickly turned his attention to his beautifully naked wife. "Nina, we're going to have to compromise if we want this marriage to work."

Nina stood up and stretched, admiring how good Travis looked. She didn't know what she was thinking almost letting him slip away. "I'm willing to do that." She walked into his restroom and rinsed her mouth with his mouthwash.

"But you're not willing to have my baby?" he asked.

Nina rolled her eyes, but tried her best not to go off. She didn't want to start a fight after they had just made sweet love. She walked over to where he was still lying and sat next to him. "Why do we have to talk about this right now?"

"Because it's the one thing I really want from you, Nina," he replied adamantly.

"Well, it's the one thing I don't want. Not right now, baby," she said as leaned down and started kissing his neck, hoping it would ease the tension between them.

When he moved his head, Nina knew that she should just give up any thoughts of him letting the situation go. Nina wanted kids, eventually but she wanted to live her life first. She looked at her friends and although they were wonderful mothers, they had lost themselves. Nina wanted to travel and have fun before she was tied down with children.

"So you're not willing to compromise with me on that? We've been married three years and I keep telling you I want a child."

"And I keep telling you that I don't!" She yelled.

"You know what? Fuck it!" Travis got up and stormed into the restroom. As he turned on the shower, he tried to relax but he was so irritated.

Nina burst in the door seconds later. "Why are you so mad? I thought we were going to try to work shit out. We don't need to be fighting over petty things."

"This isn't petty to me. This is my life. This is what I want but you don't care and I finally get it," he replied stepping into the shower.

Nina sighed and threw her hands in the air. "I don't get why you're acting like this?"

"Like what, Nina? Like a bitch? Do I need to change my tampon again?" he spat angrily. He hated that he was had so much resentment toward his wife but a man could only take so much.

"Okay, I don't want to do this. Call me when you're ready to come home," said Nina turning to walk away from the messy situation they were in. How they went from making love to fighting, she didn't know but wasn't trying to stick around to find out either.

"I am home," Travis replied coldly.

Nina thought about going off but she knew that wouldn't solve anything. She just didn't feel like it was fair for Travis to ask her to have his baby. He didn't understand all that a woman goes through during pregnancy so he wasn't trying to hear her out. She shook her head before walking out of the restroom and out of his apartment. Nina's heart told her to stay but she couldn't stop her legs from leading her to her car.

Once she got in her car, Nina instantly got an idea. She was going to get her man back and they would all be happy. She smiled a little before driving home but when she got there, the realization that her pride had left her lonely again hit her like a ton of bricks.

She walked into her dream house and headed to the kitchen to pour herself a glass of wine. She sat on the couch and turned on the TV. Nina had no clue what she was watching or what they were saying because she was too busy crying her heart out. As she sipped her wine and wiped her eyes, the mixture of mascara and Moscato was too much to bear. She placed her glass of wine on her luxury coffee table, not bothering to use a coaster. She curled up on the couch and dozed off, wishing she could rewind her whole life and start over.

CHAPTER 25

Almost two weeks had passed since Spade and Allie's beautiful night out. Allie had been walking on clouds since then. Not only did her birthday just pass, she was finally cleared for graduation. Heem reached out to her a few times but Allie didn't respond. She planned on going to the gym to talk to him soon to let him know that it wasn't a good idea for them to communicate with one another.

She cared about Heem but nothing or no one came before her family so it was in her best interest to eliminate him from her life altogether. She and Spade had been getting along very well and she was so happy to see him full of life again.

For her birthday last week, Spade flew Allie to a couples-only resort in Pennsylvania. She had the time of her life with her man. They went horse-back riding on the beach, canoeing, and they rode in a hot air balloon. It was the most romantic experience of Allie's life and she was more in love with Spade than she'd ever been. Aside from taking her places, he was becoming his old self. Charming, charismatic, and more determined than ever. Allie's head was too up in the clouds to notice that Spade had been unusually quiet that entire day.

They were headed to Chanel's all white birthday party on a yacht. Allie didn't know how Chanel could afford it and she really didn't care. She was just excited to be going on a yacht. Allie got dressed in a white crop top with matching white high-waist shorts. In true Allie fashion, she paired the ensemble with a pair of royal blue fringed heels. She pulled her hair into a bun and applied some blue lipstick. Allie was definitely feeling herself and could pull off just about anything with her newfound confidence. Spade rocked an all white Ralph Lauren unit accented with a royal blue bowtie.

On their way to the party, Allie looked over at Spade who drove silently. She reached over and rubbed his shoulder.

"What's the matter, baby?"

Spade clenched his jaw and focused on the road. He was in a bad mental space because the rehab facility contacted him and told him he would have to report to the center next week if he wanted to attend the weekly classes there. He didn't plan on leaving so soon but he knew he had to go if he wanted to change his life. It just hurt him to have to leave Allie so suddenly.

He struggled with keeping this from her but he knew he had to do it on his own. He needed to prove to himself that he could be a better man without any help.

"Spade, what's wrong?" said Allie, worried.

"We need to talk later," he replied quietly.

Allie didn't like the sound of his voice when he answered her. "About what?"

"We'll talk later baby. Let's just focus on having a good time tonight." Spade glanced over at Allie, whose face was full of confusion.

Allie shook her head and stared out the window. "How can I enjoy myself knowing something is wrong with my man?"

"Nothing is wr-"

"Cut the bullshit, Spade. I know you! Something is wrong so if you want to talk, let's do it now. Stop beating around the bush with me," she yelled.

Spade pulled over to the side of the road. Allie sat straight up and looked around, wondering what the hell he was doing. He sat silently for a few moments before putting the car in park. He didn't want to look at Allie because one look in her eyes would make him rethink the entire situation. But he needed to get help. Allie deserved better.

Spade's heartbeat sped up and his palms got sweaty. A million thoughts were racing through his mind and Spade wanted nothing more than to hold Allie until he loved all of her pain away.

"Spade, what's wrong?" asked Allie. She was becoming more and more nervous the longer they sat in the car in the middle of nowhere.

Suddenly, Allie had the urge to throw up. The last time Spade was this quiet and dull, he had gotten another girl pregnant. Allie's leg began bouncing as she folded her arms across her chest. As soon as Spade saw Allie's leg bouncing, he knew she was about to snap.

"Allie, calm down," he said calmly.

"Fuck being calm! What the hell is going on? Spit it out now before I start assuming shit," she snapped. Allie was two seconds away from going across his head.

Spade took a deep breath and started talking. "I love you, Allie."

"Yeah, yeah, fuck all that! What's going on, Jeremy?"

"Like I said...I love you. I love my kids. You've been everything to me and I've been more of a burden to you than anything. So I just need some time to get myself together." Spade looked at Allie who sat like a child with tears in her eyes.

"You're not a burden. We both have a lot to work on; we'll get through this together. I'm here baby," Allie told him.

Spade stared at the roof of the car for a few seconds. When he diverted his attention back to Allie, the tears that were being held captive finally broke free all the way down her cheeks. "That's the thing Allie. I'm holding you back. You'll never admit it, but it's the truth. I want to be the best Spade I can be and I want you to be the best Allie you can be."

"But we're better together," cried Allie. She knew where this conversation was going and she didn't like it one bit. She would do anything to keep her family together.

Spade swallowed the lump in his throat and clutched the steering wheel, trying to keep his emotions intact. The last thing he needed to do was cry and make the situation harder on both of them. "Allie, you deserve the world. I can't give you that right now."

"I don't want the world, Spade. I just want you," she pleaded.

Spade bit the bottom of his lip as two tears rolled down his cheek. "You gotta want more, Allie. I'm sorry but I gotta do this. I swear I'll come back for you, baby but I gotta let you go. And you have to let me go."

Allie couldn't believe this was happening to her. Just when things in her life were starting to come together, her relationship fell apart out of the blue. "Is there someone else?"

Spade reached over and gently grabbed Allie's hands. He softly rubbed them, tracing his finger gently over her ring finger to remind himself why he was leaving such an amazing woman. "There will never be anyone else for me, Allie. No woman walking this Earth could make me even think about leaving you. I'm leaving for me."

Allie didn't understand why Spade had to leave to get himself together but she trusted that man with everything in her body so she accepted it. She didn't agree with it but she was willing to let him fly free. She believed in her heart that Spade was the man for her so she knew that he would came back to her.

"Okay, baby. If that's what you need to do then I support you. It hurts so bad but I want whatever you want."

"I'll always love you Allie and if you still want me when I get my shit together, I'm gon' make you the happiest woman in the world," said Spade with conviction.

"I'll always want you. We were made for each other Spade."

Spade nodded his head and leaned over to kiss Allie. "You want to go home? I didn't really want to bring this up before the party."

Allie shook her head. "No, I want to go. We'll finish this talk later. I just want to enjoy myself."

Spade started the car back up and they headed to Chanel's party looking for a good time but there was no way in hell they could have been prepared for what was to come.

CHAPTER 26

"Thank you for coming with me," said Nina as she sipped a glass of wine and waited for Chanel and the rest of the guests to arrive. She and Travis arrived early and were thoroughly impressed. The gold and white décor looked so elegant and classy. Turning 25 was a big deal to Chanel and she sure was doing it the right way.

"Of course I had to come support my lil homie," joked Travis. He and Nina were still living in separate households but they talked all the time. They were working on their communication, which was their biggest issue. Travis wanted to make sure they were on the same page completely before he moved back in.

"I wonder who funded this, this is nice!" Squealed Nina, looking around.

"You women worry about all the wrong things, why does it matter?" asked Travis laughing.

"Oh, shut up!" Laughed Nina, playfully hitting her husband. He grabbed her hand and pulled her into his chest. He rubbed her booty before cupping her cheeks.

"You ain'tgot no panties on?" he asked, nibbling on her ear.

"Nope, I'm trying to make a baby tonight," she flirted. Nina wasn't having no kids and she wasn't budging on that but she wanted her husband so she pretended to be willing to give him a child. While Chanel was getting tested, Nina was secretly getting birth control so that Travis could bust in her as many times as he wanted, her eggs weren't having it.

"Get a room!" yelled Sweetie as she walked up

Nina spun around and almost ran to her friend. "Oh my God, Sweetie!" Nina hadn't seen Sweetie in so long so she was ecstatic to see her. Sweetie looked stunning in a white maxi dress. Her caramel skin was glowing as her long weave flowed down her back in perfect waves. Her smile was so bright it was almost breathtaking.

After they hugged for what felt like hours, Nina noticed a woman standing next to Noah. She was dressed in a white T-shirt with white distressed jeans. She looked less than desirable standing there with a scowl on her face.

"Who is that?" asked Nina, darting her eyes toward Ms. Attitude.

"Noah's sister," said Sweetie nonchalantly.

"Oh, okay," said Nina as she shot her one last glance. "How have you been? It's been too long."

"I know, I know! I promise to do better," said Sweetie in a confident tone. She looked around and was taken aback by how elegant everything looked. "Chanel outdid herself this time."

Nina nodded her head in agreement as she saw Allie and Spade walk into the room. Sweetie followed Nina's gaze until her eyes landed on Allie. "Damn, Allie looks good," commented Sweetie.

"Yeah, she's been working out lately. It's definitely paying off," agreed Nina. She watched Allie kiss Spade then walk over to them with a smile on her face. They all hugged and basically marveled over the fact that they were sipping champagne on a yacht.

"I feel so fancy sitting here," said Allie, laughing.

"Right! I feel like a celebrity," said Sweetie, happy to be out the house. It's been a while since Noah allowed her to go out so she planned on making the most of her day.

"How have you been, Sweetie?" asked Allie, looking at Sweetie's stomach but couldn't tell whether or not she had a bump due to the way Sweetie's dress was made. Allie laughed herself. Sweetie thinks she's slick, she thought.

"I'm doing good. I see you over there getting wine fine," said Sweetie, quickly switching the subject. Sweetie didn't have time to try to remember the lies she had been telling.

Allie blushed as she did a quick spin. "I'm trying," she winked. "How's my god baby?"

"Dallas is good," said Sweetie quickly. Dallas was a soft spot for her. She missed her daughter so much but she knew she had to stay away from the danger Sweetie faced every day. Once, Noah got so mad at Sweetie that he whipped Dallas just to hurt her. She knew at that moment that he was a monster and she needed to get her daughter as far away as possible.

Because of Noah, Sweetie had a strained relationship with her entire family so the only person she could turn to was Noah's mom. Sweetie knew that her mother in law would lay down her own life before she let anything happen to Dallas, so Sweetie knew she was in good hands. Still, she felt a piece of her dying every day that she couldn't see her baby.

Allie noticed a sad expression on Sweetie's face and even thought she saw the glitter of tears for a second. Something was up with her friend but she couldn't quite figure out what it was. Before she could further interrogate, six shirtless men in white shorts were carrying Chanel into the room.

Allie couldn't help but laugh. Just like Chanel to make the most dramatic entrance that she could. Nina and Sweetie shook their head watching Chanel being fanned by one of the men. Two of the men grabbed her gently and lowered her to the ground.

"Queen Chanel has arrived," one of them announced. Everyone cheered and clapped as Chanel posed with her hand on her hip. Out of nowhere, a few men with cameras ran up with cameras as though they were the paparazzi. Chanel laughed and posed for the camera. She even went as far as having a huge fan blowing her hair while she blew the camera kisses.

Although it was a bit ridiculous, all the girls found it amusing and cheered her on. Sweetie smiled and admired the confidence Chanel wore like a purse. She wished she loved herself that much, maybe then she wouldn't endure so much abuse.

Nina laughed hard at Chanel because she thought she looked crazy. Chanel was her girl but she was definitely doing too much. She clapped and smiled anyway, impatiently waiting for them to eat. She hadn't eaten all day trying to make sure she looked good in her romper.

Allie's smile was genuine as she watched Chanel act like the diva she is. Of all the girls, they had more issues than anyone but she felt Chanel was truly genuine underneath everything. She could be selfish at times, but hell, they all had their flaws.

Chanel looked drop dead gorgeous that night. She had on a form fitting white dress with a low cut front. Her pierced belly was flat and her round hips poked like some swangers on a '84 Cadillac. Her long legs, chocolate and toned looked fabulous thanks to the six inch gold Louboutins she wore on her feet. Her face was flawless thanks to Allie, who had hooked her up a couple hours earlier. She wore her hair in a sexy angled bob that fit her face perfectly.

After her entrance, Chanel walked around and spoke to all her guests making sure everyone was being taken care of. She then walked over to her girls, who all wore big bright smiles.

"You look beautiful," they complimented once Chanel approached them.

"Thank you! You bitches look good, too!" She squealed. After they posed for countless pictures, Chanel turned to them and smiled; just happy they were all together again.

"This is how you turn 25!" exclaimed Allie. "I wanna be like you when I grow up" They all laughed and talked for a little while.

"Where's Jah?" asked Nina, noticing Chanel came in alone.

Chanel looked around. "He's around here somewhere. She had to make her entrance alone" said Chanel pointing to herself.

Nina rolled her eyes at Chanel and looked for her own man, who was talking to Spade. Nina noticed Noah's sister standing there looking bored. "Sweetie, why won't his sister come over here? She's all in the men's face."

Chanel's head shot up and looked around until she saw the girl as well. "Who invited her? Why is she here?"

Sweetie looked at her apologetically. "Sorry, I meant to tell you. Noah felt bad leaving her home alone so he asked if she wanted to tag along."

Chanel frowned her face. "This was invite only, Sweetie. I don't know her or like her."

Nina's ears shot up like a dog. "Why don't you like her? You know her?"

"We met her at Sweetie's. Her attitude is stank," said Allie, putting her two cents in.

Chanel took a deep breath trying to calm her nerves. "I'm not going to let this ruin my day. We've already left the dock so I can't kick the bitch off. As long as she stays out of my damn way, we'll be good." Chanel looked at Sweetie, who looked like a scared puppy. She was just way too nice.

"It's fine, Sweetie. Cheer up! It's my birthday," said Chanel as she bent over to twerk. Nina and Allie followed but Sweetie stayed stiff as a board although she wore a smile on her face. She quickly darted her eyes at Noah who was giving her a look of warning. Sweetie remembered what happened last time she twerked in a room full of people. She laughed and shook her head at her friends. The headshake was also to let Noah know she wouldn't engage in those types of activities.

"Come on, y'all, let's go the ballroom where the DJ is," said Chanel walking ahead of her friends.

"This is fancy for real," muttered Allie. "I've never been in a ballroom," she said in an old English accent.

The ladies met up with their men and headed to the ballroom, which was also astonishing. The dance floor was illuminated with gold light. The glimmer of gold against the white drapes was absolutely beautiful. There were several large chandeliers dangling, almost sparkling. There was a glittery gold C emblem in the center of the dance floor. There was a projector above the DJ booth playing a slideshow of Chanel, some including embarrassing pictures of the girls in high school.

Allie could feel Spade's breath on her neck as she watched the photos of Chanel dance around the screen. She noticed that she didn't have many from her childhood. There were mainly pics of her from high school on up. Allie's heart skipped a beat when she saw an old picture of her and Spade. They were at a basketball game. Spade was standing behind her with his arms wrapped around her, laughing into her neck. She was holding his hand and laughing while looking at him. Allie suddenly felt like a stone was lodged in her throat.

Spade must have had the same feeling because he wrapped his arms tightly around her and whispered in her ear that he loved her. "Then why are you leaving me?" she asked in return. Spade tightened his grip around Allie but didn't answer her question. He simply rocked side to side and closed his eyes. Allie didn't press the issue, she just relaxed her head on Spade's chest enjoying whatever time she had left with him.

Nina held Travis's hand tight as she saw some pictures from their wedding. She looked at the joy in her face and the love in Travis's eyes and so desperately wanted to get back there. Nina just wished Travis could understand where she was coming from. She wanted to tell him the truth about why she didn't want kids, but that would mean she would have to relive all those painful memories. She gave Travis's hand a squeeze then looked up at him with a loving smile on her face. He gazed at her intensely, his smile traveling from his eyes to his lips. She puckered her lips and he gladly brought his mouth to hers.

Sweetie caught a glimpse of her and Noah at their baby shower. Tears instantly rolled down her cheeks as she remembered that moment like it was yesterday. Noah broke down crying, he was on his knees kissing her stomach. He told her he would forever be in debt to her for giving him a child. He was such a sweet and loving man who worshiped the ground she walked on. Until she made him into the monster he was. She made the biggest mistake of her life and she paid the price every day.

Chanel stood in the corner half watching the slide show and half watching her friends. She purposely put pictures of the couples to remind them what they once had. She admired them all for being able to keep a relationship. Chanel looked at the pictures of herself and remembered just how lonely she truly was. She couldn't blame anyone but herself but hell; she'd been doing that her whole life. She couldn't love anyone until she learned to love herself so she constantly pushed people away. She was afraid that everyone would see her insecurities if they got too close. After being told you're worthless so many times by the man who created you, you start to believe it. Chanel's father made her feel so low growing up. If he wasn't calling her a piece of trash or telling how black and ugly she was, he was showering her with gifts. Her dad never went a day without telling her loved her no matter how many times he'd hurt her feelings. So naturally, Chanel had a tainted view of what love was, which is why she loved Eric so much.

He could hurt and make her happy all in the same breath. But that's what love is right? She thought.

"May I have this dance?"

Chanel snapped out of her thoughts when she heard Jaheim's sexy baritone in her ear. Chanel looked at all her friends slow dancing and decided she would finally let her guard down. Jaheim was a good man to her and he deserved to have all of Chanel. That is, once she opens her results from the doctor. Chanel wasn't going to ruin her birthday for anything so she refused to open the envelope. If she did have herpes, she could wait a few more days to find out.

Jaheim led Chanel to the dance floor and wrapped his hands around her waist. They slowly danced as Maze's "We Are One" played softly in the background.

"They playing that baby making music tonight!" yelled Travis, nibbling Nina's neck. Nina forced herself to keep smiling and not roll her eyes at Travis.

"I wanna make a baby," said Jaheim, smiling down at Chanel. *With Allie*, he thought watching her dance with Spade. Her eyes were closed so she didn't notice him watching her. *Hell, she'd been so stuck to the nigga, she didn't even see me walk by*, thought Jaheim.

"Do you, now?" giggled Chanel.

"You don't want to have a baby with me, I haven't even met all of your friends," said Jaheim.

"Oh shit! You need to meet Allie and Spade. And Sweetie and Noah," said Chanel, snapping her fingers and grabbing his hand. She took a few steps then stopped. "I guess it could wait until after the song, they are all boo'd up."

Jaheim was a little pissed off. He wanted to walk in on the dance so he could the look on Allie's face. He wanted to see Spade's reaction as she lifted his head off his chest. He chuckled at the thought that Spade had no clue that he had fucked his wife all over the gym. He would find out soon enough, thought Jaheim as he focused his attention back on Chanel, who was looking at him suspiciously.

"What's wrong with you?" he asked, playing it cool.

"I was going to ask you the same thing. You got this weird look on your face," she replied, with a slight frown.

"Probably daydreaming," he shrugged.

Chanel nodded her head slowly. The look on his face was almost sinister. Chanel laughed at herself. "Sinister! I read too many books."

Jaheim shook his head trying to calm himself down. He didn't like how comfortable Allie looked with this clown ass nigga. He was relieved when Chanel grabbed his hand and led him over to where her friends had gathered around the bar.

"Hey, I want y'all to meet my boyfriend, Jah!" Announced Chanel, proudly.

Allie sipped her drink before turning to finally meet the infamous Jah. As soon as she set eyes on her trainer, she immediately began to choke on the olive she was swallowing. Allie's chest heaved in and out and she started to panic. Spade snatched the drink from her hand and patted her back. "Bae, you ok?"

Allie shook her head no, because she really couldn't breathe. Jah or Heem, as she knew him, quickly ran behind her and performed the Heimlich maneuver. Allie coughed up the olive, but was too embarrassed to look at her friends.

"I'm sorry," she coughed. "It went down the wrong pipe."

After making sure Allie was okay, Spade reached out. "Predicate that, bro."

Jaheim nodded his head and waived his hand dismissively. "No prob, nice to see you again, bro."

"Again?" asked Chanel looking at Allie and Spade.

"Oh, yeah I met him at Travis crib a few weeks ago," replied Spade nonchalantly.

"Oh, okay. Well since you know Spade, this is my friend and his woman, Allie," said Chanel. "I'm sure you'll always remember her seeing as how you saved her life the first day you met her."

Oh, I'll never forget her, he thought, but for different reasons. He extended his hand. "It was a pleasure saving your life."

Allie nervously took his hand and gave it a quick awkward shake. She refused to make eye contact with him as she folded and unfolded her arms every few seconds. She was in complete and utter shock. She cheated on Spade with a man he knows; one who also happens to be one of her best friend's boyfriend. Allie suddenly felt sick but she refused to get her white outfit dirty. She sucked in some air and let out a small smile.

"You're okay baby. You still a little shaken up, but you're okay. Relax," coached Spade.

Chanel then turned to Noah and Sweetie. "And this is Noah and Sweetie! They're like the perfect couple. They're our Jay and Bey," bragged Chanel, sarcastically.

Sweetie and Noah spoke to Jaheim and gave him their million-dollar smile. Sweetie shuddered at Chanel's compliment because it was the furthest thing from the truth.

After all introductions were in order, Chanel decided they should eat and get it out the way. Chanel had strategically picked out the tables. She sat everyone by people they knew. There was a smaller dining room where Chanel would eat dinner with her friends, while eating the appetizers on the floor with her other guests.

Once it was time for dinner, Chanel walked into the private room she got for her friends and sat in her chair, whichresembled a throne. She looked down the table with a smile. That quickly faded when her eyes landed on Noah's sister.

"Why is she in here?" Chanel asked incredulously.

Noah cleared his throat but didn't answer Chanel. Instead, he looked at Sweetie. "Nel, she doesn't know anyone out there."

"She don't know nobody in here either! Especially, not me since she walked up in my shit uninvited and has yet to say two words to me," snapped Chanel.

"I'm sorry, I'm Brandi. Happy birthday," she spoke.

Chanel rolled her eyes and turned her head. "She has to go. I'm sorry!" Chanel didn't know this bitch and she was getting bad vibes from her.

Noah discreetly pinched Sweetie's thigh under the table. Sweetie grimaced before speaking. "If she goes, I go." Her voice was shaky despite her efforts to sound stern.

Chanel put up her hand and wiggled her fingers. "BYE!"

"Chanel, come on!" Reasoned Nina. "It's your day, let's just focus on you. Don't let this ruin your night. You too cute to be acting ugly. Just continue sitting on that throne and keep giving me life."

Chanel flipped her hair and poked her lips dramatically. "I am cute, huh?" She shot Brandi an evil glare before rolling her eyes. "Fine. You can stay." She wanted to let the bitch have it but she wasn't going to let a bum bitch ruin her day. "But you can't be in none of our pictures."

Allie and Spade couldn't hold their laughter. Snickers around the table followed while Sweetie sat stone-faced, biting the inside of her jaw. She knew Noah was watching and if she looked like she wanted to smile, she would be reprimanded.

Dinner was served and everyone chatted amongst each other while they ate. Jaheim kept hoping Allie would look his way but she refused to even acknowledge his presence and it was pissing him off. What had he ever done wrong to her?

"Chanel, remember that time that big ass dog was chasing you all around the park?" asked Spade, laughing.

"Yes, I do remember that! Coach Turner tried to get me to join the track team after that," laughed Chanel. She was enjoying reminiscing with her friends no matter how embarrassing their stories were.

Noah was getting bored with all the happiness and love in the room so he pinched Brandi's leg, signaling her to put their plan in motion.

CHAPTER 27

Everyone was enjoying their dinner, reminiscing about the past when Brandi suddenly covered her face and cried silently. "Why are you crying?" Noah asked, loud enough for everyone to hear.

"Girl, what the fuck is wrong with you?" asked Chanel, rolling her neck. She looked at Nina who was giving her the look a mother would give her child if they were acting up.

"What?" Shrugged Chanel. "This ain't her birthday, she can't cry if she want to. She needs to take her ass outside somewhere. This is for me!"

Brandi's cries became a little louder, much to Chanel's dismay. "Seriously, what's her problem?"

Brandi sniffled a little before speaking. "It's just that I'm an only child so I'm naturally a loner. It's just beautiful to see how close you are. I always wanted a close-knit relationship with people. It's inspiring how much you guys love each other. And how forgiving you are! Like Sweetie forgiving Nina for sleeping with Noah before her wedding, that takes balls."

Everyone at the table gasped. Brandy's eyes suddenly got wide when she saw the look on Nina's face then back at Noah. "You told me they knew! Oh my Go-"

"What the fuck Brandi? Get your ass out!" yelled Noah, with a hard scowl on his face.

Brandi covered her mouth in horror. She quickly got up and scurried out of the dining room. Noah was gloating on the inside. They deserved an Oscar for that performance. Noah awkwardly turned back to the group. He was fully anticipating getting his ass kicked before the night was over with but it would be more than worth it in the end.

Everyone sat silently at the table. All the women had tears in their eyes as they looked back and forth between one another. Travis, whose ears were red as beets spoke in a shaky tone. "What the fuck was that about?"

Chanel stood up. "Okay, maybe we should jus-"

Travis pounded his fist on the table causing it to shake. "Somebody better start fucking talking."

Sweetie wished she could just crawl under the rock. She disagreed with Travis; she would rather no one talk. She couldn't take hearing that her husband fucked her best friend. Her best friend fucked her husband while they were engaged.

Nina's heart raced as she wondered why on God's green earth would Noah ever tell anyone about that night. She hoped like hell he would play just as stupid as she planned to.

When no one said anything, Travis nodded his head. "The silence says it all." he chuckled and shook his head. Before they knew it, Travis was grabbing for Noah. Spade, seeing it coming all along grabbed Travis before he made the biggest mistake of his life. He took the knife from Travis as Jah tried to help restrain him. "You bitch ass nigga! Came into my house, ate at my fuckin table, looked me in my muthafuckin eye and you fucked my wife?"

Travis snatched away from Jah and walked over to the dining room door and locked it. He stood in front of it with his arms folded. "Silence ain't good enough for me. You mother fuckers been silent for three fuckin' years. If y'all want to leave, I'ma get some fuckin' answers tonight."

Chanel sighed and looked around the room, not believing her eyes. How could such a perfect day take such a bad turn? And why did her birthdays always have to be horrible? Chanel was convinced she would have bad luck forever. She rested her hand on her chin and watched the scene before her. She had been so used to disappointment that it no longer fazed her.

"I told y'all that bitch shouldn't have been in here," sighed Chanel.

Travis let out another laugh. "Naw, I'm glad the bitch was here. I learned something real fucking new today."

Everyone sat silently. They knew Travis was mad because he never called women out of their name. All eyes landed on Noah as they waited for answers.

"Look man, I'm-"

"Tell me you're sorry and I'll run in your mouth, bitch!" Spat Travis angrily. He turned his attention to Sweetie. "Why the hell you just sitting there? You knew about this shit?" Sweetie was way too calm for his liking.

Travis looked around the entire room and suddenly felt played. "How many of y'all knew?" Travis tried to fight back his tears but the knife of betrayal cut so deep he didn't stand a chance.

CHAPTER 28

Nina hadn't taken her eyes off of her fingers since her secret had been revealed. Allie eyed Nina and her eyes widened. Nina looked guilty as all outdoors. Allie looked into Travis eyes sympathetically and shook her head no; she had no idea Nina had done the unthinkable.

Jah walked over to Travis to calm him down as Noah walked away from the table and stood against the wall. Chanel looked at the top of Nina's head because that's all she could see.

"Nina, what the fuck?" Chanel asked. She was no Saint but she has never and would never fuck any one of their men.

Allie, feeling guilt of her own made a choice not to chastise Nina. Instead, she walked over to comfort Sweetie, who sat silently as tears rolled down her cheeks. Allie didn't know what to say so she wrapped her arms around Sweetie and rocked her silently. She kissed her forehead and wiped her tears just like she did when they were younger. Sweetie was older than Allie, but Allie was always like the big sister.

For the first time in a long time, Sweetie had a breakdown. She was too hurt to be afraid of Noah so she screamed as loud as she could when she broke down crying. She held on to Allie like a child clings to their mother on the first day of school. She released all of her pain, anger, and resentment into Allie's chest ruining her outfit. She wanted so badly to tell Allie the hell she'd been living in so Allie could save her like she always did. But it was too late; she was in way too deep.

Nina tried her hardest to stay still as a statue each time someone said her name or tried to get her attention. She couldn't face the truth that was thrown in her face with no warning. Nina closed her eyes and wished she could disappear. Her eyes shot open as a hand forcefully lifted her head.

She was face to face with Chanel. "Bitch, I ain'tgon' play with you. What the fuck was ol' girl talking about?"

Nina slapped her hand down and stood up. "Chanel, leave me alone."

"Oh, you can talk now?" asked Travis as he marched toward her. The closer he got the softer his expression became but Spade and Jah were on his heels just in case. Travis looked around the room. "Where that hoe ass nigga at?"

Jah scanned the room and spotted Noah kneeled down with his head in his lap. "Noah, come here bro!" he yelled.

Noah hesitantly got up and walked over to where the crowd was. Spade held Travis making sure he didn't attack him again. "Y'all want us to give y'all some privacy?" asked Spade.

"Nah!" yelled Travis."Let's all sit around the table and talk about it like adults. Ain't that what y'all do, Nina? Let's gossip. What y'all call it now? Tea? Let's sip some damn tea. Let's have Mascara and Moscato in this bitch," said Travis. He sat down and stared at Nina until she followed suit. One by one, each of them sat down, not knowing what would happen next.

"So you fucked Nina, huh?"Travis asked glaring into Noah's eyes. He didn't wait for answer; he looked at Nina who was sitting next to him. "You fucked Noah, huh?" he laughed shaking his head in utter disbelief.

"Just answer the question, y'all. The sooner we get this over with, the better," urged Allie. She noticed Jaheim staring at her and it was starting to feel uncomfortable. She even thought she saw him lick his tongue at her. Although their sex was enjoyable, he was nothing compared to Spade. The sex they had was good, but the love she made with Spade was phenomenal. She focused her attention back on Nina, then Noah. "Well?"

194

"I don't want the details; just a simple yes or no. I need to hear both of y'all dirty ass say it," seethed Travis.

Noah cleared his throat and muttered a meek, "Yes."

"Yes," mimicked Travis. "Over there sounding like a lil pussy. I would have respected you more if you were man enough to come to me, but nigga you sat at my mother fuckin wedding the day after you fucked my wife. Sat on my couch, drank my beer, and smoked my weed. Gave me advice about a woman you know you fucked." Travis shook his head then diverted his attention to Nina. The tears rolling down his cheeks broke everyone's hearts.

"You looking real small right now. Where's Nina the Great? The one that has everything under control?" He balled his hands into tight fists. "Did you have sex with Noah the night before you married me?"

"Babe, I was-"

"DID. YOU. Open yours legs to this nigga before they opened for me?"

Nina sniffled as Travis looked around the room. "Y'all didn't know? Nina told me she was saving herself for marriage. So while I was beating my dick, she was poppin her pussy for this corny ass nigga." Travis grabbed a small Crown Royal bottle off the table and guzzled it.

"Answer my question, Nina," he demanded.

"Yes," she whispered.

No one could move fast enough to stop Travis from punching Noah in the nose. His white suit was stained with blood immediately.

Sweetie grabbed a napkin and brought it to his nose. "What is wrong with you? You need to be angry at your wife!"

Chanel and Allie looked at Sweetie in shock. She was right but they never thought she would ever say anything like that. Sweetie was anti confrontation.

"I'm sorry! DAMN!" screamed Nina, tears falling like raindrops.

Sweetie glared at her. "You are sorry. You are one sorry bitch. You could have chosen any other dick but instead you go for my husband. You were a slut when you fucked your boss for your management position but you've upgraded to a full blown whore!"

"You fucked your boss?" Travis asked before chuckling. "Hey, At least I hit it before he did." he shook his head, not believing what he was hearing.

"Sweetie, don't you act perfect! Getting abortions behind your husband's back!" Spat Nina, folding her arms. If Sweetie wanted to spill tea, then so could she.

Chanel looked at Nina in shock. "Nina! Are you serious? You can't be mad at her for being upset with you. You fucked her husband, you're in the wrong!"

Nina felt so cornered she had no choice but to attack. "Fuck you Chanel! Tell Jaheim how you cheated on him and contracted herpes!"

Chanel's eyes widened in horror before her eyes filled with tears. She had experienced a lot of hurt in her life, but when she looked in her friend's eye and saw nothing but hate and malice, she was at a loss for words. Nothing could have stopped that heartbreak.

Nina didn't care whose feelings got hurt. She wasn't about to feel ashamed by herself. "Y'all all want to look at me? Who in here is perfect? WHO? That's my past! We all have one so why y'all looking at me? Spade you giving me the evil eye but you fucked Genesis last year, remember that?"

Allie leaped across the table and pulled Nina's hair. Spade quickly grabbed her and pulled her back. Allie grabbed the garlic bread off the table and tossed them both in Nina's face. "Don't fuck with me! If my man was cheating, why the fuck you didn't tell me when it happened, you lying ass bitch?"

"It's not like you were ever going to leave!" Nina yelled, still sitting in the same spot. Everyone began yelling each other as Noah laughed while he covered his mouth and nose. His plan went much better than he expected. He didn't plan on leaving with a bloody nose but he was fine with that. Mission accomplished.

Chanel was fed up with the bullshit. She kicked off her shoes and ran out of the dining area. She walked into the ballroom and searched until she found Brandi. She didn't even notice that everyone ran out behind her. She ran up to Brandi and punched her in the face knocking her down. She climbed on top of her and began hitting her repeatedly.

"Chanel! No! She's pregnant!" Sweetie screamed while running toward them. Chanel felt Sweetie grab her arm and pull her off of her. Chanel fell sideways and tried to get up. She felt a strong force that caused her head to jerk forward. She quickly turned around, thinking she was being jumped but it was only Noah.

"You okay?" he asked with a look of concern.

"That bitch started this shit. She knew what the fuck she was doing," said Chanel.

"WE ARE AT THE DOCK. YOU MAY USE THE NEAREST EXIT."

Chanel was so relieved when she heard the message letting them know the cruise was over. Chanel was too ready to get off that damn boat. She spotted Travis running towards her. "I'm sorry, Chanel. Let me know the cost of damages. I'll pay them all and even refund you whatever this party had cost."

197

Chanel rubbed her head not even thinking about the fact that she would be responsible for the mess that was made on the yacht. She exhaled and figured she would let her father pay for it. Money wasn't an issue to Chanel. She just used it as an excuse to give Eric hell. Chanel had plenty of money and was living proof that it didn't buy happiness.

Chanel cried as Travis tried to console her. "I'm sorry I ruined the party." If only he knew it had nothing to do with the party. It was the realization that everyone's life was about to change. These girls and even Travis and Spade were the closest thing to family she had. They all cared about each other, but after tonight, there's no telling what their futures held.

All she knew was that it would NEVER be the same between them.

CHAPTER 29

Two weeks passed since Chanel's party, but it felt like a year to Nina. She knew she let her embarrassment get the best of her and now her friends weren't speaking to her. She had tried to reach out to Travis several times but to no avail.

After they left Chanel's party, Travis ignored her the entire ride back to her house. Once they arrived, he didn't even park in the driveway. He pulled up on the curb and waited for Nina to exit his car. As soon as she stepped out and closed the door, Travis sped out without making sure she made it in the house safely.

Nina knew she fucked up. She was angry with herself but more so angry with Noah. Why did he have to open his big fucking mouth? They swore to keep that night a secret because it was an accident. Nina had got so wasted that she could hardly stand. She was passed out on Sweetie's couch when Noah came down to check on her. One thing led to another and Noah was pounding her doggy style while Sweetie was sleep upstairs. As soon as it was over, Nina cried her heart out, overwhelmed with guilt. Noah promised her that they would keep it a secret. He said neither of them was in their right mind and she agreed. Since that day, she had buried those thoughts so deep in her mind that she'd almost forgot it happened.

Nina pried herself out of bed and showered. It's been so long since she's felt this alone but she knew there was nothing she could do about it. She thought about Travis and how hurt he must be. She promised herself to make it right with him. Once Nina got dressed, she planned on getting her hair and nails done. She had been sulking around and quite frankly, she was tired of it.

When Nina opened her front door, she saw a woman walking up holding an envelope in her hands. Nina frowned her face wondering who this woman was and what she wanted. Nina stood in her doorway waiting for the lady who was taking her sweet time.

"Hello, is this the St. Claire residence?" asked the lady, as she got close enough for Nina to get a better look. At first glance, she was worried that she was holding divorce papers but she was dressed to casually in a t-shirt and a pair of skinny jeans. The woman had a very beautiful face. She had a smooth, blemish free caramel tone. She had large eyes that were full of sadness. Her Senegalese twists were neatly pulled into a bun at the top of her head.

"Yes, this is. How may I help you?" Nina shifted her weight and folded her arms, waiting for an answer. She was growing impatient with this woman who looked timid as hell standing before her.

"Is Travis home?" she asked quietly.

"No he's not. But I'm his wife so any business you have with my husband can be handled through me in his absence," replied Nina.

After a moment of hesitation, the woman finally spoke. "My name is Gabi. Travis and I had a relationship about seven years ago."

Nina looked at the woman in shock. This was the woman who had broken Travis's heart in a million pieces by lying to him about her pregnancy. "I've heard of you. Why are you here?"

Gabi clutched the large envelope as if she was holding some type of top-secret information. She let out a sigh and slowly began to speak. "Well, as you may know, Travis and I had a horrible break up and we haven't spoken since. So I came here hoping to speak with him and clear a few things up."

"Don't take this personally, but you and my husband don't have a damn thing to talk about," replied Nina.

"We actually have a lot to talk about. My husband and I just split and I'm in sort of a financial bind, so-"

"What does that have to do with my man?" interrupted Nina.

Gabi tried her best not to go off. If Nina actually let her speak, she could get to the point. "Long story short, my husband isn't my son's father. Travis is."

Nina shook her head and tried her hardest to not fall out. "Excuse me?"

Gabi stood nervously as she took in Nina's reaction. "I know this may be a lot of information to take in but it's hard for me too. I really believed Phil was the father of my child, but he went and got a DNA test behind my back. I guess I never paid attention to how much Aiden actually does look like Travis."

Nina folded her arms and scowled at Gabi. "The nerve of you to walk up to my home to reveal some bullshit information like this. What is it that you want, huh? To be a big, happy family? It's not happening. You just told me you were having a hard time financially so you expect me to believe anything you're telling me right now?"

"Listen, I don't want to be here doing this. It's embarrassing for me to be standing here right now but Travis deserves the truth. I could have kept this secret for the rest of my life but that would be selfish on my behalf. If Travis doesn't want to be involved in our son's life, I understand but I just wanted him to know." Gabi handed the large envelope she was holding out to Nina, who snatched it out of her hand.

"Get the hell off of my property," said Nina through gritted teeth. Gabi didn't argue or put up a fight; she simply turned and walked away. Nina watched the home wrecking bitch as she walked back to her car. As soon as Gabi was gone, Nina rushed into her house and made it to the restroom in time to throw up.

Nina was beyond stressed and this situation made it ten times worse. After cleaning herself up, Nina walked into her kitchen to pour herself a glass of pink Moscato. She stared at the envelope for what felt like hours before she finally opened it. The first thing she retrieved was a birth certificate. Aiden Christopher Jacobs, born December 12, 2008. The certificate shows Gabrielle and Phillip Jacobs as the parents. Nina assumed the birth certificate was included to verify that he was indeed born around the time she was with Travis.

The next document was the DNA test results, which excluded Phillip from being the father of Aiden. Nina's heartbeat sped up but she wasn't convinced of anything. Who knows how many men Gabi was sleeping with at the time? The next thing Nina pulled out confirmed her every doubt. The picture she was holding spoke a thousand words. That little boy was Travis through and through.

Aiden was a light brown color with the same shaped eyes as Travis, though his eyes weren't hazel. The structure of his nose resembled Travis's but most of all he possessed the same small freckles that every man in Travis's family had. Nina hung her head and cried until she was all cried out. Her marriage was already on the rocks and this information would only drive a deeper wedge between them. All Travis wanted was to be a father, so if he found out about Aiden, she knew that their chances of reconciliation would be slim to none.

Nina couldn't take the chance of losing Travis forever so she quickly devised a plan to get her husband back. She picked up the phone and called one of her co-workers.

"Hey, Charlie, this is Nina. You want to make some money?"

CHAPTER 30

"Mommy, Bubba hit me!" yelled Jerricka as she ran towards Allie. Allie laughed at Jerricka, who couldn't pronounce the word brother.

Jeremiah ran in the room behind his sister. "She hit me first, mama!"

"Jeremiah, what did I tell you about hitting your sister? You're a boy. You don't ever put your hands on a girl, you hear me?"

Jeremiah nodded his head. "Yes ma'am." he walked over and hugged his little sister. "I'm sorry." Jerricka smiled and hugged her brother back. Allie watched her kids in amazement and was glad that the shared such a close bond.

"Are y'all ready to go to the park?" asked Allie.

"Yes!" They said in unison. "Is daddy coming to the park, too?" asked Jeremiah.

Allie hesitated but gave him a big smile. "Daddy can't make it to the park this time, big boy but Aunt Chanel is bringing E.J and Dante and after the park, we'll go eat ice cream!"

"Yeah," he cheered. "I haven't seen Dante in like, ten years!"

Allie laughed uncontrollably, which caused Jerricka to laugh. "Boy, you haven't even been alive ten years!" She grabbed him and began tickling him. He giggled loudly and kicked his feet and Allie was satisfied that she had taken his mind off of his dad.

Spade moved out a few days after Chanel's train wreck of a party. They sat down and had dinner as a family and explained to Jeremiah that Spade would be living somewhere else. Of course, he didn't fully understand so every morning he woke up asking for daddy. Spade called the kids everyday to talk to them and he picked them up from daycare everyday, but she knew that it was a big change. Jeremiah was Spade's shadow. He loved the hell out his daddy, so Allie did everything in her power to keep him distracted.

"Can I take my football to the park, mama?" Jeremiah asked after he was all tickled out.

"Yes, hurry and go get it." Allie got their stuff together and texted Chanel to lether know that they were headed to the park. Once she loaded the kids and their belongings in her car, Allie put the Kidz Bop CD on for her kids and drove silently to the park. Allie was doing the best she could to be strong for her kids but she was slowly breaking down on the inside. She didn't think that it would be so hard living without Spade but it was torture. Every time she saw his name pop up on her phone, she wished he was calling to tell her he was coming home. Instead, it was the same routine. He talked to the kids, asked how she was doing, told her he would talk to her tomorrow. Allie felt her lip quivering and quickly snapped out of that painful mindset.

Once they arrived to the park, Allie allowed her kids to play at the playground while she sat on the bench, watching them waiting on Chanel. Allie desperately tried to keep Spade off her mind but he was all she thought about.

"Hey stranger."

Allie looked up and saw Jaheim standing in front of her. She quickly cleared her throat and looked away. "Hey. Chanel didn't tell me you were coming, too."

"I didn't come here with Chanel. She didn't tell you that we broke up?" he asked, surprised.

Allie shrugged her shoulders. "We haven't talked much."

Jaheim sat down next to Allie, causing Allie's body to stiffen. "Allie, what's wrong? I thought you said you didn't want things to be awkward between us."

"That was before I found out that not only were you dating my friend, you knew my boyfriend!" said Allie with an attitude.

"I was just as shocked as you were! I had just found out my damn self. I texted you and told you to call me ASAP but I never got a call or a reply," Jah pointed out.

Allie shook her head. "I feel awful, and I'm sorry for the way I've been acting towards you. I'm just under a lot of pressure right now."

"It's cool. I'm still the same dude though Allie. We were cool. We were close. I care about you and I just want my friend back. What happened between us will stay between us," said Jah, flashing Allie a charming smile.

Allie nodded her head but didn't respond to what he said. "Chanel's on her way, you might want to leave."

Jah nodded his head and stood up. "Call or text me if you need me Allie," he said over his shoulder as he walked away. Allie's stomach turned as she watched Jah strut off. Of all the men she could have cheated with, she had to choose Chanel's man. What kind of shit is that? The bad part about it is that Allie actually liked Jaheim. She knew she could be herself around him, which is why she needed to avoid him at all costs. She was too vulnerable to have him so close.

"Slow down Dante, stop that running!" yelled Chanel.

Allie looked to her left and saw Chanel's godson darting towards the playground with EJ following. Allie smiled watching his short, chunky legs try to keep up. Chanel shook her head at her boys as she took a seat next to Allie.

"I thought I just saw Jah ass," said Chanel, removing her shades. "Did I tell you we broke up?"

"No, you haven't told me anything," said Allie.

"Oh, well yeah. We broke up the night of my birthday. He played it cool all the way, until we made it home and he let me have it. I deserved it though," said Chanel as she watched the kid's run freely with no care in the world. She wished she could go back to those worry-free days.

"Are you okay?" asked Allie, looking at Chanel. She wore a blank expression on her face so Allie couldn't tell how affected she was.

"Yeah, I knew it was coming. I need to focus on getting my shit together, anyway," she said. "I let him open the results. He read for his self that I don't have herpes but he still left. He said he just didn't see us going anywhere."

Allie sat silently not knowing what to say. "Spade left me, too."

Chanel whipped her head around so fast she almost broke her neck. "Bitch, what?"

"Yeah. We still co parent but he has his own place and we don't speak much unless it concerns the kids," said Allie solemnly.

Chanel reached over and hugged Allie. "I'm so sorry to hear that. Why didn't you call me?"

"Girl, we all have been going through so much, I just needed to deal with it internally first," replied Allie.

"I can't believe that. Did he say why?"

Allie caught Chanel up on everything that happened between her and Spade before they arrived at her party while Chanel listened intently.

"I have faith that y'all will work it out," said Chanel trying to sound hopeful. She loved Allie and Spade together but Allie looked like a lovesick puppy.

Allie smiled at the thought. She wished she was as sure about that as Chanel was. She sighed and changed the subject. "Any word from Nina?"

"Fuck her! She had the nerve to text me and tell me that I pushed her to her limit. All I did was tell the bitch that she was wrong because she was! She fucked her friend's husband, where they do that at?" asked Chanel.

"She threw everybody under the bus because she got exposed. That was fucked up and I don't respect her ass for that."

"Bitch, you hopped across that table so fast," laughed Chanel.

Allie shook her head. She regretted putting her hands on Nina but the bitch crossed the line coming from her family. Allie hadn't even addressed what Nina revealed about Spade simply because she had just had an indiscretion of her own.

"She almost got her ass whooped that night," Allie laughed. "All because of a messy bitch who had no reason being there."

"She started that shit on purpose," said Chanel, rolling her neck.

"You think so?" asked Allie, tilting her head.

"Bitch, think about it. She started that bullshit speech talking about how she didn't have no siblings. Bitch, you're Noah's sister! How the hell you don't have siblings?" Exclaimed Chanel.

Allie didn't even notice that before. "You're sho right! Damn, so you think she did that on purpose?"

"Hell yes! She knew damn well Sweetie didn't know about that shit," said Chanel shaking her head.

"We need to get to the bottom of this. We're going to have to do another pop up because Sweetie hasn't returned my calls."

"Mine either," retorted Chanel.

Allie couldn't believe how much everything in her life was falling apart. No amount of mascara or moscato could fix the damages that had been done to their friendship. Allie felt like Chanel was one of the most consistent friends in her life and who knows how long that would last if Chanel ever found out about her and Heem.

"I do have some good news, though. I got a job at a beauty shop," said Chanel proudly. "And I haven't slept with Eric!"

"You better werk!" Allie was proud of Chanel. "Well, you know I'm doing my externship but in two weeks, I will officially be done with school. I won't walk across the stage until December, though."

"Yaassss! You know we're going to be-." Chanel stopped herself mid-sentence. Things had changed so much, she didn't even think about how different it would be. Neither of them had spoken to Nina and Sweetie had completely shut them out. Chanel sighed and thought of a way to get all them back together. Allie had been working so hard to finish college and Chanel wanted to make sure she was celebrated the right way.

Allie and Chanel sat silently, watching their children play, lost in their own thoughts.

CHAPTER 31

"You want me to do what?" asked Charlie, one of Nina's old employees. They were seated in Nina's living room eating fruit.

"I need your piss. Pee in this pill bottle for me," said Nina holding a small prescription bottle in her hand.

"You're going to pay me for letting you use my pee?" Charlie asked, still confused.

"Yes. And I need you to find a way to print me an ultrasound that has my name on it. Sneak into your husband's office and do what you have to do," said Nina with a serious look on her face. "These are two very simple requests for five thousand dollars. Can you do it or not?"

After mulling it over for a couple seconds, Charlie agreed to the terms. Nina slid over an envelope. "Here is twenty five hundred. Once Travis buys the fact that I'm pregnant or you produce the ultrasound, whichever comes first, you'll get the rest."

Charlie nodded her head excitedly. Nina knew the money would entice Charlie; that's why she chose her to help her with her mission. Although Charlie was married to a doctor, her money was tight. Her husband monitored her spending very closely. Nina knew that having money of her own would be all the motivation Charlie's pregnant ass needed.

Charlie got up and went to restroom once she finished snacking. She returned with the pill bottle in her hand wrapped in toilet tissue. Nina motioned for her to take it back to the restroom where pissed belonged. Nina thanked Charlie for her services and walked her outside, handing her the envelope.

Nina walked back into her house and headed straight to the restroom. She opened her cabinet and pulled out the pregnancy test she had purchased earlier. Covering her nose, Nina dipped the pregnancy test in the pee for a few seconds before putting the top on and laying it flat. She took out her phone and called Travis. Just as she expected he ignored her call, so she called back and got the same result. Nina looked over at the positive pregnancy test and smiled. She took a picture of the test, making sure she got her tattoo in the picture so he would know that it was really her holding the pregnancy test.

I'VE CALLED YOU TWICE AND GOT NO ANSWER SO I GUESS I HAVE TO TELL YOU VIA TEXT MESSAGE THAT WE ARE HAVING A BABY.

Nina attached the picture to the message and hit send. She knew it was only a matter of time before her husband was back in her arms again. Travis wanted nothing more than to be a father so Nina needed to give him that hope until he fell in love with her again.

Nina walked into her bedroom and got her purse. She pulled out a little card that was included in the envelope Gabi sent. The card contained her contact information so Nina decided to give her a call.

"Hello?"

"Hey, this is Nina St. Claire, Travis's wife," said Nina in a polite tone. "Is this Gabi?"

"Yes, it is."

"Hey, I was calling to apologize to you about the way I acted toward you. The entire situation just caught me off guard as you can imagine," said Nina, all the while rolling her eyes.

"Of course," agreed Gabi. "I'm just going through a really hard time right now since my husband left. We live in Atlanta now, but we may be moving back to Houston with my mom. She doesn't stay far from your place so out of respect, I wanted to give Travis a heads up."

Nina had no idea that they lived in an entire different state. That was perfect! She pretended to care about what Gabi was telling her. "Well, thank you for that. I'll talk to Travis tonight, I haven't told him about this yet but he needs to know. But I'm going to tell you now that you can't expect for him to be jumping for joy."

"I know. I even understand if he doesn't want to be involved in his life at this point. It's just a messed up situation," replied Gabi.

"Aiden is the most important person in this situation. Travis will do what he feels is best for him," said Nina said, sounding so sympathetic there was no way Gabi could know she was being played.

"Thanks, Nina. Travis is lucky to have such an amazing woman for a wife," complimented Gabi.

"Bye, now," said Nina hanging up the phone. Nina walked into the kitchen and grabbed a bottle of wine. Wine had become her best friend in the last few weeks but she wasn't complaining.

Travis sat at his desk rubbing his temples. They were on a tight deadline to complete a project and he felt like his team was moving too slow. Travis had been on edge since everything had gone down between him and Nina. It really fucked his head up knowing that Nina not only fucked someone he knew, she slept with her manager for a promotion. He asked himself time and time again, who the fuck did he marry?

Even finding out all that information, Travis couldn't stop thinking about Nina. She was so flawed but he loved that woman to death. He made a vow to his wife, his family, and most of all to God to be there through the good and the bad but he was at his wit's end with her. The disrespect, the lies, and now the cheating was too much for Travis to handle.

"You need anything?" asked Wendy as she poked her head in his office. He shook his head no and went back to reviewing his paperwork. It was getting harder and harder for him to fight temptation when it came to her. She was throwing it at him every chance he got, but as long as he was a married man, he was going to try his best to dodge it.

Wendy smirked and walked into Travis's office and placed her hands on her hips. "So, we're just never going to talk about what happened?"

Travis looked up from his desk. His eyes landed on Wendy's cleavage before moving up to her face. "What you mean?"

Wendy rolled her eyes playfully and tilted her head. "Are you kidding me? You really don't remember?" Her face got serious and Travis was more confused than ever.

"Remember what?"

"The night we had sex," she hissed. Wendy knew Travis wouldn't remember but she needed him to believe he initiated the sex. She hardly remembered the night her damn self, but her pussy was sore the next day so he obviously tore it up.

"What?" Travis leaned back in his chair and studied Wendy's face waiting for her to crack a smile. When her lips remained pressed together tightly, he knew she was serious. "When did this happen?"

"The night Nina called. You kept wanting to take shots so we did. After about four, we started watching a movie. You started feeling on me, telling me you wanted to feel me at least once before you went back to Nina. One thing led to another and we fucked," Wendy explained.

Travis wrecked his brain trying to remember what she was talking about. He briefly remembered taking shots with Wendy, he even remembered them sitting on the couch but he did not remember sleeping with her. He shook his head and tried to find

212

words but he fell short. Suddenly, he recalled feeling like he was getting head but he thought he was dreaming.

Wendy covered her face and shook her head. Travis stood up and walked over to hug her. "I'm sorry that I don't remember. I normally don't get that fucked up. It's cool, you don't have to cry."

Wendy looked up at him. "You don't understand," she cried. "You told me that Nina didn't want to have your baby so you wanted me to. You nutted in me, Travis."

Travis quickly released his grip on Wendy and took a few steps back. Wendy was so proud of herself. By the look on Travis's face, he was caught all the way off guard. She continued to sob. "I had a doctor's appointment next week that I thought you wanted to go to. Now I just feel so stupid."

Travis looked at how distraught Wendy looked and pushed his feelings to the side. As shocked as he was, he couldn't let Wendy beat herself up. "I - I'm sorry. I'm just thrown off like a motherfucker. Stop crying, we gon' work this out."

"I should have known you were vulnerable that night. I can't believe I fell for your words about us having a family," said Wendy. She knew she was pushing it but she needed him to feel bad.

Travis let out a deep breath. Damn, he had fucked up royally. "I didn't lie to you on purpose! I don't even remember any of this but I am truly sorry and I'll be here for you through whatever you choose to do."

"Can we just talk about this another time?" asked Wendy as she stood straight up and wiped her face. She gave Travis a look of disappointment before walking away.

"Fuuuuuck," groaned Travis as he slammed his fist against his desk. He then brought his fist to his chin and tried his best to remember that night. He couldn't remember sleeping with Wendy. Travis always had a small tingle feeling in his balls the day after he had sex. It had been that way since he started having sex and he

213

didn't recall having that feeling when he woke up the next morning. But he wasn't one hundred percent sure. Travis instantly felt a migraine coming on and decided to take off early.

He grabbed his hard hat and walked into the warehouse to let Mike know he was leaving for the day.

"Mike! I'm gone. Make sure your men complete all their tasks today because we pushing it close," said Travis.

"I got ya boss," replied Mike who was carrying boxes. "You good?"

"I'm anything BUT good, nigga. I'll lace you up later, I gotta go figure some shit out," replied Travis. One of the employees who was driving one of the machines backed up too far and hit a stack boxes, causing the shelves to rattle.

"Travis!" Screamed Wendy who appeared out of nowhere, running to him pointing. No sooner than he looked up, he felt a powerful force that knocked him off his feet. Travis attempted to open his eyes but every muscle in his face hurt. Travis relaxed his head and succumbed to the darkness that surrounded him.

"Travis, shit!" said Mike as he raced over to where was laid under a huge box. A few other employees ran over as the pushed the box off him. Wendy cringed as soon as she saw blood, still she ran over to his side.

"Call the ambulance, now!" She cried, kneeling down next to him. Her heart raced when she noticed that he wasn't moving. "Travis!"

She saw his eyes flutter so she leaned in and noticed that the blood was coming from his nose. "He's breathing!" Wendy was afraid to touch him because she didn't know where he was hurting but she whispered in his ear letting him know he was going to be okay.

When the ambulance arrived, Travis was conscious but in too much pain to speak. He saw Wendy's teary eyes and realized how much she cared about him. As they were putting him into the back of the truck, Wendy stopped at the curb. Travis nodded his head letting her know he wanted her to ride with him. Travis dozed in and out the entire way to the hospital but every time he opened his eyes, he saw Wendy's face.

CHAPTER 32

Mike was on the phone with their corporate office informing them of the incident when they took Travis out so he didn't see Wendy get into the back of the truck with Travis. Mike went into Travis's office and called Nina. He was sure that is what Travis would have wanted. All he talked about was his wife.

"Hello, Mrs. St. Claire? This is Mike, I work with Travis," said Mike nervously.

"I know who you are, how can I help you?"

"I was calling to let you know that Travis had an accident today at work. He's okay," he added quickly. "They think he may have a dislocated shoulder. He's on the way to Memorial Hermann now so I just thought I would give you a call."

"Thank you! I appreciate that," said Nina calmly. She texted Travis over an hour ago about her pregnancy and she has yet to receive a reply. Now all of a sudden, he dislocated his shoulder? Nina rolled her eyes, not buying that sob story.

She decided to call the hospital anyway. "Hi, I'd like to be transferred to Travis St. Claire's room please."

"Sure, one moment." The line went silent for about ten seconds. "Ma'am, he was just admitted he is not in a room yet."

Nina's heart stopped as she grabbed her purse and her car keys. She sped all the way to the hospital. Although, it was only a minor injury, Nina needed to show Travis that she was willing to become a better woman for him.

By the time she made it to the hospital, Travis had been assigned a room. She stopped by the gift shop to pick him up some chocolates. Nina walked into Travis's room and was surprised to see another woman sitting next to him.

216

Travis was surprised to see Nina walk through the door but not as surprised as she was to see Wendy. Nina looked Wendy up and down but focused her attention on her husband. She sat the chocolates on the stand next to him and leaned down to kiss his lips.

Travis was thrown off by this sudden display of affection, especially since he hadn't talked to her in weeks. "You feeling okay?"

"I'm straight."

"Are you going to introduce me to your friend here?" said Nina, smiling.

"It's my receptionist Wendy," said Travis dryly.

Nina looked at Wendy and wondered when she became so bad. She didn't look anything like that when Nina first met her. She would have been gotten her fired if she knew she blossomed the way she did.

Wendy smiled. "Nice to see you again."

Nina smirked. "You, too. Thank you for coming but I'm here now so you can leave."

Wendy looked at Travis, then back at Nina. Travis lay silently, irritating Wendy. Why couldn't he stand up to that bitch? Instead of causing a scene, Wendy stood up and patted Travis's hand. "I'm glad you're okay. Are we still on for next week?"

Travis nodded his head. "Yeah. Thank you for coming Wendy and for everything you said. I heard you."

Nina watched Wendy blush at Travis's words and had to stop herself from slapping the smirk off of her face.

"Nice seeing you again," said Wendy, giving Nina a fake smile before walking out.

217

"She's rather friendly, isn't she?" said Nina, turning her attention to Travis who has yet to look at her. She sighed. "Travis, I'm sorry. I feel so horrible about what I did to you. I hurt you in so many ways and you didn't deserve that. I just need one more chance to prove myself to you."

When Travis didn't answer, Nina kept talking. "I miss you Travis. I'll do anything to make it up to you. Whatever you want, you got. Before my past was brought up, we were doing good, Travis. We're finally pregnant so I just want to make this work."

"Pregnant?"

"Yes, didn't you get my text message?" Nina asked. Travis struggled to sit up so Nina quickly helped him retrieve his phone from his pocket. Nina watched his face closely waiting to see his eyes light up. Instead, his expression was blank. Nina frowned her face slowly.

"What's wrong? Aren't you happy?"

Travis closed his eyes to fight off the headache that was coming again. How did he go from praying for a kid his whole life, to find out that he was having two in the same day? Travis didn't understand why this storm cloud was hovering over him. He tried to do right by everybody but he always got fucked over in the end.

"Of course, I'm happy. Today has just been a rough day. I'm in a lot of pain, right now," Travis replied.

"I understand that, but I just-"

"Knock, knock," said a nurse as she stepped into the hospital room. "I'm coming to check your vitals Mr. St. Claire."

Travis had never been so happy to see a nurse in his life. After checking his vitals, the nurse informed him that his blood pressure was high. He gave Nina a hard stare. She was the reason for all his stress.

After the nurse made her notes, she told him that the doctor would be in soon to try and put the bone back in place.

"How long is recovery?" asked Nina.

"If surgery isn't required, about three weeks as long as he wears the sling and don't do any tasks to re-injure it," she replied before leaving the room.

Nina looked at Travis and rubbed his arm. "Let me take care of you. Come home while you recover so I can show you that I'm serious about moving forward in our marriage."

Travis wanted to tell her no so badly but his heart wouldn't allow him to. Even through all her flaws, Nina was the woman that he loved so deeply. "This is the last straw for me Nina. If we can't get it together this time, we're done."

Nina smiled and kissed him softly. "Thank you, thank you!" Nina was overwhelmed with gratitude. She had to figure out the best way to continue to fake her pregnancy all while being a super wife. Nina pulled out her phone and texted Gabi letting her know they needed to meet up as soon as possible.

CHAPTER 33

Wendy walked out of the hospital with a smile on her face. Miss Nina thought she was going to wiggle her way back into Travis's life but she had another thing coming. Wendy was carrying Travis's baby and she couldn't wait until he found out. She had an ultrasound scheduled so that Travis would get the full experience. There was no way he would put up with Nina's bullshit once he got the taste of having a real family.

Wendy was so preoccupied with her thoughts that she walked right into someone's chest. "Oh, sorry!" She apologized.

Noah looked into Wendy's face and smiled. "No, problem. Nice to see you again."

"I'm sorry, do I know you?" asked Wendy, taking a step from the man whom she didn't recognize.

"You actually know me quite well," retorted Noah. "We met at Travis's."

"Oh, okay," said Wendy, trying to walk around him. Noah slid over and stepped in front of her. "What do you want with me?"

"Some more of that pussy," he growled.

Wendy looked at him with disgust. "You wish you could get this pussy. Please move out of my way." She brushed past him and continued her trek to her car.

"I had that pussy several times that night. On the couch, the floor, your car," he called after her. She stopped dead in her tracks and spun around. "I think I might have left my shorts in your backseat."

Wendy stormed towards him with her fists balled. "What the fuck are you talking about?"

220

Noah smiled at how angry she was. "Well, while you were busy drugging Travis, you left your drink unattended. I had just so happened to have forgotten my keys in the apartment so I went back for them. You dummies forgot to lock the door so I just walked right in to enjoy the show. You were riding the hell out of Travis when you passed out. I sucked your pussy until you woke up then I fucked the shit out of you. Coke makes you freaky because you came every time I choked you out."

Wendy stood with her fists balled, chest heaving rapidly. Tears burned her eyelids as she stood feeling naked in front of this monster. "Did you just admit to raping me?"

Noah shrugged. "You looked so bored fucking a man who was sleep so I helped you out. You never told me to stop so I wouldn't call it rape by a long shot."

"I'm calling the police and you will pay," threatened Wendy.

"Ahh," said Noah, pulling out his phone. "I figured you would say something of the sort. This video here shows you drugging Travis. This video shows you telling me to give it to you deeper." Noah played a few seconds of each video before winking at Wendy.

"You had me blindfolded, you sick fuck!"

Noah shrugged. "Hey, we're into freaky shit."

Wendy felt sick to her stomach as she turned around and nearly ran to the car. Once she was in, she locked her door and sped off. She pulled into a convenience store parking lot and cried. She knew being lowdown and sneaky would backfire but she was only trying to give Travis the love he deserved. Now, she was pregnant with the baby of a sick stranger. She felt so violated and she planned on getting revenge on the motherfucker who ruined her perfect plan.

CHAPTER 34

Sweetie sat in the car and watched Noah talk to some woman through the window. She was very uncomfortable with their encounter for some reason. Their body language said they had tension, which meant they had some type of history. She started to wonder if she was the woman who sent him home with scratches on his back a little while back.

Sweetie grew impatient waiting on Noah to finish his conversation. She was even more bored with waiting on Brandi to get out of her doctor's appointment. She didn't know why Noah wouldn't just let her stay home alone if he was just going to make her wait in the damn car. After finding out that Noah slept with Nina, Sweetie's attitude was on ten constantly. She talked back to Noah all the time, not caring about the consequences.

Brandi strutted out of the hospital doors with a smile on her face. Noah saw her coming out and followed her to the car. Sweetie climbed back into the backseat as Noah helped Brandi in the car. Once he got in, he asked her how the appointment with.

"It went good, everything is good but I am pressing charges on Chanel," said Brandi, proudly.

"What? Why would you do that knowing you were wrong?"

"Because she attacked me and I'm pregnant," spat Brandi.

Sweetie scoffed. "She didn't know you were pregnant."

"Which is why you'll testify that she did know," said Noah, looking at her in the rearview mirror.

Sweetie shook her head defiantly. "I won't do that to her."

Noah let out a hearty laugh. "You will."

"I'm not going to do it and no matter how much you beat me, my answer won't change," said Sweetie.

"Jameka, Jameka," said Noah, shaking his head. "Well, I'll just take a trip to CPS to get sole custody of Dallas. And you can go live with Chanel since that's where your loyalty lies."

Sweetie bit her lip and tried not to cry. Noah was a monster who played dirty and she was tired of fighting a losing battle. She wondered where Noah kept his gun. If she killed him, she would go to jail and she wasn't built for jail. She could always kill herself after, she thought. She quickly dismissed all of those evil thoughts and tried to think of an escape plan.

Once they arrived at home, Sweetie noticed Allie's car parked on the curb. She and Chanel were in the front seat talking. Sweetie couldn't be more excited to see them. They literally picked the perfect time to pop up at her house. Noah pulled in the driveway and walked into the house with Brandi behind him. Sweetie waited until Noah was in the house. She turn around and ran to Allie's car. She opened the backseat door and slid in.

Allie and Chanel screamed before realizing it was Sweetie.

"Drive! Now!"

Allie started her car and drove off wondering why Sweetie was acting so strange." What is wrong with you?"

"Did you run to the car?" Inquired Chanel, looking at Sweetie through the rearview with raised eyebrows.

"Yes. I had to get away without Noah knowing where I went," replied Sweetie looking out the window. Chanel had a million questions to ask but remained silent. She would wait until they were face to face to address her concerns.

Once they arrived at Chanel's place, they all sat on the couch quietly. Chanel stared at Sweetie who refused to make eye contact with her.

"What's up with you, Sweetie? You've been acting really weird," said Chanel.

Sweetie shifted in her seat, not knowing if she should come clean to her friends. Before she could answer, Chanel continued talking.

"I'm trying to figure out why you feel the need to lie to us," Chanel said. "I was at work this morning and heard some interesting news. Brandi is not Noah's sister, she's his baby mama?"

Allie looked at Sweetie, waiting for her answer. She was just too through when Chanel gave her the tea. She couldn't understand why the hell Sweetie was still with Noah.

Sweetie hung her head and began softly sniffling. Allie and Chanel walked over to comfort her, which made her cry harder.

Allie rubbed her back gently. "Talk to us."

Once Sweetie calmed down and caught her breath, she looked at her friends with sad eyes. "It's true! She's his baby mama. She got evicted so he invited her to stay with us."

"And you went for that? It's bad enough he cheated on you, but you have to look his infidelity in the face every day?" exclaimed Chanel.

Sweetie felt like a fool sitting before them but they didn't understand her fear. They didn't understand how weak and worthless she felt knowing she could never escape the wrath of him. She continued crying as Allie rocked her back and forth.

Chanel looked at Sweetie and pulled her hair from her face. As she moved the hair behind Sweetie's shoulder, she noticed what looked like a bruise on her neck. "Sweetie!" She exclaimed pulling her shirt down to get a better look.

Sweetie jumped off the couch so fast it looked as though she flew. Chanel's eyes filled with tears as Allie looked on in confusion. "What did I miss?"

"Sweetie, take your shirt off," ordered Chanel. Sweetie stood looking like a kid. Her eyes were wide and full of fear; she was holding herself and shaking her head as if she was pleading with Chanel.

Chanel wasn't moved. "Don't make me come snatch it off of you." Sweetie was trembling but she slowly removed her shirt.

Allie gasped and looked at Sweetie in horror. There were bruises covering her entire body. Sweetie folded her arms over her body and closed her eyes.

"Is he putting his hands on you?" asked Allie, jumping to her feet. Chanel circled Sweetie and grimaced. She had one bruise on her back that stretch from her shoulder to the middle of her back.

Sweetie nodded her head slowly. She felt ashamed but she also felt a sense of relief knowing that she no longer had to hide it. Allie walked over to Sweetie and softly touched her side. Sweetie flinched and let out a small groan.

"Your rib may be fractured," she whispered, not believing her eyes. Sweetie's odd behavior finally made sense to Allie. "We need to get you to a hospital."

"No! It will heal on its own, it will just take a while," Sweetie answered, pulling her shirt back over her head.

Chanel shook her head slowly. "Sweetie, you're being tortured. Why didn't you say something?"

"I knew something wasn't right," muttered Allie.

"Well why didn't you help me?" cried Sweetie. "You know me better than anybody, Allie. Why didn't you notice that I was suffering? Why didn't you save me?"

Sweetie doubled over and cried out. She was in so much pain mentally, emotionally, and physically. She had been living in her personal hell for almost two years and no one noticed.

"I'm so sorry, Sweetie. I'm here now, though. You have to get away from that man immediately," warned Allie.

"It's too late now. I'm in way too deep," said Sweetie dreadfully. "He'll ruin me."

"Fuck that bitch ass nigga," snapped Chanel. "He didn't swing back when Travis was in his face but he has the nerve to beat you like a dog? I can't believe you let him do this to you!"

Allie glanced at Chanel and gave her a stern look. She was sure Sweetie felt bad enough as it is she didn't need anyone making her feel worse. Chanel caught Allie's look and rolled her eyes.

"How long has he been hitting you, Sweetie?" asked Allie softly.

"Almost two years, now. It's become a lot worse since we moved back," she admitted. "He wasn't always this bad. It's all my fault."

Chanel threw her hands in the air. What the hell did she mean it was her fault? "Your only fault was marrying a bitch ass nigga. Please don't let me hear you saying that again!"

"He used to be good man. He was gentle, he was kind, and he was everything to me." Sweetie looked at her friends with teary eyes. "Remember I was pregnant when we moved away the first time?"

Allie and Chanel both nodded. "You told us you got an abortion," remembered Chanel.

Sweetie took a deep breath. She said a silent prayer asking God to help her get through the painful story she was about to reveal. "Noah and I had somewhat of an open marriage. He would bring women into our bedroom and sometimes he would want me

226

to sleep with someone. Usually, it was investors or businessmen. Well, this one man got carried away and he nutted in me. When I found out I was pregnant, Noah moved us away. If the baby turned out not to be Noah's, we would give it up for adoption and no one would ever know."

Sweetie looked up briefly to see the stunned looks on their faces before dropping her and continuing. "Well, the baby was Noah's. Noelle Janae is what we named her. I suffered from postpartum depression really bad after having her. I was lonely and I was miserable but I loved my baby to death. She was beautiful, looked just like me. I wanted to keep her close to me at all times. One day, I was extremely tired and decided to take nap. When I woke up, I looked to my right where I had her lying next to me but I didn't see her. I sat up in a panic, and there she was, lying underneath me. But she wasn't my baby anymore, she was cold and blue."

Sweetie began to cry hysterically. Allie and Chanel both ran to her side, tears running down both of their faces.

"I killed my baby," cried Sweetie. "I promise I didn't mean to do it, I swear. Noah said I did it on purpose but I didn't! He began whipping me after that. He said I needed to be punished since he didn't send me to jail. He got one his friends to list her cause of death as crib death. If I leave him, he will expose me and take Dallas away from me forever."

"We won't let that happen, it's okay," said Allie.

As all three ladies sat and cried together, they realized that they needed each other more than they thought. And though Nina did them dirty, they needed her too especially if they wanted to save Sweetie from the nightmare she was living in.

CHAPTER 35

Nina woke up at the crack of dawn to cook Travis's breakfast. This was his first morning back home and Nina wanted to prove to him that she was serious about repairing their marriage. She made him some pancakes, eggs, grits, and bacon. Once she made his plate and sat it on the tray, she poured him a glass of water and a glass of juice. She brought the tray into their bedroom, where Travis was sleeping peacefully. She wrote him a note telling him she had some business to handle and that she would return soon.

She took the week off of work to cater to Travis's every need. She was more determined than ever to make sure he was satisfied. Nina quickly got dressed and headed to IHOP. Once she was seated, she browsed the Internet waiting on Gabi to show up.

Fifteen minutes later, Gabi walked in with her son in tow. Nina's heart sped up as she looked at a younger version of Travis. She could tell by the pictures that they resembled, but face-to-face, there was no denying the fact that Travis was this kid's father. Nina took a gulp of her water and cleared her throat. Her nerves kicked into overdrive when Gabi and Aiden sat directly across from her.

"I'm sorry, I'm late. My mama wasn't able to watch Aiden as planned, so I had to bring him along," said Gabi apologetically.

Nina's stomach began to turn flips. She let out a nervous laugh. "I don't think he should hear what I'm about to tell you."

Gabi's facial expression quickly changed from a smile to a frown. She nodded her head, understanding where the conversation was headed.

"He just feels that it's in everyone's best interest if they didn't meet. He's already missed out on so many years and the kid already has a clear idea of who their father is. He doesn't want to confuse the kid," explained Nina trying her best to not make it obvious to Aiden that they were talking about him. He was wearing headphones but Nina didn't want to take any chances.

Gabi put her head down and nodded her head. "That's understandable. I don't know - I just. I know he really wanted a kid so he deserved to know that he has one."

"I'm sorry, I tried to get him to reconsider but he felt like it was selfish of you to just show up all these years later," Nina lied. She reached into her purse and pulled out an envelope. "This is a check for ten thousand dollars. It's not much but I hope it will help you so that you don't have to pick up your whole life and move here."

Nina tried to look as sincere as possible when she handed Gabi the envelope. Gabi peeked inside the envelope and stared at the ten thousand dollar check. That money would definitely help her get back on her feet. "Travis definitely missed out an awesome kid. But I'll take this money and invest it in his future. Thank you for trying Nina," she replied, standing. "Let's go Aiden."

Nina watched them walk away and a felt a brief twinge of guilt knowing that Travis had a son in this world that he would never know about. Nina was too insecure in her marriage to allow a kid to come into the picture. Travis's life would be complete and he would no longer need her so she did what she felt was best. He had been missing from his life all these years so a few more wouldn't hurt.

After finishing her omelet, Nina grabbed her purse and headed out the door. As she was walking out, Chanel was walking in holding E.J. Nina froze when she saw her because she didn't know how Chanel would react. Chanel looked her up and down and attempted to walk past her.

"Chanel," called Nina.

Chanel raised an eyebrow and stared at Nina. "Oh, you still know my name?"

"Can we talk, please?"

Chanel stepped back outside and waited for Nina to begin speaking. "I know y'all are probably tired of hearing my apologies, but I truly am sorry for the pain that I've caused. It was very selfish of me to throw any of you under the bus and I feel horrible about it. I love all of y'all and I want to make it up somehow."

Chanel moved EJ from one hip to the other as she listened to Nina's apology. She wasn't sure how genuine it was, but she accepted it anyway. She loved Nina and missed her so much. "I can think of a few ways for you to make it up but in the meantime, I need to fill you in on what's been going on."

Although Nina had just eaten, she still took a seat with Chanel to catch up. Nina's jaw dropped as Chanel told her what had been going on with Sweetie. Nina couldn't believe Sweetie was enduring such abuse and didn't talk to her friends about it.

"I can't believe she never told me about the baby," said Nina, feeling her heart break little by little. Sweetie didn't deserve the way she was being treated.

"She never told any of us. It's like she was living a double life right under our nose. I just hate that Allie and I didn't look deeper into the signs because we knew something was wrong," replied Chanel, feeding EJ a pancake.

Nina shook her head sadly. "Where is she now?"

"She stayed with Allie last night and I think she's staying with me tonight. We can't let her go back to Noah."

"We won't. Ugh, I've been such a horrible person to everyone. I would have never been able to forgive myself if something happened to her." Nina gazed off in the distance regretting every bad decision she had ever made.

After making plans with Chanel to meet up with the other girls to apologize, Nina drove back home to her husband. She decided in that moment that she would put her fears aside and truly let Travis lead her. She had a good man and she was so close to losing him all because of her pride.

She walked into her bedroom, where Travis lay watching TV. He saw that his tray was empty so she took it to the kitchen. When she returned, she crawled into bed next to him and began stroking his penis. Once it began to harden, Nina took him in her mouth and bobbed her head slowly. Travis let out a groan and began thrusting his hips. She allowed him to make love to her mouth until he was almost about to cum. Nina looked at Travis and smiled as she straddled him. She rode him slowly, staring him in the eye the entire time. His hand cupped her ass as he matched her rhythm stroke for stroke.

Nina picked up her pace as Travis gripped her waist tightly. Seconds later, Travis's eyes were rolled back and his hot cum was released inside of her. Nina collapsed on top of Travis and rested her head on his chest. "I love you, baby."

"I love you, too," he whispered. "I can't believe you're finally having my baby."

Nina closed her eyes on his chest. She was too far in to back out now. Travis would never forgive her if he found out that she was lying about being pregnant so Nina planned on telling him she miscarried when she got her cycle next month. He would be devastated but he would at least believe that she was willing to give him the family he always wanted.

Allie and Sweetie sat on her couch watching their children play and sipping wine.

"We haven't had Mascara & Moscato night in forever," commented Sweetie.

"I know. Things have changed so much in the last couple of weeks," replied Allie, shaking her head.

"I know, right," said Sweetie, staring at her daughter who was focused on the blocks she was playing with. She turned to

Allie with a serious expression on her face. "If anything happens to me, promise me that you'll take care of Dallas."

Allie was caught off guard by Sweetie's statement. "Nothing is going to happen to you, Sweetie."

"Promise me," said Sweetie sternly. "You're her god mother so I hope you take that role seriously."

Allie didn't like the sound of Sweetie's tone but she made the promise anyway. She loved Dallas like her own and would do anything for her. "Are you scared?"

Sweetie thought about Allie's question for a while before answering. "No. I'm not afraid anymore. I'm just anxious now. I'm waiting on him to come for me because I know he will."

"Why did you stay?"

"I felt like I had to. Noah is a very intimidating man and I felt so much guilt and remorse for what happened to Noelle. I had alienated myself from you all so I felt like he was all I had," Sweetie replied.

"You need to go to the hospital," suggested Allie, shuddering at the thought of all the bruises that looked as though they were tattooed on Sweetie's body.

Allie's doorbell rang and Sweetie breathed a sigh of relief. Allie walked to the door wondering who it could be. She looked out the window and saw Chanel's car. She opened the door with a smile to greet Chanel, but it quickly faded once she saw Nina standing next to her. Allie rolled her eyes and walked away, leaving the door open for them to enter.

Sweetie's eyes widened when she saw Nina enter the room. She didn't know how to react so she just sat quietly. Nina walked over to Sweetie with tears in her eyes. "I'm so sorry, for everything."

Sweetie wanted to hate Nina for what she had done, but her heart wouldn't allow her to hold on to that resentment. She embraced Nina and they hugged for a long time, sobbing softly. Nina looked up at Allie, who also had tears in her eyes. "I'm so sorry, Allie."

Allie walked over and hugged Nina. They had been friends for over ten years and they needed each other now more than ever.

"Why is everyone crying?" inquired Dallas as she looked around the room.

"We're crying happy tears, baby," replied Sweetie smiling at her daughter.

Jeremiah let out an exaggerated sigh and shook his head. "Women," he muttered.

Laughter filled the room, temporarily erasing all the secrets, lies, and betrayal amongst them. They relished in that moment for a while for they wasn't sure just how long it would last. Soon after, Nina was in the kitchen cooking, Allie was making drinks, Sweetie was cleaning up and Chanel sat on the couch talking shit just like old times.

Allie's phone vibrated in her bra where she had it tucked away. She pulled it out and noticed it was Spade. "Hello?"

"Hey, what you doing?" asked Spade.

"Nothing, cooking. You?"

"Chilling. I was going to stop by there today if that's cool with you. I wanna see you and the kids for a little bit," he replied.

"That's cool. The girls are over here, but I would still like for you to come," Allie answered.

"That's a bet, I'll be through there in about an hour."

233

Allie couldn't help but smile. "Okay. See you then." She ended the call and went back to mixing their drinks. When she looked up, she noticed all eyes were on her. "What?"

"Do we need to leave? We don't want to mess up nothing with you and baby daddy," joked Chanel.

Allie waved her off. "Girl, please. It's nothing like that."

"Your whole face is red, Allie. Stop trying to play us!" laughed Nina.

"Okay, fine. I'm excited to see him. I haven't saw him since he moved out. His brother always gets the kids and drops them off. I miss him so much," said Allie. She hoped that he was coming to tell her that he was ready to come home.

"Awww," said the girls in unison. Jerricka mocked them causing all of them to laugh again.

"It's been a while since I've did this with you guys," said Sweetie. "I'm really enjoying myself."

Knocks at the door interrupted their conversation. Allie felt her heart rate speed up. Nina smiled at Allie. She looked like a schoolgirl who was going to talk to her crush for the first time. "We're going to take the kids outside to the backyard so y'all can have a little privacy."

Allie waited for the house to clear out before she went to the door. She fixed her hair in the mirror that hung in the hallway. She took a deep breath and opened the door with a smile. The person on the other end forcefully shoved the door, hitting Allie and causing her to fall backwards.

Noah entered the house looking like a mad man. "Where the fuck is she?"

Allie quickly tried to stand but Noah shoved her back down and rushed into the living room. "Jameka! Where the fuck are you?" he yelled.

Sweetie froze in place. Sweat particles immediately formed on her forehead. She felt herself becoming dizzy. "He's here," she said quietly. "No, oh my God! He's here." Sweetie became hysterical as she paced back and forth.

"Allie!" screamed Nina as she ran toward the house. Dallas looked up at her crying mom and started to cry as well. Chanel walked over to Dallas trying to calm her down.

"Who wants to be a superhero?"

Jeremiah raised his hand first, followed by Jerricka and finally Dallas. "Okay good. Let's pretend we're trying to escape from the bad guys. Let's run out of this gate and go to our super car, okay?"

They nodded their heads excitedly, and when Chanel said go, they all took off running and made it to Chanel's car where she planned to call 911. Panic set in once she realized she left her phone in the house. She didn't know what Noah was capable of, but the girls had a 3-1 advantage so she hoped that would be enough.

Chanel tried to stay as calm as possible for the sake of the children but her nerves were on edge. "Okay, y'all lay down in the backseat to hide from the bad guys." The kids giggled but did as they were told. "Whoever stays quiet, gets ice cream."

Back inside the house, Noah was yelling at Sweetie demanding that she bring their daughter home. "I'm the custodial parent of Dallas, so you need to bring her home before I call the police."

"And we'll let them know that you beat your wife," retorted Nina.

"Ooh, I'm so scared," mocked Noah. "There's no way out of this Jameka. We can do this the easy way or we can do it the hard way."

Sweetie shook her head defiantly. "I'm not letting you leave with my baby." Noah pounced on Sweetie like he was lion and she was his prey. He grabbed her neck and began choking her while Allie and Nina ran over and began trying to get him off of her.

Noah pushed Allie backwards and tripped Nina, all while still holding Sweetie's neck with one hand. The front door bust open and Spade shot through the living room like lightning. He ran over and began throwing punches. Noah quickly lost his balance and shielded his face instead of fighting back.

"Bitch ass nigga, get up and fight me," spat Spade as he stood up and kicked Noah in the stomach repeatedly.

"You're going to kill him, Spade! Stop!" cried Allie.

Spade kicked him one final time before snatching him up like a rag doll. "Don't you ever step foot on my property again or I will kill your ass."

Noah ran his tongue across his teeth and laughed. He broke free of Spade's grip and shot Sweetie an evil glare before walking out of the house. He limped back to his car, coughing promising himself that Jameka would pay for disobeying him.

Spade looked at Allie with angry eyes. "The fuck was that about?" As soon as Spade pulled up, Chanel screamed and told him to hurry inside so he did.

Sweetie looked at Spade with terror in her eyes. "I'm sorry. This was all my fault." Nina grabbed Sweetie's hand and led her out the front door so Allie and Spade could talk in private.

Allie was trembling as she sat on the couch. She spoke slowly, filling Spade in on everything that happened in the last few weeks. Spade sat silently as he took in everything Allie revealed to him.

"She gotta find somewhere else to stay," he said once Allie finished talking. "I can't risk putting my kids in danger because she

236

don't want to go to the police. And I want you to stay away from her."

"What? I can't do that! She needs me now more than ever," replied Allie.

"No, our children need you. Sweetie needs professional help. If Noah is as dangerous as she says, you need to stay away from her because there's no telling what he is capable of," said Spade in a serious tone.

Allie understood what Spade was saying but she didn't want to cut Sweetie off. Sweetie needed all the support she could get.

Spade stood up and stretched. "A'ight, I'm about to burn off. I'll stop by this weekend to get my kids."

"You're leaving already?" asked Allie standing up as well. They hadn't even got the chance to really talk; she didn't understand why he was in such a rush to leave.

"Yeah, I have somewhere to be," he lied. Spade needed to get back to the sanctuary of his apartment before he slipped back into a dark space. On top of working on his smoking and drinking, Spade was working hard to get his anger under control.

Allie folded her arms and stared at the floor. She blinked away her tears before looking back up at Spade. "You don't want me anymore, do you?"

Spade was taken aback by Allie's question but he kept his cool. "Let's not do this right now Allie. I'll be back this weekend."

He leaned over and pecked Allie's forehead. "Make sure you look out the window or peep hole before you open this door. Don't worry about Noah, he won't be back."

Allie avoided Spade's gaze as she walked him to the front door. Spade lifted her chin and looked deep into her eyes. "I love you."

A small smile spread across Allie's lips but she wasn't satisfied. She knew Spade loved her but she was unsure about whether or not he was really coming home to her one day. Allie watched Spade get into his car and drive away to his new life.

Nina and Sweetie walked over to Allie with smiles on their faces. As soon as they got a look at her, the smiles vanished into thin air.

"He don't want me no more," cried Allie. She shook her head not wanting to believe the words she just spoke but she could feel it in her heart that Spade was no longer interested.

Nina hugged Allie and wiped her tears. She had never been so emotionally drained in her life. "We're going to take the babies out for ice cream, get some rest. I'll bring them back tomorrow."

Allie nodded her head and walked back in the house. After she packed the kids' overnight bags, she decided to head to the gym. There was no better way to relieve stress than getting a good workout in. Without thinking, Allie drove to the gym where she slept with Jaheim. She was so lost and she could use a listening ear.

Allie walked in the gym and was a bit disappointed to find that Heem wasn't in his usual spot. She solemnly put in her earphones and started on the treadmill. She ran for twenty minutes before stopping to catch her breath.

"Your stamina has improved significantly," complimented Heem, standing behind Allie watching her ass jiggle in the tights she wore.

Allie turned around, surprised to see Heem. Her eyes lit up seeing him because he was such a breath of fresh air. "I learned from the best."

"I'm surprised to see you here. You've been dodging me for weeks," he replied, smiling." Once I signed that paper, it was fuck Heem."

"It was nothing like that. You know, things just spun out of control so fast. I'm sorry. You didn't deserve that."

"It's cool. I knew you were a heartbreaker from the start so I was ready for it," he laughed, holding his heart.

Allie laughed loudly. "You're so crazy."

"What's been up with you? How have you been holding up?" asked Jaheim.

Allie stepped off the treadmill and wiped her forehead. "I'm trying to be strong but it's only so much a person can take."

"You look so unhappy," noted Jaheim, staring into Allie's eyes trying to find the truth behind them.

Allie didn't want to admit the truth so she didn't answer his question. "I just want to know if there's someone else. The not knowing is killing me! I can't fight to save our relationship if I don't know what I'm up against."

Jaheim hated to see her so upset. "Allie, some things are better left unknown. You'll drive yourself crazy thinking about that shit."

"I'm driving myself crazy now. Wondering if I'm waiting on a forever that will never happen," Allie replied sadly.

Jaheim stood still for a few moments before speaking again. "Do you really want to know?"

Allie's heart skipped a beat and she felt her entire face become hot. She looked at Jaheim with pleading eyes.

"He was with some chick the other night. Brought her to my crib. He didn't look like he was serious about her, he was just...you know?"

Allie couldn't breathe for a second. "He was what?"

Jaheim hesitated before pulling out his phone. There was a picture of a half naked girl sitting in Spade's lap. His arm was around her waist near her ass. He slowly handed the phone to Allie. Allie quickly grabbed the phone and looked at the picture. She gasped as tears made the picture blurry. Spade's face wasn't visible but she knew her man when she saw him. And that was definitely him with a bitch on his lap.

Jaheim seized his opportunity to hold Allie again. He held her tightly as she sobbed quietly. He hated to be the reason that she was in so much pain but it was a part of his plan. He invited Spade and Travis over to play cards and dominoes with some of his other boys. He also invited a few strippers over although he pretended to be shocked when they arrived.

As soon as the girl sat on his laps, he pulled her off of him. Jaheim snapped the picture right on time because it looks like Spade is groping her.

Allie suddenly stepped backwards. "I have to go." Allie quickly wiped her face and damn near ran to her car. She held her tears in the entire ride to her house. Once she made into her house, she went and poured herself a glass of wine. Allie sipped her Moscato as mascara ran down her face. She had almost reached her breaking point and that wasn't good for anybody.

CHAPTER 36

Travis had been home for over a month and Nina couldn't be happier with the way things were going. She was being the wife he always wanted her to be. She cooked, cleaned, and slept with him almost every night.

She stood in front of the TV as she ironed Travis's work clothes. He was finally cleared to go back to work. Nina had his lunch ready and she planned on surprising him during his lunch break and giving him some dessert. After she was finished ironing, Nina went into the restroom and peed on a stick. She impatiently waited on the results and was disappointed to see the negative sign. She let out a frustrated sigh. She would just have to plan a miscarriage. She felt like they were strong enough to handle that.

Nina quickly wrapped the test in tissue and stuck it in a plastic bag. She swung the door open and was startled to see Travis standing there. She clutched the trash bag tightly as she jumped backwards.

"You alright?" asked Travis as he walked into the restroom to relieve himself.

"Yeah, you just scared the hell out of me," Nina quickly walked toward the door,.

"What's in the bag?"

"Tissue. I threw up again and you know how I hate that smell," she squeezed her eyes shut and prayed he didn't press the issue.

"I'll take it out for you," offered Travis.

"I need the exercise baby, it's fine," replied Nina as she quickly walked away before Travis could protest any further. Nina

241

quickly threw the evidence away in the large garbage can in their garage. She took a few deep breaths before heading back inside.

Travis turned on the faucet and pulled out his phone. He called Wendy for the fifth time in two days but he luck didn't change. She didn't answer the phone or return his calls and he couldn't figure out why.

Travis found himself thinking about Wendy more often. He had been back with Nina for a month but he didn't feel a connection with her. She was pretending to be this perfect wife and that's not what Travis wanted. He didn't want a whole new woman. He wanted the woman he fell in love with to get her shit together. Nina just couldn't do that and Travis started to feel fed up.

He was happy that Nina was carrying his child but he knew she this would be something she used to throw in his face later. Then there was Wendy. He still didn't remember what happened between them but he could clearly see the love she had for him.

Travis put his phone back in his pocket and walked out of the restroom. He walked over to the window and saw Sweetie getting out a car and running into their house. Since her incident with Noah, Sweetie had been staying in one their guestrooms with Dallas. Travis looked at the time and noticed it was almost midnight.

"Hey, why aren't you lying down? You gotta be up in the morning!" said Nina as she entered the room.

Travis walked over and flopped down on the bed. "I think it's time for Sweetie to leave."

"Why?" asked Nina, scowling.

"Because I said so. I don't mind helping nobody but I won't be used," Travis stated.

"What are you talking about?"

"I just saw Sweetie creep in the house. Noah dropped her off," he responded.

Nina twisted her face up. "You're a damn lie! She is terrified of that man."

"I'm telling you what the fuck I saw! She playing you, Nina. She still fucking with that nigga so let her take her ass home to him!" he yelled.

"No, Travis. He beats her ass!" exclaimed Nina.

"She must like it! That ain't my business, Nina. But this is my house and I say she gotta go," said Travis dismissively.

"This is OUR mother fucking house and I say she stays!" defied Nina.

"There you go! I was wondering when you was going to take your mask off. You so far up your friend's ass that you didn't realize that you were losing a good man. You may want to downsize because I'm not paying the bills in a house where I have no say so. Sweetie can stay, cus I'm out." Travis grabbed his keys and stormed out of the house.

Travis cursed Nina out in his mind at least ten times before he made it to his apartment. Something told him to keep paying the bills there and he was glad he did. As Travis got closer to his apartment, he noticed Wendy's car in the parking lot.

He walked up and knocked on the window, startling her. She sat still for a few moments before opening the door and stepping out.

"How long have you been sitting out here?"

Wendy shrugged her shoulders, not really knowing the answer. "A few hours maybe. I drive by every night just to see whether or not you're here."

"Why didn't you call me? I've been blowing your phone up," admitted Travis.

"I didn't want to talk to you while you were under the same room as your wife. So, I came here every time you called to see if you were here." Wendy looked away and fought back tears,

Travis looked at her with concern. "Did you go to the doctor? I really wanted to be there."

"It would have been a waste of time. There's no baby," she answered hoarsely. Travis didn't know how he felt about what Wendy had just said to him. It was somewhere in between relief and disappointment.

He reached out and pulled her into his embrace. "Come on." he grabbed her hand and led her into his apartment. He showered in the master bathroom while Wendy freshened up in the guest restroom. Wendy lay on Travis's bed wearing a sexy silk nightgown. Travis licked his lips as he lay down beside her but he willed himself to behave. He pulled Wendy's body until her ass was resting on his penis. He wrapped his arms around her and planted a small kiss on the back of her neck.

"Goodnight, Wendy."

"Night, Boss," replied Wendy getting comfortable within his arms. Travis didn't plan on having sex with Wendy because he was still legally married to Nina. He knew he had no business even being that close to Wendy but Travis couldn't help but enjoy the feeling of falling asleep next to someone who truly appreciated him.

CHAPTER 37

"Chanel, you said the caterers are good to go, right?"asked Nina.

Chanel smacked her lips. "Yes, for the fifth time! Damn!"

"Just making sure, you know you tend to forget a lot of things," Nina pointed out. Chanel shrugged her shoulders.

"Relax, Nina. Everything will be fine," reassured Sweetie. They were planning a surprise party honoring Allie, who had just completed her externship. She was one step closer to becoming the nurse she always dreamed of being.

"Should we send Spade an invite? I know Allie has been super pissed with him," said Nina.

"I sent him one already. That's her kid's father. He needs to be there," said Chanel.

Nina was hesitant about that but the damage had already been done so she shrugged it off. Travis crossed Nina's mind and reminded her to ask Sweetie a very important question.

"Sweetie, you haven't been in communication with Noah, have you?"

Sweetie shook her head and frowned her face. "No, why?"

Nina shrugged her shoulders. "Just asking. Making sure you're staying strong." She studied Sweetie's face but her expression never changed.

"Fuck Noah."

Chanel stayed silent but looked at Sweetie and shook her head. She saw for herself that Sweetie was back in contact with Noah. A few days prior, she passed by their house to have a talk with Brandi and noticed Noah leading Sweetie in the house, holding her hand. She wanted to help her friend but why should she care if Sweetie didn't?

"Chanel, look in that drawer and hand me that notebook in there. It's yellow," said Nina changing the subject.

Chanel opened the drawer but all she saw was a big envelope. She picked up the envelope and sure enough, the tablet was under it. As Chanel went to put the envelope back, the contents of it slipped out. She didn't notice that she had grabbed it at the wrong end.

Chanel kneeled down and looked at the birth certificate and photo. "Nina, what the hell is this?"

Nina looked up and saw Chanel holding up the contents of that awful envelope. How did she forget to get rid of it?

"Why are you going through my shit? It's nothing," said Nina walking towards Chanel. As soon as she was close enough, she tried to snatch the picture out of Chanel's hand but it was no use. Chanel had already seen the boy who was undeniably Travis's twin.

"Oh, bitch it's something. What the hell is going on?" Chanel quizzed. Sweetie peeked over at the picture and was stunned.

Nina sat down at her kitchen table and massaged her temples. "That's Aiden. Apparently, he is Travis's son with his high school sweetheart. She showed up a few months ago while Travis and I were going through a rocky time. I told her Travis wanted nothing to do with the baby and paid her off. I've never mentioned it to Travis."

"Nina!"Exclaimed Chanel with disgust. "How could you?"

"What? A woman just pops out of the blue with a baby and I'm supposed to accept it?" Nina scoffed.

"It's not even about you, Nina. It's about that child who is out in the world without a father because of you!"

"He has a father! He was raised by the man for almost eight fucking years!" Nina yelled.

Sweetie normally stayed out of these things but she didn't agree with Nina one bit. "What about Travis? All he ever wanted was to be a father and you're taking that away from him."

"I will give him a child! One day! But for now, we need to focus on fixing our marriage," Nina said defensively.

"You're so insecure about your marriage that you're jealous of a kid. You're scared Travis is going to care about something more than he cares about you. You do a lot of fucked up things, Nina St. Claire, but this took the cake. You're more of a selfish bitch than I thought." Chanel got her purse and walked to her car. She could deal with a lot of things, but a scandalous female wasn't one of them.

Chanel called Allie to vent about what just happened, but before she could call, she saw a text message from her saying they needed to talk. Chanel sent her a quick text letting her know she was on the way over.

"Is everything okay," she asked once she was seated on Allie's couch.

Allie nodded her head and sat across from her. "Something has been weighing on my mind for a while now and I can't continue to hold it in. Jah, well I knew him as Heem, was my trainer. I didn't know he was the same person as your Jah until your party. He was a good friend to me and he was a great trainer so we've been kind of hanging out a little lately."

Chanel looked at Allie with bored eyes. "You're friends with my ex, so what?"

"We had sex once while he was training me," Allie admitted.

"Are you serious? So you're out fucking my ex behind my back and smiling in my face?" asked Chanel, raising her voice.

"I only slept with him once and that was before I knew that he was your man. You called him Jah, he introduced himself to me as Heem, so there was no way I could have known," explained Allie.

"But when you did find out, you said nothing," Chanel said, curling her lip.

"When I told you ladies that I needed a trainer, you never mentioned that you were dating one," Allie recalled.

"Because I didn't want this to happen," Chanel shot back,

"I feel so bad, believe me I do. That's why I had to tell you face to face. I hope you're okay with us still being friends because that's all we are. I will never sleep with him again," promised Allie.

"I'm done with all you bitches," muttered Chanel as she walked out of Allie's house. "Kiss my ass, Allie you can keep your apology."

Allie didn't chase after Chanel as she was leaving because she knew she deserved it. She was just tired of hiding her friendship with Jaheim. He had been there for her through everything and she didn't want to continue to push him away.

Speaking of Jaheim, Allie was headed to meet him at a bar for drinks to celebrate the fact that she had completed her externship. She quickly showered and dressed in a crop top paired with distressed denim blue jeans. She decided to throw on a pair of heels just because.

As she was getting ready, Allie heard her doorbell ring. She walked to the front door and peeked out the window but didn't see anything. She cracked her door open and saw a big bouquet of flowers. The note on the card read, "Congrats Nurse Allie. See you soon."

Allie smiled and headed to the bar to meet Jaheim. As soon as she arrived, she spotted Jaheim who was wearing a bright smile. "Well if it isn't the world's sexiest nurse."

"Stop it," Allie replied, hugging Jaheim before sitting down next to him.

"Congrats, girl. You worked hard for that," he acknowledged.

Allie blushed and ordered an apple martini. "Thank you for the flowers, they were beautiful."

"No problem," he replied. "You're an exceptional woman Allie."

"You're so charming," Allie smiled. "You're going to make some woman really happy one day."

"I want to make you happy, Allie. I want to see that beautiful smile every day. You're too precious to walk around looking miserable. You're worth way more than a part-time relationship."

Allie shifted in her seat. "Jaheim you're a great guy. You helped me overcome so many things so I will always care about you. But when it comes to my heart, it's with Spade and always will be. It may sound crazy but that's just how I feel. There may come a time when those feelings no longer exist but as long as he is in my heart, there's no room for anyone else?"

Jaheim tried his hardest to hide his frustration but he didn't understand what else he had to do to change her mind. He had to eliminate Spade for good if he ever wanted Allie to be his. "Even though he has moved on and found somebody new?"

Allie let her drink trickle down her throat before she answered. "I'm not threatened. If he was serious about the bitch, he would let me know. He respects me more than that."

Allie spoke with much more confidence than she had. She really wasn't sure where she stood with Spade but she would continue to stand firm until her heart told her otherwise.

"All that love in your heart for someone who doesn't even deserve it," Jaheim replied shaking his head.

Allie didn't respond. She wasn't comfortable having this conversation with Jaheim. She didn't need to defend her love.

"I'm sorry Allie I just hate to see you so down while he's out living his life freely. I try to stay in my place but after I made love to you I knew that we had a connection much deeper than I imagined."

Allie couldn't stop her jaw from falling. "We didn't make love, Heem. We fucked. I appreciate you for being kind to me but there's no deeper connection. I want us to be friends but please understand, we will never be anything more whether Spade and I get back together or not."

Jaheim's eye twitched but he held his composure. "Aight."

"I'm not trying to be mean but I don't want to lead you on in any way," she reasoned.

"It's too late for that," he seethed. Jaheim stood up and left some money at the bar. "Congrats again."

Allie watched him walk away in shock. She had no idea he was secretly falling for her. Otherwise, she would have ended their friendship a long time ago. Allie decided to stay at the bar and have a few more drinks. She deserved to drink to her accomplishments.

"What's your name, sexy lady?"

Allie spun around and saw Spade smiling from ear to ear. Her first reaction was to jump up and hug him. "Hey, what are you doing here?"

"We should be asking you the same thing young lady," joked Travis. Allie was so caught up in seeing Spade that she hadn't even noticed him standing there.

"I'm celebrating," replied Allie, raising her glass. She looked back at Spade and got butterflies in her stomach. It was something so different about him but she couldn't put her finger on it. She hadn't seen him since the incident with Noah so she was taking all of him in.

Spade looked at the empty glass next to Allie. "You on a date?"

"No," Allie replied quickly. "Drinks with a friend, but they left about ten minutes ago."

"Well, can your baby daddy buy you a drink or two?" he asked, sheepishly.

"Of course you can."

Spade and Travis took their seats. Spade ordered a hot wing basket but skipped the drink. Allie was just happy that he was there. She didn't even notice he wasn't drinking.

"So, did you like the flowers I sent? They didn't have any blue ones so I sent roses instead."

Allie's eyes widened. "You sent those flowers?"

"Yeah, who else would have sent them?" Spade stopped chewing his food for a minute. "Are you seeing somebody, Allie?"

"No, I should be asking you that," she shot back. She was feeling her drinks and the ratchet would soon find its way out.

Spade put both his hands up. "I've been chilling. I don't have time for no bitches."

"Hmph," Allie said, rolling her eyes.

"He ain't bullshitting. Jah brought some strippers over, right? Soon as she sat on Spade lap, he grabbed her and tossed her ass," laughed Travis. He then stopped and looked at Spade. "Too much info?"

Spade chuckled but shrugged his shoulders. "Bitch shouldn't have come into my personal space."

Allie listened quietly thinking about Jaheim tried to twist the story to make it seem like Spade had been messing around with the girl. It all made sense. He tried to take credit for sending the flowers too in an attempt to squeeze his way into Allie's heart.

Allie leaned over and kissed Spade. It was the first time in over two months that their lips touched and Allie felt like she was melting away. Spade wrapped his arm around her waist and kissed her back, biting her lip gently just the way she liked.

"Check, please!" said Travis, laughing. "These niggas need a room."

Allie looked into Spade's eyes and smiled. He returned the smile and held her for a few moments. "I'm proud of you."

"Thank you, baby. When are you coming home?" Allie saw the hesitation in his eyes before he tried to blink it away.

"Let's take it one day at a time, okay?"

Allie nodded her head and took a seat back on the stool. She was in and out the rest of the time they were there. If they weren't talking about getting back together, Allie didn't want to talk. She was drunk and horny and Spade was doing nothing more than pissing her the fuck off.

CHAPTER 38

Nina walked around the venue making sure everything was in place for Allie's surprise party. Her black and gold color scheme screamed elegant and chic. She knew Allie's favorite color was blue but she refused to throw a tacky party.

She told Allie that she got a promotion at her job and she was throwing herself a celebration dinner so she wouldn't suspect a thing. It was a grown and sexy all black affair so she hoped that everyone cooperated. Nina had invited all of Allie's family just so she would know how proud of her everyone was. So many people counted her out after she had her kids, but she didn't let anything stop her from getting what she wanted. She was truly an inspiration to everyone around her.

Slowly but surely, guests started to arrive and before Nina knew it, she had a full house. Allie's sister texted Nina to lether know they were about fifteen minutes away. Nina quickly grabbed the mic from the DJ. "Everyone, Allie is in route. She should be here in ten minutes so be sure to be quiet when the lights dim."

Nina scanned the crowd and only saw Sweetie. She and Chanel weren't speaking but she didn't understand why she wasn't there. She continued looking around and her heart stopped when she spotted Travis. He had his receptionist with him as if they were on a date. Nina politely sat the mic down and walked over to where he was standing talking to Jaheim.

"What are you doing here with this bitch?"

Travis glanced at Nina dryly. "Why are you being disrespectful, Nina?"

"No, you're being disrespectful by showing up with her," fumed Nina, pointing in Wendy's face. Wendy wanted to slap the hell out of Nina, but it wasn't the time nor the place for the drama.

She looked at Nina's stomach and rolled her eyes. The bitch just looked fat to her, she didn't see anything close to a baby bump.

"I didn't plan on bringing her. She needed me to take her somewhere but I didn't want to miss this for Allie so I told her to just ride with me," replied Travis calmly.

Wendy looked away, not understanding why he was explaining anything to the bitch. The lights dimmed suddenly, which meant that Allie had arrived. Nina gave Wendy one more nasty look before walking away. She looked around making sure her camera men were in place and that the band was ready. Once she was satisfied, that everything was good to go, she text Amber letting her know to send Allie in.

Seconds later, the door opened. "SURPRISE!" Surprise was the perfect word for Allie's face as she walked in saw her friends and family all in one room.

"Oh my God, who did this?" cried Allie. She spent a lot of time on her makeup and she was about to ruin it already.

Nina and Sweetie stood with smiles on their faces as they watched Allie look around the room in awe. Nina noticed a slight look of disappointment on her face as she looked around the crowd and didn't see Spade.

Nina walked over and hugged her. "He said he was really sorry he couldn't make it. He sends his love."

Allie's heart broke a little but she was determined to have a good time. She was tired of letting Spade be in control of her emotions. If he didn't want her, she would just move on simple as that.

"Chanel didn't come either, huh?" Allie shook her head but understood why she did not attend. She just didn't believe that Chanel would care that much.

"Now you know I wouldn't miss this day for the world. Even though you did fuck my man," said Chanel from behind

254

Allie. They hugged each other for a long time as Sweetie and Nina tried to figure out what they missed.

CHAPTER 39

The entire night went smoothly. Allie was so happy to be around her loved ones and she was so grateful to Nina for making it happen. Halfway through the night, guest after guest stood up during dinner to honor Allie and give her words of encouragement.

Chanel stood up and took the mic. "I've known Allie since high school and since high school, I sort of hated her. Me and Amber almost fought a thousand times because she didn't play about her baby sister." Everyone chuckled, including Allie's parents.

Chanel took a deep breath. "I hated Allie because she was all that I wanted to be. On top of being beautiful, she's such a loving and caring person and she just draws you into her. Growing up, that's what I always wanted not realizing that I was seeking the wrong attention by being over the top, negative, and slightly promiscuous. These last few months, Allie and I have become extremely close and she's been such an inspiration. She's taught me so much about loving myself and she didn't even know it. I watch her bust her ass every single day with not one complaint and it made me realize what a woman should be. I'm extremely proud of you Allie and I love you so much. You're the mascara to my Moscato for life."

"Awwwww" echoed throughout the entire room as Allie dabbed her eyes. She stood up and blew Chanel a kiss before sitting back down.

"We have one more person who would like to speak on behalf of Allie," announced Chanel with a sly smile. Spade walked on the stage from the back and Allie almost passed out.

"You look beautiful tonight," he complimented once he got the mic. "Can you come sit up here, I wanna talk to you."

Once Allie was seated on the stage, Spade pulled up a chair in front of her so that they were face to face. "First, I want to tell

256

you that I love you and I knew you could do it. You work so hard and I owe you so much for all that you've done and sacrificed for me and our children. It's been nine years and they all haven't been easy but you stuck it out with me gracefully and I appreciate you for that. I can't repay you for all that you've done but I do have a few things to show you."

Spade reached into his pocket and pulled out a necklace. "This reads sixty days sober. I've wanted to come home and hold you every night for sixty days but I had to get myself together so I could be the man you deserved. I felt you slipping away so I did what I had to do to make sure that you'd never feel unappreciated or neglected again."

The crowd cheered as Allie blushed and cried.

"For nine years, I've called myself your man but the truth is, I was nothing more than a boy. I was prideful, selfish, and sometimes just irresponsible. I stand before you today as a man. A man who wants to give you the winter wonderland wedding of your dreams. I want to give you the blue hydrangeas, the icicle chandeliers, and the caged blue jays. I want to see you walk down the aisle in the Vera Wang dress. I saw the magazine picture you hide in your panty drawer," he said. Allie thought Spade was ignoring her each time she talked about her dream wedding but he listened to every word she said. He just didn't want to get her hopes up knowing he wasn't in the position to be the man she wanted.

Spade got on one knee and pulled out a Tiffany box. "With this 18 CT, white gold ring with the blue sapphire that you've talked about since high school, I humbly ask you to be my wife. Alyssa Denise Spencer, will you marry me?"

Tears filled Spade's eyes as he waited for her to answer. He saw Allie staring at her dream ring with tears in her eyes as she jumped into his arms. Spade smiled proudly and noticed there wasn't a dry eye in the room. He looked over at Allie's dad who nodded his head with approval.

"Yes! Yes!" cried Allie. She held on to Spade tightly as she cried. "I love you so much."

Spade smiled and slipped the ring on her finger before posing for pictures. Allie's smile was so bright that nothing could ruin that moment. Not even Jaheim, who was standing with a scowl on his face. Allie hoped and prayed that he would keep their secret but that night, she didn't care. Her life was finally falling into place and she couldn't be happier.

Travis watched Spade and Allie slow dance and was overcome with heartache. He was genuinely happy for them but he couldn't help but think of how just three years ago he was happily in love. Now, Travis just felt empty. He had given so much of himself that he was mentally exhausted.

"You okay?" nudged Wendy.

"Yeah, I'm good," he replied.

Wendy nodded her head but didn't speak. She saw that him and Nina kept glancing at each other and realized she was fighting a battle she just couldn't win. "Go talk to her."

"Who?" asked Travis.

Wendy smiled at him and stood up. "Your wife."

Travis shook his head before he spoke. "I don't have anything to say to her. I'm done with her."

"You can't even stop looking at her, Travis," Wendy pointed out.

"Don't get me wrong, I still love her. But I'm done with her. I just want to be a father to my kid, that's all," he replied. Travis was done fighting for Nina's attention; he would find a woman to love him for all that he was and all that he was not.

"Can I steal your date for a minute?" Chanel asked as she approached them.

Wendy smiled politely. "Sure."

Chanel smiled back and turned to Travis. "May I have this dance?"

Travis laughed but agreed. "What are you up to?"

"Nothing, I just really need to talk to you," replied Chanel.

Travis frowned when he saw the serious expression etched on Chanel's face. "Are you okay? Do we need to step outside?"

"No, it will draw too much attention, Chanel reasoned.

Travis looked around the room. "You don't think us slow dancing will cause attention?"

"Not nearly as much as it would if we disappeared together," retorted Chanel. She sighed before talking again. "I love you like a brother and Nina is my sister so this is hard for me."

"What? What's going on?"

"You have a son that lives in Atlanta. His mama, Gabi, I believe came looking for you. Nina paid them off to never contact you again. I just couldn't let that sit on my conscience knowing how badly you want to be a father."

Chanel regretted her words as soon as they left her lips. Travis was staring at her with an expression that she couldn't make out. Maybe she should have just kept her damn mouth closed.

"When was this?" he asked still trying to process what she was saying.

"A few weeks ago, maybe. I don't know I just ran across the picture of the kid and the birth certificate and asked her what it was about," answered Chanel.

"A picture?"

Chanel nodded her head. "He's your twin, Trav."

Travis shook his head and chuckled. "A son, are you serious? He must be around seven or eight if it's the baby that Gabi told me wasn't mine. Wow!"

Chanel saw the joy on Travis's face and some of her guilt subsided. She loved Nina to death but she was wrong for what she did.

"So Nina never planned on telling me?'

Chanel looked at him with sympathy but didn't answer. Travis bright complexion turned red as he thought about how selfish Nina was. If he had never been over her, he was definitely over her that day. Not only was he disgusted by her actions; he'd also lost all respect for her. He hated that both of his kids would be raised in broken homes but as long as he got to be a father, he was good with it.

"Thank you for telling me, Chanel. I know that must have been hard for you," said Travis.

"It was; but living with the guilt of knowing that was much harder. I just wanted you to know the truth," she responded before walking away.

Allie was overwhelmed with joy after Spade proposed to her. It was a moment that she has dreamed about her entire life and she couldn't have picked a better time or place for it to happen. She was surrounded by so much love that she had been crying the entire night.

Allie snuck away to the restroom while Spade danced with her mother. She retouched her makeup in the mirror because she refused to look crazy in her pictures. Once she finished, she looked at her reflection and loved the woman smiling back at her. It took so much pain, disappointments, and lonely nights to finally get her happily ever after but it was worth it. She knew exactly what she wanted and she didn't let anything stop her from getting it. She thought about Heem and the mistake she made with him. Although she wished it never happened, she was glad it did. Besides getting her confidence back, she realized that no one in the world could hold a candle to what she had with Spade.

Allie smiled at her reflection before walking out of the restroom. As soon as she stepped out, she bumped into Jaheim. They stared at each other for a few seconds making Allie uncomfortable.

"Excuse me." She quickly looked away and tried to walk pass him but he didn't move.

"Allie, talk to me," he pleaded, reaching his arm out to her. Allie took a step back and scowled at him.

"I don't want to talk to you. I don't even know why you're here," she retorted as she glared at the man she once trusted.

"I wanted to support you. I really am proud of you," he answered as he jammed his hands into his pockets. He looked at Allie with sincerity in his eyes and hoped she would soften up.

Allie saw the desperation twinkling in Jaheim's eyes but felt nothing. "It feels weird, okay? Chanel knows what happened between us. She's hurt and you being here don't make it better. I can't be cool with you, Heem. You lied to me. You wanted me to believe that Spade had moved on. You even took the credit for those flowers, knowing you didn't send them."

"You were so unhappy," he muttered with pleading eyes. "I hated seeing you like that, Allie. I care about you so much."

"If you care so much, then leave. Now. Stay away from me and my fiancée. I understand that Travis is your friend so we may see each other in passing, but I want nothing to do with you." Allie folded her arms in front of her and tilted her head slightly to the right. "I don't even want to think about what else you lied to me about."

Jaheim stepped forward again causing Allie to jump back. "Don't fucking touch me," she warned.

"I'm a sincere man. I let my feelings for you get out of control so I made some bad decisions, but I'm still the man I was when I trained you and made you feel beautiful again, Alyssa."

"Call me Allie," she reiterated. "And I don't care what kind of man you are anymore. Please leave now." Allie hated to be so mean to him, but she no longer respected him.

Jaheim fixed his face into a tight scowl before stepping out of Allie's way. She shook her head and stepped closer to him. "FYI, don't even think about threatening me with telling Spade. He'll forgive me, but he'll kill you."

She rolled her eyes and brushed pass Heem, leaving him and his drama behind her. She was a newly engaged woman who planned on enjoying the rest of her night.

Sweetie snuck away during the slow dances and walked outside. She looked around until she spotted Noah's company car. She quickly ran over and got in. "Circle the block," she ordered.

Noah smiled and did as he was told. He reached in the backseat and pulled out a bouquet of flowers and handed it to Sweetie. "You look beautiful tonight."

"Thank you," replied Sweetie, blushing. Noah had been so sweet and charming the last couple of weeks and she loved it. He apologized profusely for the things he had done to her. He explained the amount of pressure and stress he was under and Sweetie understood.

"I've been taking my meds again, I'm praying again, I'm a changed man, Sweetie," said Noah, proudly.

Sweetie's heart fluttered when he called her by her nickname. She was so accustomed to him calling her Jameka like she was his child, so it warmed her heart to hear him speak to her so affectionately. "I can see the change, babe. I really can."

He placed his hand on her chin and leaned in and kissed her softly. "I've missed you so much. Just come home. I promise you I'll do better."

"Give me a few weeks and I'll be there. I want a fresh start without all the judgment and ridicule from my friends," she explained.

"True friends wouldn't judge you. Those girls are only looking out for themselves, how many times do I have to tell you that?"

"I know," she said sadly.

"Let's move. Let's start over, baby. It's been nothing but drama since we moved back. Let's go live our life the way we want to," suggested Noah.

"That sounds good," agreed Sweetie. She loved her friends but they did cause a lot of chaos in her life. Noah was doing better and she saw the progress in him so if saving her marriage meant leaving everything behind, then that's what she planned to do.

Noah crawled in the backseat and smiled seductively. "Come to daddy, babe."

As always, Sweetie did as she was told.

CHAPTER 40

Chanel moaned softly as she dreamed about Idris Elba's head between her thighs. Lawd, that man looked good to her. Her eyes fluttered when the sensations started to feel much too real. When she saw a figure's head buried in her vagina, Chanel shot up.

Eric looked up at her and smiled. "Rise and shine, sweet stuff."

Chanel snapped her legs closed and screamed. "Eric! What the hell are you doing here?"

Eric twisted his face and pointed to her sweet spot. "It's sort of obvious what I'm doing, Chanel."

Chanel used her long legs to push Eric's weight off of her. "Why, asshole? And where is my son?"

Eric sighed as he stood up. "He's in the room sleep. Why are you acting so funny?"

Chanel cocked her head to one side and scowled before speaking. "I'm not acting funny; I'm acting annoyed; because I am."

"Well, I think it may cheer you up to know that I'm leaving Talia. Now you and I can finally work things out," he answered with a small smile.

Chanel shook her head slowly as she glared at the man that she once loved dearly. "Never."

Eric's smile quickly faded. "What?"

Chanel stretched before she stood up. "You heard what I said. N-E-V-E-R," she spelled slowly. "Not in this lifetime."

Eric shook his head in pure disbelief. "All this time, all you've wanted was to be with me. Now I'm here telling you that I want to be with you and you're giving me attitude?"

"I'm giving you attitude because you're a triflin' excuse for a man," she snapped. "You lead me on for years, making false promises to me, and dogging me out every chance you got. Now you want to walk up in here like I'm supposed to be jumping for joy because you claim to want to be with me? Nigga, fuck you!"

Eric chuckled at Chanel's outburst. He rubbed his chin and licked his lips as she ranted. "Chanel, stop the act. Just let your guard down and let daddy take care of you. Let me get some of that good stuff."

Chanel threw her head back and laughed. "Fuck you! You will never get close to me with that sick dick of yours. You running around giving bitches herpes and you want me to fuck you?"

264

Eric stood still as his eyes grew big. Chanel folder her arms and nodded her head. "Yeah, I know about you. How dare you know you have this shit and not even tell me?"

Eric put his hands on his face and sighed. "I never slept with you during an outbreak so that I wouldn't give it to you. I was careful. I respect you more than that."

"But you don't respect your wife? Because she has it," Chanel countered.

Eric sat down at the edge of the bed. "Chanel, we're talking about us right now."

"There is no us, Eric. I'm tired of chasing behind your ass. I'm tired of sneaking around and I'm damn sure tired of you treating me like shit. You weren't careful, you were a coward. You wasn't man enough to tell me the truth so fuck you!"

Eric looked into Chanel's gorgeous face. "I love you, Chanel. Who is going to love you more than me, huh? You're a mess. You're insecure and lonely and you lack ambition. Who will love you, Chanel?"

He stood back up and got into her face. "WHO?" He screamed. "Sure, you'll find plenty of niggas to fuck you but nobody is going to love a woman like you."

"You've beat me down for a long time Eric and for a while, I believed that you actually cared about me but it's clear that you don't. So I'll be all that you said that I was but what I won't be, is a fool for you. I'm done, Eric."

Chanel walked over to her bedroom door. "So you can leave, now. I will be getting the locks changed tomorrow so you can throw away that key."

Eric shook his head and walked out of her bedroom. "Chanel Almighty," he laughed. "We'll see how long this lasts before you start feeling lonely again and want some of daddy dick."

Chanel rolled her eyes. "Nigga, please. Your stroke game is weaker than your hair-line, get the fuck out of my house." Chanel followed Eric to the front door and watched him leave.

"Fuck you, bitch," he seethed.

"Right back at ya!" she smiled, waving. "And Eric... I'll love me more than you ever did and so will my son. That's all I need."

Chanel closed the door and smiled to herself. She had a long way to go to become the person she wanted to be, but getting rid of Eric was definitely a big step in the right direction.

CHAPTER 41

Travis sat nervously as he waited for Gabi to arrive at the restaurant. As soon as he found out he could possibly have a son in the world, he went into overdrive trying to make arrangements to meet him. The day after Allie's party, Travis returned to his old neighborhood and visited Gabi's mother house since he didn't know how to get in touch with her directly. After speaking with her mother, Travis arranged a sit-down with the mother of his child.

Travis tapped his fingers on the cold table as his stomach turned flips. He had an idea of what he wanted to say but he knew once Gabi got there, it would be much more difficult.

Travis stared at the entrance of the restaurant until finally, he saw Gabi appear. He eyed her intensely as she walked towards him. It's been nearly eight years, but Gabi didn't look like she had aged a bit.

Travis stood up and embraced Gabi when she got close enough to him. Gabi felt anxious, nervous, but a bit relieved to be able to talk to Travis herself.

"Good to see you, Gabz. You look great." Travis shot Gabi a small smile as she sat down into the booth.

Gabi felt a warm sensation through her body when she heard Travis call her Gabz. It gave her a sense of comfort, so to speak. "You too."

"Do I? I feel like an old man. I've been going through a lot lately," he confessed.

Gabi nodded her head slowly. "You and I both."

Travis shifted in his seat and stared at his menu. "You hungry?" He didn't wait for her answer. "Of course you are. Eating was your favorite thing in the world."

"It still is," she laughed. Travis joined her as they briefly reminisced on their past life together.

They ordered their food and sat silently before Travis finally broke the ice. "Why didn't you tell me?"

Gabi took a deep breath and took a sip of her water. "I didn't know at the time. When I cheated on you with Phil, I felt so bad but I knew in my heart I was carrying your child. I was young and didn't know anything about conception and pregnancy, so when they gave me a conception date, I traced it back to Phil. I thought I was doing the right thing by telling you what I thought was the truth."

Travis nodded his head as he listened to Gabi speak. He heard the sincerity in her voice and no longer felt angry with her.

"My mama said she knew the truth from the start that he was yours, but I didn't. Aiden looked like me when he was born," she explained. She handed him a photo album, with photos of Aiden over the years. "It wasn't up until a few years ago that I started having doubts. He just reminded me so much of you. At first I thought it was because I still loved you, but when he became obsessed with baseball, I knew. And then, he started to look just like you."

Gabi picked with her food for a while, before continuing. "I talked to my mama who told me that you were happily married so I didn't know how to tell you so I avoided the truth. Phil found our prom picture and also noticed how much Aiden looked like you. He went behind my back and got a DNA test and proved what we all knew."

When Gabi looked back up, she had tears in her eyes. She shrugged her shoulders. "I understand why you don't want anything to do with us, but I just wished you would have talked to me instead of having your wife do it."

Travis thumbed through the photos of his son and felt so proud. He didn't need a test of his own; he had no doubt that Aiden was his son. "Gabi, I just found out three days ago. Nina didn't tell me anything, one of her friends did. I would never pay you to disappear with my son. I've always wanted to be a father; you of all people should know that. Does that sound like me or something that I would do?"

Gabi gazed sadly into Travis's hazel eyes. "Time changes people, Travis. After all the pain I caused you, I just didn't know."

"Well, I would never be the type of man to abandon his responsibilities. You can keep whatever money Nina gave you, but I would like to meet my son. Our son."

Gabi smiled as the tears rolled down her face. "We're going back to Atlanta. Our flight leaves at 5 today."

Travis gulped and cleared his throat. He hadn't even entertained the fact that they had an entire life outside of him. He was the one with unrealistic expectations.

"We can set something up for us to come back. I need to talk to him and let him know what's going on because his life is going to be affected, too." Gabi wanted to hold Travis as she watched his heart break in front of her. She saw the same look in his eye when she told me she wasn't carrying his child.

Travis nodded his head and put his head in his hands. He took a deep breath before finally muttering okay. They continued to eat in silence before parting ways.

Travis drove home with a heavy heart. He didn't know how he would through each day knowing he had a son that he couldn't see or play with. As soon as he walked into his apartment, he went into his room and threw himself on the bed.

Wendy walked out of the restroom with a towel wrapped around her. She stopped when she saw Travis sprawled across the bed. "Everything okay?"

Travis let out a groan. Wendy walked over and sat down next to him. "Travis, what's wrong?"

He stared at the ceiling to avoid looking at Wendy's almost naked body. He was feeling so frustrated and he wanted nothing more than to flip her over and take all his anger out on her walls. "I don't want to talk about it right now."

Wendy pulled at Travis's pants and started to unbuckle his belt. She felt his hand grab hers in an attempt to stop her. "Travis, just relax. I'm going to temporarily relieve your stress, and then I'm going to get my things and go home so you can make things work with your wife."

"Wendy-"

"Travis," she whispered before taking him into her mouth. Travis stopped fighting and just laid back and enjoyed Wendy's skills. She performed her task with precision and swallowed once she was finished.

After getting cleaned up, Travis pulled Wendy into his chest. "If the circumstances were different, you'd be the perfect woman for me. I wish I could have been the man for you. "

She bit her lip and wrapped her arms around Travis. "I don't deserve a guy like you." She looked into his eyes. "You're such a good man with such a big heart. You love your wife and everyone can see that. So go fight for that love."

Travis kissed Wendy's forehead and held her tight. Once they finally let go of each other, he helped Wendy take her things to her car. He stood and stared at her for a while wishing he could merge her and Nina into one person.

"I really thank you for everything. If you ever need me for anything, you know I got you."

"Well, I could use a raise," Wendy laughed as she hugged Travis one last time. "See you at work tomorrow, boss!"

"Your ass better not be late," he joked. Travis watched her drive away before retreating back to his apartment. Before he could make it to the door, he received a text message that made him happier than he'd ever been.

CHAPTER 42

Nina walked into Pappadeaux Seafood and took a seat in what used to be her and Travis's favorite booth. Travis was already seated and looked happy to see her, which caught her by surprise.

"Someone's happy today," commented Nina.

Travis stood up to hug her. "What can I say, life's been good."

Nina accepted Travis's embrace then sat down. "That's good to hear."

"Well, I wanted to meet you here so we can talk about our marriage. It's been in shambles for a while now and I won't completely blame you. I felt like a piece was missing from my life and I put a lot of pressure on you to fill that void and it wasn't fair. I feel like I'm missing out on everything during your pregnancy and I don't like that. I shouldn't be receiving ultrasound pictures via text. I should be there. I ran out on you and you didn't deserve that."

Nina listened to his words and was glad that he finally understood that he was wrong, not her. "So this mean you and your little girlfriend are on bad terms. Because just last week at Allie's party, you were singing a different tune."

Travis leaned back in the booth and shook his head. "Nina, really? I'm trying here. Work with me, please."

Nina sighed. "Okay! I love you Travis and I always will. Of course, I want our marriage to work. I want you to come back home so we can continue living our lives the way we planned to." Just not today, thought Nina. She was on her period and she had no way to explain that so he needed to stay away for at least another week.

"I'm with that. I want us to make it work. Wendy is a beautiful girl with a beautiful soul but she is not Nina Marie St. Claire. I just ask that you put me before your friends. Allow me to be the man of my household."Travis looked at his wife and hardly recognized her. After he found out that she paid Gabi to pretty much disappear, Travis began to re-evaluate his life. He was a very traditional man so he didn't believe in walking away without a fight so he promised himself to give his marriage one last chance. He planned on telling Nina that he knew about what she did, but he decided to wait until they were in a private place in case things got out of hand. He did a lot of soul searching and praying, and all signs led right back to Nina. He knew he was a fool in love but all he ever wanted was a family. He loved Nina with every breath in his body no matter how many times she pushed him away. He knew deep down that he would always go back to her.

"I learned my lesson, I promise to do better."

Travis and Nina had a beautiful dinner discussing how they would move forward with their lives. They planned on going to counseling to get their communication back on track so that they could raise their baby as a family. Nina pretended to listen to Travis but all she could think about was how was she going to fake her miscarriage.

They were about to order dessert when Nina's phone rang. "This is Sweetie, one sec babe." Nina answered the phone and heard a lot of commotion in the background. She couldn't make out what was going on but she heard Noah yelling and screaming at her.

"Hello? Hello?" Nina said repeatedly.

"What's going on?" Travis asked concerned.

"I don't know, there's a lot of yelling in the background, I can't hear," said Nina holding one ear.

"Just hang up, that has nothing to do with you. Sweetie is grown and can handle her own. Besides, you're having dinner with me." Travis said.

"You're right," said Nina, sitting her phone in her lap purposely not hanging it up. She was so pissed at Sweetie for going back to Noah after all that he put her through.

"Look and see what dessert you want while I run to the restroom real quick," said Travis getting up. He walked over and gave Nina a kiss. "I can't wait to hold you and rub your belly tonight."

Nina smiled at him as he walked away. As soon as she could no longer see him, she put the phone back to her ear. The next thing she heard was a loud crash and Sweetie's screams. Nina quickly grabbed her purse and keys and darted out of the restaurant. Noah had her and her friend fucked up.

Moments later, Travis returned from the restroom to find an empty table. He walked over to the waiter. "Have you seen my wife?"

"She just ran out of here not too long ago, we thought she skipped the bill."

Travis pulled out his debit card and handed it over to the waiter as he called Nina's phone. "Where are you?" he asked when she answered.

"On my way to Sweetie's. He over there beating her ass again."

"You gotta be kidding me. That's not your business. Do not go over there! The fuck is wrong with you?" Travis yelled, not caring about the attention he was getting from the other patrons.

"No, what's wrong with him? Always putting his hands on a fucking woman!" Nina as she weaved in and out of traffic.

"She keep going back to him, when will you understand that? You can't help someone who don't want to be helped. Nina, I'm begging you to come back here or drive home."

"No, Travis. I'm not about to let my friend go through that." Nina wasn't trying to hear anything Travis said.

Travis balled his fists and paced back and forth. "Nina, as your husband I'm asking you to not go over there."

"As your wife, I'm telling you that I'm going!" she yelled

"You're pregnant, Nina. What can you do?" he asked. The waiter came over and handed Travis his card. He quickly signed the receipt and darted out of the restaurant to his car.

"I'm going to tell that nigga about his self and march my damn friend out of there," Nina replied.

"Your so called friends are going to be the reason you end up alone," Travis warned.

"What you going to do, huh? Leave again? Cus they were the only ones there when you abandoned me so fuck you!" Nina hung up the phone and put the pedal to the metal. Travis had some nerve telling her she would end up alone because of them when she was alone for months because of him.

Travis was so frustrated but he headed to Sweetie's house against his better judgment. He wanted to teach Nina a lesson so badly but he would never let her put herself or their child in harm's way. He would later wish he never made that decision.

274

CHAPTER 43

"Noah stop!" yelled Sweetie as he continued to throw blows.

"Then eat her pussy like I said, bitch!" yelled Noah.

Sweetie looked at Brandi in disgust, then back at Noah. "I'm tired and I always do her. Why can't she do me for a change?"

Sweetie was used to Noah making her have threesomes with Brandi but she was getting more and more disgusted the bigger Brandi's belly got.

"Cus I taste better, bitch," laughed Brandi, as she spread her legs open.

Sweetie wasn't a fighter by any means but she sure wanted to slap that stupid ass smile from Brandi's face.

"I'm not doing it," Sweetie defied, Noah ran over from where he was seated and grabbed Sweetie's neck.

"Listen you worthless piece of shit, you will do what the fuck I say do or I will snap your neck."

When Sweetie didn't move, Noah tightened his grip around Sweeties neck. Sweetie tried to deal with the pain for as long as she could but when she got dizzy, she knew he wasn't bullshitting. She nodded her head so he could loosen his grip.

His bucked eyes and wicked grin made Sweetie's flesh crawl. She didn't understand how a person could be so evil. She felt so naive for believing that he was a changed man. The only cure for his sickness was death.

He finally released her from his grip as she gagged and gasped trying to catch her breath. She touched her neck and flinched from the pain. For some reason, Sweetie became angry.

She grabbed the statue that was sitting on her coffee table and hurled it at Noah's head.

He moved just in time for the stone to crash against the mirror on the wall instead of his skull. He snapped his head around. His demeanor was that of a madman as his eyes nearly bucked out of his head. He charged her, causing her small frame to fall backward. He lifted his leg and sent a powerful kick to her torso. Brandi stood and watched in fear. She knew that one day; she too would become Sweetie so she stood silently, afraid to move. The fact that she was pregnant was the only thing stopping Noah from beating her to a pulp also.

Pain waves shot through Sweetie's body. She curled over and cradled her head in the crooks of her arms. He violently grabbed her by the hair and swung her, making her fall through the glass table in their living room.

"Oh my God, Noah! You're going to kill her!" screamed Brandi, but she didn't move. She was too afraid that he would hit her too.

"The bitch must want a death wish, throwing a fucking statue at me," yelled Noah. He kneeled down and grabbed Sweetie's face, bringing it closer to his.

As bad as Sweetie wanted to cry, she refused to let her tears fall. She refused to show any type of weakness. Noah thrived on feeling powerful but Sweetie spat on him like the coward he was.

"Bitch!" he growled. Noah was so taken aback; he couldn't keep his rage under control. He stormed into his bedroom and grabbed his Glock 40 before returning to the living room. He cocked it and jammed it in Sweetie's face. Sweetie's eyes widened and she felt a hot gush trickling down her leg. She started to shake when she came to the realization that she was about to die. She just hoped and prayed that Ruthie wouldn't let anything happen to Dallas. Sweetie was tired of fighting, she was tired of being abused, and most of all she was tired of living in fear. If Noah wanted to kill her, she wouldn't try to stop him; she just hoped he kept his promise and killed his self too.

Brandi screamed and covered her mouth. "Shut the fuck up!" he yelled, pointing his finger at her. Brandi feared that she would go into labor watching the scene before her. She wished she would have never got involved with Noah because she saw her future right in front of her. Like Sweetie, Brandi had allowed Noah to manipulate her and alienate her from her entire family so she had nowhere to go. Brandi continued to cry silently as Noah held his gun in Sweetie's face.

Noah kneeled down and jammed his gun in Sweetie's mouth. He wiped her spit off his face and slapped Sweetie in the face. "Bitch, you gon' pay for that. But I'm going to make you suffer long and hard before I kill your stupid ass. You fucked up now!"

He kicked her again before walking away to grab some tape. Brandi cried, encouraging Sweetie to call 911 but Sweetie could barely move. She knew her phone was in her back pocket but she didn't have the strength to grab it. She wouldn't have called the police even if she could. She would be dead by the time they made it, anyhow.

Sweetie watched in shock as she saw Nina rush into the house. "Sweetie!" She screamed. Nina looked at all the glass surrounding Sweetie and was afraid to get closer. "Shit!" She picked up her phone to call 9-11 but her hands were trembling so bad she dropped it. She leaned down to pick it up but a black boot crushed it before she could get to it.

Nina looked up and into Noah's eyes and almost cried. The deranged, evil face he wore let her know that this man was capable of anything. "Well if it isn't Nosey Nina."

Nina was terrified but she tried her best to keep her composure. "It sure is, Bitch ass Noah."

"I wasn't a bitch when I had you bent over in my restroom," he laughed loudly.

"You was an even bigger bitch then with that baby dick," she spat, disgusted.

He pulled out his gun and pointed it at her. Nina gasped loudly. Noah smiled and winked at her. "You ain't so bad now, are you?"

"I have someone on the way to handle you so you might want to make your scare tactics quick," Nina said rolling her eyes. She looked confident but she was bluffing her ass off. Nina instantly regretted leaving the restaurant. She glanced over at Sweetie who looked like she was in a trance.

"Go sit your fat ass on the couch," ordered Noah waving his gun. Nina quickly scurried to the couch, bracing herself the entire way there. The last thing she wanted was to be shot from the back.

"Lord, please lead me. I need you now," she prayed silently. Sweetie sat emotionless like she knew death was coming and welcomed it. Nina was scared out of her mind. She looked around for Brandi, who had disappeared. Nina hoped she was calling for help.

Noah walked over to the ladies slowly. Suddenly, there was a loud noise followed by footsteps. Noah quickly turned around and without thinking, fired two shots.

Nina's eyes widen and her entire world stopped. Everything moved in slow motion and the only sound she heard was the bullet piercing her husband's heart. She didn't hear the gunshots or her screams; she heard her husband's gasp as the bullet burned a hole through his chest.

"Traaaaaaaaaaaaaaaavis! NOOOOOOOO!" Nina instinctively ran towards her husband. She didn't even think about Noah or his gun. Her heart thumped against her chest as she ran to her husband's side. "Baby, baby."

278

She quickly grabbed his face and kissed him. "You're okay, baby. Stay with me, baby."

Travis's eyes were blank, as he appeared to choke on his blood. "Stay with me, okay?" Nina cried. Travis nodded his head slowly as he struggled to breathe.

Soon, there were sirens in the distance and Nina felt a glimmer of hope. As the EMTs rushed in and pulled her away from her husband, Nina wished those bullets were hers. Travis was such a good person with such a good heart. He didn't deserve that. He had only showed up to Sweetie's house to protect her.

Nina didn't remember her conversation with the police, she didn't even remember the ride to the hospital. She felt as though she was trapped in some horrific nightmare and she wanted so badly to wake up and make it go away.

CHAPTER 44

Word spread like wildfire about what happened to Travis so the entire crew was all gathered in the waiting room anxiously waiting. The silence in the waiting area was almost crippling. Besides an occasional squeak or a door opening, it was mute as everyone remained trapped in their thoughts.

Nina sat between Chanel and Allie as they all held hands. Chanel said a prayer as she tried her best to comfort her friend without breaking down herself. She loved Travis like a brother and she hated that this happened to him. She saw Jaheim sitting alone, breaking down and walked over to him. She silently sat next to him and held him as he prayed for his best friend. She sat with him for about ten minutes before he finally spoke. "I'll be okay. Go make sure Nina is good."

Chanel kissed her ex on his forehead before heading back toward her girls.

"I've never talked about the way my mama died," said Nina. "I didn't even tell Travis." Her gaze was far off and her eyes were small. Her jaws were tense as if it was painful to speak of those memories. "My mama died giving birth to me. Her mama died giving birth to her. When I was little, my cousins would tease me by saying I'd killed my mama. All throughout my childhood and even through my teens, I had horrible nightmares about that."

Nina wiped her eyes but couldn't stop the river of tears from flowing freely. "I was so scared to give birth to a child then not be here to watch them grow. I wanted Travis to have a little more time with me before I succumbed to the same fate as my mother and grandma. I didn't know how to tell him without him giving up his dream of being a father for me, now I may never get the chance."

"You'll get to tell him because he's going to be okay. His blood transfusion will go smoothly and in a few weeks, we'll all be laughing and joking again," Allie said in a hopeful tone. She tried to stay strong for the group, but she was trembling inside. She had so much love and respect for Travis for being such a standup guy. She knew that her friend was a handful but that man loved him some Nina. No matter what the situation was, he had his wife's back.

Nina rocked back and forth and cried until there were no more tears left to fall. Her heart was so heavy that even breathing was unbearable. One hour turned into three and she grew more and anxious. She had been back and forth to the restroom continuously vomiting. Never in a million years did she think something like this would happen to her.

"I'ma fucking kill that nigga when I see him," Jah yelled suddenly, referring to Noah, who had disappeared from the scene of the crime. Sweetie was still at the precinct for questioning. "That was my right man, my ace, man. He would give anybody the shirt off his back. Why him?"

Jah glared at Nina, hating that he blamed her for this. He wanted to hate her, but the love he had for Travis wouldn't allow him to. He loved her too much.

"That's if I don't get to him first," muttered Spade, who had been silent the whole time. Travis was more than his friend; he was like a brother to him. At his lowest points in life, Travis was there. When he couldn't buy his kid's Christmas gifts, Travis bought them and told Spade all he wanted in return was for him to keep being the best father he could be. Spade promised his self he would make Noah pay. He wouldn't get his hands dirty but he knew plenty of niggas who would do anything for a couple thousand bucks.

At 11:37 p.m., the nurse finally came into the waiting area. Jaheim quickly jumped out of his seat and went to grab Nina's hand. After he helped her up, they walked over to the nurse while Chanel, Allie, and Spade watched in anticipation.

281

Allie's heart stopped when she saw Nina collapse in Jaheim's arms. She let out a sigh as Spade squeezed her hand.

Nina turned around walked back to where she was seated. "He pulled through. We have to wait to see him in the morning."

Sighs of relief traveled across the waiting room. Travis was one of the sane ones in this group filled with craziness and they didn't know what they would do without him. Nina thanked God for sparing his life and she made a promise to herself to come clean with him about everything. Even if it meant losing him, Nina wanted a clean slate and if she had to fight to get her husband back, she was prepared to do it. She smiled as she thought of their future. Maybe once she told him about Aiden, she wouldn't have to have a child of her own. She figured being a blended family wouldn't be so bad.

"So, I guess we're camping out here all night?" Spade asked in much better spirits.

Nina nodded her head and smiled, happy that she still had her man and her real friends. She vowed to herself to find the balance between the two.

CHAPTER 45

ONE WEEK LATER

"I don't think I'm ready for this," muttered Allie as she walked into the doors of the church. Travis's funeral was packed already so she hoped Chanel saved her and Spade a spot like she asked her to. Travis died hours after his blood transfusion. The doctors said his body might have rejected the blood and there was nothing that they could do. Allie could hear still Nina's scream echoing in her ears. The doctors allowed them to go in to say their final goodbyes to him but Allie couldn't take it. Nina had crawled in the bed beside him and was begging him to wake up. Allie's eyes watered at the memory and she shuddered. She quickly blinked her tears away and gave Spade's hand a squeeze.

He wasn't taking Travis's death well either. Before his death, Travis hired Spade at his construction company once Spade finished rehab and paid him extremely well. Travis was one of the few people Spade considered friends and he even asked Travis to be the best man in his wedding. Spade swallowed the lump in his throat as he slowly walked into the funeral. He was glad Allie was next to him because he felt weaker than he'd ever felt.

Allie looked around the church and noticed that Sweetie was missing. She had been missing in action since the night of the shooting, along with Noah. Allie and Spade slowly walked down the aisle as Spade broke down.

"Why him, man? He didn't deserve that. He was a good dude," he sobbed. Allie held tightly on to his hand as he shook his head and cried. Allie wanted to pull him toward their seat but she knew Spade would want to see Travis one last time. Allie braced herself as she looked into the casket. Surprisingly, she didn't feel scared.

Travis looked just like himself. He looked like he was sleeping peacefully and that gave Allie a sense of comfort. It was when Nina and Travis's mom entered the church that Allie lost it.

Nina screamed and cried asking God to give him back to her. She stood in front of his casket and kissed his face so many times.

"I cooked your favorite meal last night, baby. I made the meatloaf the way your mama does. I made the mashed potatoes you like and I even made greens. Not the canned ones because I know you hate those. Just wake up and come eat with me one last time. Please, Travis. Please!"

There were sniffles and sob all throughout the church. Watching Nina cling to the casket was painful for them all. "Give him back, God! Please give him back and I promise I'll be the best wife I can be. Just give him back to me. Travis, please come back. You said you wouldn't leave me again, you promised!" Nina looked at Travis lying in the casket and wished it was her instead. It should have been her. Nina bawled her eyes out thinking about the last few months of their lives. They could have been so happy had it not been for her pride. She continued screaming as she held on the casket for dear life.

Finally, Jah walked to the front and escorted her to her seat. Travis's mom sat stoic on the front row, shaking her head in disbelief. Her only son was now gone.

As the service moved on, people stood in line to talk about Travis and how he was such a great cousin, boss, friend, and worker. It was evident that he had left his mark on everyone he met. Everyone had such nice things to say about him and how helpful he was. Nina learned things about her husband that she didn't know; probably because she was too busy to ask. He'd helped one of his employees get a car, he loaned another one of his co-workers one thousand dollars to get a lawyer, he even sent one of his employees on an all expense vacation when she found out her husband cheated on her. All in all, everyone talked about how giving he was, how respectful he was, and lastly how much he loved Nina St. Claire.

After much hesitation, Spade finally stood and walked to the podium. His heart was heavy but he had to speak on his friend's behalf, he owed him that. Spade looked at Travis for a few minutes before he started to speak.

"Everyone had such beautiful memories to share about Travis and they all made this so much harder for me. We heard about Travis the man, Travis the boss and Travis the friend; but I was one of the only ones who got to experience Travis the father."

Spade could see some people whispering and others looking plain old confused but he continued his speech. "Travis recently found out that he had an 8 year old son living out in Atlanta. It just so happened that his son, Aiden, was out here for a few weeks. Travis asked me to come with him to meet him. Of all the people he could have asked, he asked me because he said he respected me so much as a father. He asked me to drive his car to meet Aiden because he was too nervous. The entire ride he kept saying how he couldn't believe he had a son out in the world. Anyway, when we got there, Travis walked to the trunk and pulled out a big bag. It was a ball for every sport imaginable in that bag," laughed Spade. "Probably even a bowling ball, that's how excited he was."

Laughter spread through the church and Spade paused for a moment, catching his breath. "He wasn't sure what the kid liked so he bought everything he could think of. When he first laid eyes on his son, the look of pride and joy on his face was priceless. I wanted to cry just standing there watching him. He grabbed and wrapped him tight in his arms and kept telling him he was sorry. Aiden didn't know what he was sorry about, so instead he just hugged him back. Travis held him for so long that I had to break it up. Within a week's time, Travis knew everything about the kid from his favorite color to his first teacher's name. He called me every day and bragged on what a smart son he had and how fresh he was with the ladies. He was a proud father. Anyone who knows

Travis knows he was a baseball fan and so is Aiden. The morning he passed, we took Aiden to his first baseball game. When we got there, Aiden's eyes lit up like Christmas lights. He ran and jumped into Travis's arms and told him he was the best dad in the world."

Spade paused and tried to swallow the lump in his throat. "The look on Travis's face will stay with me for the rest of my life. He was overwhelmed with love and gratitude. He told me for the first time in his life, he felt complete. Travis hardly even watched the game that day, he just kept looking at Aiden, making sure he was okay. Although we are all sad right now, Travis did what he wanted to do in life. He was successful, he married the woman of his dreams, and he got to be a father, even if for a week. He was happy. The last time I saw him he was smiling from ear to ear and that's how I'll always remember him. He is, he was, and will always be my best man. Thank you."

When Spade left the podium, everyone was bawling their eyes out. Nina felt so guilty about not telling him about his son so he would have known sooner. She just always believed that they had time. As she watched them close the casket on her husband, she screamed out in pain.

"Nooooooo!" she tried to run to him, but Jaheim's grip was too tight on her. He had to be strong for Nina because that's what Travis would have wanted. Jaheim held her for the remainder of the services. He didn't tell her it would be alright because he truly didn't know if it would.

Allie and Chanel held Nina tightly as the pallbearers, including Jaheim, Spade, and Mike carried Travis out of the church. As the girls reached the back of the church, Nina saw Sweetie. She couldn't control her anger as she charged at Sweetie.

Sweetie saw Nina coming and quickly ducked her punches. Chanel grabbed Nina and pulled her away while Nina screamed. "Bitch! This is your fault! You thought Noah whipped your ass, you ain't seen nothing yet!"

"Nina, stop. Come on," urged Allie as she pushed her out of the church.

Nina's mascara stained her cheeks as she sobbed. "He begged me not to go over there, Allie. He begged me time and time again to put him first and I didn't listen."

Allie rubbed Nina's arm softly as she guided her out the church away from the stares that were burning through her.

"Why didn't I listen? He told me this would happen!" screamed Nina. Travis's words echoed in her mind. *Your loyalty to your friends will be the reason you end up alone.*

After they made sure Nina was okay and settled, Chanel and Allie went back to search for Sweetie. They saw her sneaking out the back.

"Sweetie!" yelled Allie. Sweetie turned around but quickly tried to walk away. Chanel took off running to stop her, with Allie walking quickly behind.

"Where have you been?" quizzed Chanel.

Sweetie looked at them nervously. "Around. I've been laying low."

"With Noah?" asked Allie. Sweetie shook her head no but they both knew she was lying.

"Sweetie, really?"

"What, Chanel? You wanna beat me up, too? Come on! I've been abused sexually, mentally, physically, and emotionally so bring it on! I beat myself up every fucking day of my life when Noah isn't doing it for me," Sweetie countered.

"Is it true that you told the police it was an accident?" asked Chanel, disgusted.

"It *was* an accident," replied Sweetie. Noah was already on edge and he didn't know it was Travis walking through the door.

Chanel shook her head and folded her arms. "What the fuck is wrong with you?"

"What's right about me? After being told that you're worthless for so long you start to fucking believe it! It's either I get my ass beat or he takes my daughter and abuses her and I will die before I let that happen! I already caused one of my babies to die I won't let it happen again," cried Sweetie. She knew she looked stupid to her friends, but they would never understand how hard it is to walk away from that situation.

Chanel's demeanor instantly softened. If no one understood how Sweetie felt, she definitely did. She knew what it was like to almost hate yourself. "Sweetie, we are here for you."

"It will never be the same now. I'm the reason Travis is dead," Sweetie sobbed.

"You're not, okay? Everything happens for a reason. God gave you a second chance because it could have easily been you in that casket. This is a sign that you need to wake up and get the hell out. If he kills you, do you really think I will be able to take Dallas from him?" asked Allie. "You are her mother, your job is to protect her but protecting her is not being abused. She will grow up thinking that's love and the cycle will repeat. You need to get out now Sweetie."

"It's not that easy! If it were, then I would have done it a long time ago. Me and the hundreds of other women who deal with getting their asses kicked on a regular basis. It's HARD. I have a daughter that I would not be able to gain custody of if I left him. I would have had nowhere to go. I didn't want to get y'all involved because I didn't want to drag y'all into it. But look what happened! My best friend lost her husband because she wanted to save me when I didn't even want to save myself."

Sweetie cried as Allie and Chanel comforted her. They were all hurting because of her situation. Their love for her outweighed the love she had for herself and she hated that.

"Where is he?" questioned Allie "He deserves to be in jail for what he did."

Sweetie hugged herself tightly, slightly shivering. She wasn't sure what gave her the chills because it was a fairly sunny day out. "I haven't heard from him all week," she answered. "I've been staying in a shelter."

"Sweetie, you can come stay with me," offered Chanel.

Sweetie wiped her tears and shook her head. "I'll find my own way out of this." She sighed and looked at her watch. "I have to go, now but I'll keep in touch. Dallas is safe with Mama Ruthie so I'll be okay."

Allie and Chanel said their goodbyes and walked slowly back over to where Nina was standing alone.

"This is all her fault," Nina whispered when her friends got close enough. "I believed her when she said she was done with him. I went against everything he told me for her."

"Nina, I know you're hurting but you can't blame Sweetie. You left that restaurant that day. You went against your husband because you wanted to," Chanel said softly. "You can't blame everyone else for your mistakes. It won't bring him back. That man lived for you and he died for you, he wouldn't have wanted it any other way."

CHAPTER 46

Wendy sat in her car and cried for hours after Travis's funeral. She took his death really hard because he was truly her only friend. He showed her so much love and compassion without even trying to. She sat in the back of the funeral, not wanting to be seen. She listened to every story told about him and knew his death couldn't be in vain.

Wendy sat and thought about how much she hated Noah. She hated him for what he did to her and what he did to Travis. She promised herself that one day soon, she would make him pay. One day came quickly as she spotted Noah walking out of the barbershop. She wondered what he was doing on the north side of Houston where she lived, but those thoughts quickly faded.

Wendy saw nothing but red as she slammed her foot on the accelerator. Noah's terrified expression caused her laugh as he realized what was happening. He didn't have enough to react before her car came barreling at him full speed. The sight of his body bending like a doll caused Wendy's adrenaline to race. She heard a thud as Noah's limp body collapsed on the hood of her car before sliding to the cement. Instead of backing up, Wendy continued to drive without a care in the world. When her car felt like it went over a hump, Wendy hoped it was Noah's heart being crushed by the wheels of her car. She wanted to break his heart like he did hers.

Wendy drove up a few feet before putting her car in park. She turned on her Tupac CD and lit up a cigarette. She smoked and rapped along to her favorite artist as she waited for the police to get her. Unlike Noah, she wasn't a coward; she was fully ready to pay the price for killing that monster. She wasn't even afraid of what would happen to her, she'd lost the only person in the world that made her want to be better. If it weren't for Travis pulling her off the street and offering her a job, she would have been dead a long time ago. Now that he was gone, she didn't have anything to motivate her so she figured she would end up dead or in jail anyway.

Wendy reached in her glove compartment and pulled out her stash. She looked in her rearview mirror and saw the crowd that was gathered around Noah's crushed body. She watched people point at her car while talking on the phone. She smoked her last blunt then rested her head on her steering wheel. When she heard sirens in the distance, Wendy knew it was over for her too.

EPILOGUE

A year after Travis's death, Spade kept his promise and gave Allie her Winter Wonderland dream wedding. Spade was currently working as the manager of Travis's construction company. Allie worked as a RN at a children's hospital. They purchased their first home right before their wedding and were finally living their fairytale.

Chanel was the maid of honor in Allie's wedding, with her sister, Nina, and Sweetie being her bridesmaids. Dallas and Jerricka were her flower girls, and Jeremiah was the ring bearer. Spade's brothers were his groomsmen. Aiden took Travis's place of being Spade's best man in their wedding. At their reception, they played a short video in Travis's memory and even left a seat open for him at their table. Spade made arrangements with Gabi to get Aiden a few times out of the year. He knew Travis would have appreciated that very much.

Chanel enrolled in beauty school and was one semester away from having her license. She planned on opening her own beauty shop in the next few years. She had been Eric free for almost two years despite his numerous attempts to reconnect with her. Talia had left him and took half of everything he had like she said she would. Chanel was happy that he was finally getting what he deserved. She even took him off of child support, so he would have no reason to contact her. Eric's parents picked EJ up every other weekend so she never had to see Eric face-to-face. Though Chanel was single, she did have a guy in mind that could possibly tame her but she was taking things slow. She was much more focused on being a better mother to her son, a better woman, and a better friend to her girls. Chanel finally started to love herself and it showed in all aspects of her life.

Sweetie was currently working on repairing her relationship with her family and friends. She finally got the strength to leave Noah right before Travis's funeral so when she heard he was killed a few weeks later, she felt relieved. She didn't attend his funeral, but she did visit his gravesite to say her final goodbye. Instead of being angry and bitter, she prayed that God would have mercy on his rotten soul. Sweetie worked part time as a receptionist but she spent most of her days talking to domestic abuse victims. Her goal was to let them know that domestic abuse doesn't only affect you; it also affects those you love. She and Nina were still working on their friendship; there was still a lot of hurt and animosity between them, but they both knew they needed each other to survive.

Wendy planned to plead guilty to the murder of Noah but surprisingly, a girl she didn't even know testified that it was an accident. Being that Wendy didn't leave the scene, the jury didn't have a reason to doubt the story. She was only sentenced to eight months in jail due to the marijuana that was found in her car. After she completed the drug program and the community service hours that she was required to do, she moved back to her hometown to start a new life. She couldn't bear going back to work without Travis being there.

Brandi also moved away from Houston after Noah's death. She testified on behalf of Wendy because she owed her life to her. Brandi knew Noah would eventually kill her, so she was grateful for Wendy, although she'd never met her. Brandi gave birth to a healthy baby boy and was currently focused on being the best mother she could be.

Jaheim moved to Austin after Travis's death and became the manager of a gym. He tried to reach out to Allie for a few months, but to no avail. He decided to let that situation go because he heard her warning about Spade loud and clear. He still texted Chanel from time to time to check on EJ out of respect. He decided to go to counseling because he just couldn't stop himself from preying on naïve women with self-esteem issues.

Nina was still dealing with Travis's death every day of her life. She was stuck on the what-if's and couldn't let them go. She got to the point where she finally accepted her role in everything that happened, which was a tough pill to swallow. Although she didn't understand why Travis had to die, she learned a valuable lesson about pride and taking people for granted. Nina talked to Gabi often and loved to hear stories about Aiden. She even loved to hear Gabi's old stories about Travis's younger days. He wasn't with her physically, but she could feel Travis's presence with her everywhere she went. Sometimes she could even smell his cologne and she knew that he would be with her forever, as he promised. Nina opened a community center for young kids in the neighborhood called Travis's Treasures. Although she never got a chance to give him kids physically, every child that walked through those doors each day belonged to her because of him.

Mascara & Moscato night resumed a few weeks after Travis's death. The girls didn't miss a Friday, no matter the circumstances. Despite their differences and all the drama that occurred, each girl knew that they needed the other for their own reasons. They were nowhere near perfect and it would probably take them years to repair everything that had been broken, but they were willing to take it one day at a time. It's not often that you find a group of women that love and support each other genuinely, even throughout the lies and secrets that tried to tear them apart.

This particular night they sat in the living room of Allie's new home in their pajamas as if they were kids again. Allie was doing their makeup, while Chanel did their hair. Instead of Nina driving herself crazy making sure everything was perfect, she was too busy getting ready to hit Sweetie with a pillow.

She was too slow because Sweetie got her first. All the girls giggled and hit each other with pillows like they were in high school and for just one moment; the perils of life didn't matter because they knew for certain that they would always have each other.

THE END

NOTE FROM THE AUTHOR.

Domestic abuse is never okay. It is NOT a form of love. If you or someone you know is being abused, please seek help immediately. It will not only help the victim, it will help their loved ones well.

Not everyone has a group of friends that they can talk to, but you're not alone and you are NOT at fault. The domestic abuse hotline is available 24/7, with professional advocates waiting to help you. 1-800-799-7233 or 1-800-787-3224. No cost, no judgments; strictly support.

This book is dedicated to all the Ninas, Allies, Chanels, and Sweeties of the world. There will always be light at the end of the tunnel. Allow yourself to be vulnerable sometimes and you will see that we all go through similar things but with the right support system, you will always push through.

I hope this book inspires someone to appreciate their loved ones more because tomorrow is never promised. I hope someone takes a good look in the mirror and find that beauty that we all possess; my hope is that you fall so deeply in love with yourself that you won't have to rely on someone else to do it for you. I hope this book inspired someone to fight through those hard times if you see that your spouse is trying. The road won't always be easy but in the end it will be worth it. Most of all, I hope someone reads this book and finds the strength they need to walk away from any abusive relationship whether it is mental, verbal, or physical abuse.

Thank you all for reading! I hope you enjoyed it as much as I did while writing it!

CPSIA information can be obtained
at www.ICGtesting.com
Printed in the USA
LVOW10s2258190917
549289LV00020BA/488/P